Paris is a Ghost

75

FSG

PARIS IS A PARTY,

PARIS IS A GHOST

PARIS IS A PARTY,

PARIS IS A GHOST

DAVID HOON KIM

FARRAR, STRAUS AND GIROUX New York

Farrar, Straus and Giroux
120 Broadway, New York 10271

Printed in the United States of America
First edition, 2021

Library of Congress Cataloging-in-Publication Data
Names: Kim, David Hoon, [date] author.
Title: Paris is a party, Paris is a ghost / David Hoon Kim.
Description: First edition. | New York : Farrar, Straus and
    Giroux, 2021.
Identifiers: LCCN 2021008598 | ISBN 9780374229726
    (hardcover)
Subjects: LCSH: Paris (France)—Fiction. | GSAFD: Love stories.
Classification: LCC PS3611.I45297 P37 2021 |
    DDC 813/.6—dc23
LC record available at https://lccn.loc.gov/2021008598

Our books may be purchased in bulk for promotional,
educational, or business use. Please contact your local
bookseller or the Macmillan Corporate and Premium Sales
Department at 1-800-221-7945, extension 5442, or by email at
MacmillanSpecialMarkets@macmillan.com.

www.fsgbooks.com
www.twitter.com/fsgbooks • www.facebook.com/fsgbooks

10 9 8 7 6 5 4 3 2 1

For Bosie

For my mother
홀륭하게 키워주셔서 고마워요

That time, that sorrow.

—Danish proverb

CONTENTS

I

FUMIKO

Sweetheart Sorrow

Fumiko had locked herself in her room. No amount of pleading or bargaining seemed to sway her resolve not to come out. We hadn't argued. One minute she was sitting on my bed; the next minute she wasn't. She lived three doors away, coming and going as she pleased, and it took a whole day for me to notice that anything was amiss. On the third day, I went to see the concierge; I had gotten as far as his door when it occurred to me that I could be making a terrible mistake. I was living illegally in my residence hall, a crumbling twelve-story building named for a dead postwar French writer I had never read. My student identification card having expired a long time ago, I could not afford to get expelled from my room. Fumiko had locked herself up before, though she always emerged from her self-confinement after a night or two. There was a word my father sometimes used, back in Denmark, *kærestesorg*— sweetheart sorrow—to describe the sadness one feels at the thought of a love affair nearing its end. A sadness one is not yet ready to face. As I walked away without knocking, I could almost hear my father's voice in my head.

Back at Fumiko's door, I called out her name, as loudly as I dared, not wanting to attract the attention of the other residents.

Her voice, when it came to me from the other side, sounded impossibly far away: "I'm sorry."

"I know," I said, pressing my ear against the wood. "Just open the door, OK?"

"I can't."

"Why not?"

"I can't."

Another long silence. Then I heard her say, *"J'ai froid"*— "I'm cold." Or it could have been *"Ta voix"*—"Your voice." The fact that so many French words rhymed with each other, coupled with Fumiko's difficulties in pronouncing them, resulted in frequent misunderstandings between us.

"What did you say?"

"Your voice."

"My voice? What about my voice?"

But she had gone silent again.

I decided to take the air, visit the Latin Quarter. It wasn't yet evening, and the métro was abnormally quiet—a lull between rush hours. After getting off at Saint-Michel, I lingered a few moments at the station entrance. Thanks to the heat from the subway tunnels, the nearby trees hadn't yet lost their leaves and the air smelled of mimosa and chestnut, even though winter was well underway. The guard at the entrance of the Sorbonne let me through, barely glancing at my expired identification card. Students loitered in groups in the main courtyard, bulky scarves wound elegantly around their necks. The marble-floored corridors were unheated. In the snack bar, empty white plastic cups stained with coffee littered the countertop. It was as if I had never been away. I walked past Philosophie, Histoire, Littérature française, stopping at Littérature générale et comparée, my former department. The benches were empty, no one waiting to see his thesis director. I scanned the walls. Among ads for au pair girls and cheap health insurance was a handwritten note covered with uneven, badly formed letters: "Theoretical physicist seeks Anglophone to translate treatise. 200 pages. 10 euros / page." Since abandoning my dissertation, I'd earned what money I could by giving English lessons to French high-school students, teaching unruly adolescents how to pronounce their "h"s and haggling with their stingy parents over my hourly rate. I knew nothing about physics, theoretical or not; yet the prospect of translating something—of not having to churn out anything in the way of original thought—appealed to me. I checked to see if anyone was watching, then tore off the piece of paper.

On my way home, I pictured my employer-to-be presenting me to other colleagues—i.e., hypothetical physicists of theoretical physics—in need of a translator. A beggar making the rounds growled because I didn't drop anything into his grubby outstretched hand. Closing my eyes, I imagined myself earning two thousand euros a month, sitting in the back seat of a taxi with Fumiko next to me, as we cruised down the avenue de la Grande Armée. The Grande Armée was the B side of the Champs-Élysées, radiating from the opposite edge of the place de l'Étoile. I was, if nothing else, a modest dreamer.

At a telephone booth, I dialed the number. I could see my hall of residence from the booth, and I tried to find Fumiko's room among the tiny mirrored squares, her last words to me—*your voice, your voice, your voice*—echoing in my head. Near the top, I noticed a solitary blind eye, one of the windows failing to reflect back the sun's dying rays. An open window in the middle of winter? I was counting off squares when, on the ninth ring, a man finally answered, introducing himself as Raoul de Gadbois. "Clarisse has seen fit to move the telephone yet again," he went on, "thence my difficulty in answering it." His French, ponderous and antiquated, was straight out of the Littré. Turning away from the building, I told him I was calling about the ad; I was convinced it had been there for months. We talked. He inquired if Blatand, my name, was English, and, resisting the urge to say yes, I admitted that I was from Copenhagen. "Where," I added, trying to give my French "r"s a British lilt, "everyone speaks the King's English." Gadbois suggested an hour and a date (one-thirty, tomorrow), then gave me an address: quai Louis-Blériot, in the sixteenth arrondissement.

"You need only to tell Clarisse that you are having lunch with me, Monsieur Blatand."

"Clarisse?"

"The maid."

After hanging up, I cast a sidelong glance at my profile in the glass booth. I could feel it. This was a turning point. The reflection in the glass nodded with me. If I hadn't yet gotten the job, I had already gotten a free meal. My luck was changing, and I was almost convinced I would find Fumiko waiting for me at my door. Stepping out of the elevator on the seventh floor, I ignored the peeling wallpaper, the occasional graffiti. The hallway was empty. No Fumiko. I felt a wave of sadness at the thought of returning to my room, to my single bed, my drawerless desk, my requisite antediluvian sink with two faucets: scalding hot and bone-numbing cold.

I stopped at Fumiko's door and knocked. Two quick raps.

"Fumiko, can you hear me? I know you're in there."

Gradually, I became aware of a muffled flapping noise. As though she were at her window, airing out the bedsheets.

"You can't keep this up forever," I said, more to myself than to her.

I had met Fumiko a year ago, in the métro. She was not the first to mistake me for one of her countrymen. To anyone seeing me walking around in Paris, I probably looked about as Scandinavian as the Emperor Hirohito, even if the only thing I was able to say in Japanese was "I don't speak Japanese."

"But you look so Japanese!" an exasperated Fumiko told me that day, her French much more foreign-sounding than mine. Words, in her mouth, always seemed to have one syllable too many. We stood facing each other, surrounded by commuters, in the stale air of the subway car.

When I told her where I was from, she screamed. Several people looked at us.

"*De-eh-enmark?* Wouah!" A pause. "So you speak"—another pause—"Danish?" She even managed to give "Danish" an extra syllable.

"Yes."

Fumiko was from a small town in northern Japan; she was auditing courses at the École des beaux-arts. She smoked Marlboro Lights, or *Maru-boro Rai-to*, as she pronounced it. She owned an Aiwa mini-disc player, which, she told me, used a special lithium-ion battery. The friendlier she became, the more I found her friendliness irritating, presumptuous. I had met people like her before, Asians who thought I had something in common with them. In Denmark, I had grown so used to looking different from everyone around me that I was able to forget what I looked like. In France, I was made aware, all over again, of my appearance: from French students frowning over my un-French, un-Japanese name to panhandlers in the street who shouted "*Konnichiwa!*" when I walked past, no doubt the only Japanese word they knew.

I didn't think I would see Fumiko again, but I ran into her a few days later, at the student cafeteria. She insisted on sitting with me. On the way out, we discovered not only that we were both headed for the same building, but that we both lived on the seventh floor—like something out of an Ionesco play. After that, we kept bumping into each other: at the cafeteria, in the hallway, by the elevator. (Only later did it occur to me to wonder if she had planned these "accidental" meetings.) I learned that Fumiko had left for Europe after recovering from a nervous breakdown, the way wealthy Scandinavians went to the Mediterranean to convalesce from respiratory ailments. A drastic change in environment, a doctor had said, could only do her good. Her parents wired money to an account at the BNP every month. She had chosen Paris because she had studied French in secondary school.

I in turn told her about my thesis—I hadn't yet abandoned it—on the influence of Sir James Frazer in the works of Samuel Beckett and Flann O'Brien. I was (as I used to tell my thesis supervisor) interested in the manifestations of magic; I said this to Fumiko with none of the self-consciousness that I displayed in front of my professor. She asked me how long I'd been in France, and I gave her my usual line: "Long enough to feel like an exile, not long enough to feel French." I told her about being adopted as an infant, about growing up in Copenhagen, my childhood fishing trips with my father to the Faroe Islands, my grammar-school years spent in Sweden. Fumiko asked me why Scandinavians always sounded like they were mumbling, and I told her it was mostly the Danish. Even Swedes and Norwegians had trouble understanding us. There was a saying that Danes spoke with potatoes in their mouths—"*Danskerne taler med kartofler i munden.*" When she heard me speak the language, she couldn't stop laughing, yet I understood that she wasn't mocking me. Her reaction, I told myself, would have been the same with a blond-haired and blue-eyed Dane. Who would have thought that the laughter of a Japanese girl would make me feel Danish again?

I don't know when I fell in love with Fumiko, with her boyishly cut black hair, her sputtering French, her habit of washing her underwear in the communal kitchen sink, even with the way she had of entering a room, so quietly and unobtrusively that I often glanced up to find her reading one of my books or staring at a picture on the wall. An unforeseeable side effect of communicating in a language foreign to both of us was that it allowed me to forget, sometimes, that she was Japanese. A foreign language allows one to rename the world and everything in it. Perhaps I was able to do so with Fumiko as well—that is, I was able to see Fumiko herself with new eyes. Watching her inspect the carcass of an insect on my windowsill one afternoon, I found myself thinking, I have fallen in love with your strangeness. That same day, I told her she was beautiful: "*Vous êtes belle*"—the formal *vous*, in contrast with the *tu* we normally used with each other, underlining the solemnity of the occasion. Fumiko, from across the room, smiled, as though suddenly understanding something.

"What's so funny?" I asked.

"In Japanese, the *vous* is used by the wife to address her husband. The wife says *vous* and the husband says *tu*. I never thought about it until I came to France."

I went to where she was sitting, a book open in her hands. "Is that why you said *vous* to me for such a long time?" I asked.

She slapped me lightly on the arm with her book. "I said *vous* because we didn't know each other very well."

"And now?"

She didn't answer. That night, as we lay in bed together, I told her I loved her. (In French, it was easier to say such things.) But the words, even buffered by a foreign language, nearly caught in my throat.

"*Moi aussi*," Fumiko answered, after a while. "*Je vous aime.*"

I believe she was in love with me from the very beginning. Not long after we first met, I found on my doorstep two Fuji apples and an old Grundig transistor radio. All because I had mentioned, in passing, the persistent silence of my room. The accompanying note said, "A ghost in your room can make the silence disappear." I puzzled over the words for several minutes, until I realized that she had probably meant *en revenant* (coming back) instead of *un revenant* (a ghost). Later that evening, there was no answer when I knocked on her door, and, assuming she was out, I left a note of my own, signing it, "A fellow ghost." We'd been going out for a few weeks when she told me she had been home the day I came by but had been unable to leave her chair.

"Why?"

"All of a sudden, I felt afraid. I couldn't move. I sat there, listening, for a long time." She gave an embarrassed laugh. "When I opened the door, you were already gone."

Had it only been three days? I was unlocking my door when I heard someone step out into the corridor. With a quickness in my chest, I looked up. It was Pascal, a psychology student who lived a few doors down. After hesitating, he waved. I had first met Pascal in the cafeteria. He had wanted me to take part in his research on pathological disorders affecting East Asian natives. "Some routine questions, nothing elaborate, so I can get an idea of your psychological makeup," he had told me that day, even after I had informed him of my background. Caught off guard, I had suggested Fumiko, hoping she would refuse. But Fumiko was only too happy for an occasion to practice her French with a native speaker. A week later, Pascal came to my door.

"I don't know if I should be telling you this," he said.

"Telling me what?"

"It's about Fumiko."

"What about Fumiko?"

"Normally, I never reveal information given to me during an interview, but"—he glanced up and down the corridor—"I thought you might want to know."

"Know what?"

"In Japan, the majority of nervous breakdowns occur in the late teens. That's when you have your university entrance exams, your pre-entrance exams to qualify for the entrance exams, your preparatory classes for the pre-entrance exams . . ." Watching him talk, I recalled the morbid enthusiasm he had displayed in the cafeteria while telling me about *hwa-byung*, a stress syndrome that affected middle-aged Korean women, and the dreamy look in his eyes as he went on about a Japanese malady in which the sufferer grew obsessed with his own body odor. "There's even an exam to get into the preparatory classes, if you can believe that. It's no wonder so many of them kill—"

"What's your point?" I said. I knew that Fumiko had found life in Japan exhausting.

He cleared his throat. "Your girlfriend came to France as a cure. But one of the conditions of her recovery was that she avoid things, *elements*, that might remind her of Japan. At least, for the time being . . ." His voice trailed off.

"So? I don't see what the problem is." I stared down at the floor, where a corner of one of the tiles had been chipped away. Pascal didn't say anything. I looked up at him. "You mean me?"

"I've been trying to decide whether it was worth telling you."

"But I have nothing to do with Japan!"

Pascal lifted his hands, palms out. "I only told you because I thought you should know. You can take it or leave it."

But I couldn't. I could neither take it nor leave it. Although I looked Japanese on the outside, I didn't *feel* it, had never felt it. At the same time, the doubt always remained that I was not who I thought I was, that, unbeknownst to myself, I was an impostor, a fake. I feared I was no one, in the end.

Now I called out to Pascal, who had reached the other end of the corridor, "How's the research going?" When he turned around, I noted, not without a certain satisfaction, the dark circles under his eyes.

"Could be better."

"Oh? What's wrong?"

"My theories aren't holding up." Pascal walked slowly towards me. "A recent study on cultural imprinting weakens what I've been proposing in my . . ." He stopped walking, then smiled thinly. "In other words, I'm in a bind."

A beat passed in silence.

"Can I ask you something?" I said.

"Sure."

"Is there a disorder where, uh, the patient locks himself in his room?"

"*Hikikomori*. Modern-day hermit syndrome." Pascal's face lit up. "Most live with their parents, who leave food by the door. In some rare cases, it can get ugly, but they usually live quietly in their rooms and only come out after dark." He winked. "That is, if they come out at all."

My body felt hot all over, the way it did at the onset of a fever.

Pascal was looking at me strangely. "Why do you ask?"

"Just testing your knowledge."

Raoul de Gadbois lived on the last floor of an apartment build-ing overlooking the Seine. Despite the excessive heat of the radiators, I sensed something cold, a chill in the air. The fur-niture, the fixtures all seemed old but barely used. Everything was brightly lit. My head ached. After a mostly sleepless night, I had woken up in a sorry state, my throat full of phlegm and my tongue covered with little bumps: the fever had blossomed. Clarisse—a squat, middle-aged woman—led me past the study on the way to the dining room. I noticed an ornate glassed-in cabinet where small octavo volumes of Greek and Latin inter-mingled with yellowing physics tomes. On the hallway wall hung a black-and-white photograph of a young woman with penetrating eyes and a mouth too large for her face.

Gadbois stood up from the table, and we shook hands. He looked to be at least seventy, a reasonably ugly man with a fleshy face and a perfectly bald head. His ugliness was subtle: it took a moment to realize, and fully appreciate, its scope. He didn't seem the slightest bit surprised that I was not "Euro-pean," as though it were a given, to him, that all Danes looked like me, and vice versa.

He said, gravely, "Bonjour, monsieur."

"Bonjour," I said. "Monsieur."

After we sat down, Gadbois asked about my life in France, the weather in Denmark—but the usual inquiries about my background did not come. I knew that a sneeze could strike at any moment, but I nevertheless forbade myself from asking for even a tissue, convinced that the smallest show of ill health would jeopardize my prospects. Feverish and delirious, I was about to tell him, just to have it done with, that I had been adopted, when Clarisse came in with a bottle of wine on a tray. It was only as I watched her fill Gadbois's glass that I understood, with a start, that the old man was blind.

The main dish was brought in. With slow, practiced movements, Gadbois's hand swept across the tabletop and closed over the fork and knife. Clarisse, as though waiting for something, stood in the background. At that moment, a strange and ridiculous thought entered my head: that Gadbois had intentionally kept his blindness from me on the phone, and in the laconic phrasing of his ad. He took a bite and said, "This isn't mackerel. Are you trying to trick me?"

I could tell, simply from looking, that the fish was mackerel; I had helped my father inventory the catch on our summer fishing trips.

"It's a mackerel, monsieur," Clarisse said, unfazed by Gadbois's reprimand.

He took another bite. "Herring. You went out and bought a herring."

"Herring is more expensive, monsieur. You gave me only enough money for mackerel."

Gadbois turned away from his plate with calm disdain. "Is this mackerel, Monsieur Blatand?"

I sensed Clarisse, in the corner, fixing me with her imperturbable gaze.

"You're right," I finally said. "It's not mackerel."

Gadbois, dignified and triumphant, turned to Clarisse and nodded once, gravely, his honor restored.

In addition to the mackerel, other items on the menu—the roast potatoes, the buttered artichokes with shallots—were systematically contested by Gadbois. Clarisse responded to each accusation with equanimity and patience. At last Gadbois acquiesced, resigning himself to the impostor food. It was the best meal I'd had in months, and yet I couldn't taste a thing. Each time Clarisse came around to fill my glass, I kept my eyes on my plate, unable to look at her.

"You are not a student of physics," Gadbois said, staring off into space, as though it had just dawned on him.

I stared at his stained, grayish teeth. "Well, no."

"Have you translated physics texts before?"

"Not exactly."

"Have you studied physics at all, Monsieur Blatand?"

"Well . . ." A memory resurfaced: dropping mold-encrusted coins onto the roof of the bicycle shed from my bedroom window in the Stockholm suburb of Rinkeby. "Some studies on gravitation, a long time ago."

Gadbois's gleaming forehead shifted. "What do you think of the theory of relativity?" he asked, slyly.

I stared at him. Was this a trick question?

"The fact is," he went on, "scientists have suspected for years, even decades, that there might be an inconsistency somewhere. No one has been able to prove it."

Gadbois stopped. I watched his flabby, brown-spotted hands smooth out the napkin, as though acting independently of their owner. I felt a painful, almost physical longing to see Fumiko, to hear her voice, feel her hand on my shoulder. Gadbois started talking about the inherent difficulties of describing something called a black body. I tried not to sneeze as I stared at the vacant seat next to him. A knife and fork had been set out alongside an empty plate, as though for a guest who had not come. Under the glare of electric lights, I saw that the porcelain was coated with a layer of dust, the silverware dulled by tarnish.

After the meal, Gadbois suggested we go to his study. I walked beside him, matching my steps with his, which were cautious but never unsure. Suddenly, he halted in the middle of the hallway, and I was trying to decide whether to tell him that the study was still a few feet away when he pointed at the photograph I had noticed earlier.

"My wife," he said, reaching out and brushing his fingers over the wooden frame, "in 1963."

That afternoon, I stood outside Fumiko's room with a plastic bag full of food. Day four, I told myself, ear pressed against the door. Five, if one counted the evening she had locked herself in.

"Fumiko?" I waited. "I brought you some food."

Some fruits, cheese, a *boule de campagne*, her favorite bread, from the nearby Franprix. I knew the exact contents of Fumiko's cupboard, having glanced inside it the day before her self-confinement. Since then, each item had engraved itself in my memory, frozen in time: a bag of dried chickpeas, a canister of salt, a withered Fuji apple, the rock-hard stump of a baguette. The human body, I knew, could go up to three weeks without food. And Fumiko had all the water she could drink from the faucet.

Back in my room, I wrapped all my blankets around me to keep warm—thinking wistfully of the dense, heavy comforters found in Danish country hotels—and sat down at my desk to start work on the twenty pages Gadbois had given me to translate. Instead of paragraphs on physics, it turned out to be a series of letters between Gadbois and the Académie des sciences. "After consultation by an expert, we must regretfully refuse your articles for publication. It appears that your work rests on principles that no experiment has justified. Your theories, in addition, do not contain any experimentally verifiable element."

Over the next few days, in between checking to see if Fumiko had left her room, I allowed the twenty pages to become my obsession, the cynosure of my day-to-day life, as all-consuming as a new love affair. I even caught a grammatical error Gadbois had made, writing *une* instead of *un hémisphère*, which, unlike *une sphère*, was masculine. (It was the kind of error native speakers rarely made, although rarely didn't mean never, and I found such lapses strangely fascinating, like hearing a renowned pianist miss a note during a concert.) Sometimes, looking up from my work, I thought, *At last I've found my calling*. Once an indefatigable library rat, I no longer waited in line at Beaubourg or the bibliothèque Sainte-Geneviève, whose vast ribbed interior made me think of a whale's belly; I stayed in my narrow, cramped room and worked on Gadbois's text. "R. de Gadbois's definition of gravity, based on a modification of Planck's law of black-body radiation, ignores the effects caused by the disintegration of electrons near a rotating black hole." "I insist that you seek the opinion of another expert. If my articles do not appear in the Academy's reports, I shall include, in the English translation of my treatise, this potentially incriminating correspondence in its entirety." "The articles submitted for publication by R. de Gadbois show great ambition. His substantial program is reminiscent of the articles published by Albert Einstein in 1905. Unfortunately . . ."

At night, hoping to lull myself to sleep, I tried to recall what little physics I'd gleaned from magazines and science-fiction novels. Gravity was not a physical force but caused by a curvature in space-time. The density of an object determined its gravitational pull. Around a black hole, near the event horizon, the pull became so strong that time crawled along at a snail's pace, a minute lasting several millennia. I imagined everything inside Fumiko's room slowing down—the decomposition of atomic particles, radioactive emissions, transmigratory thought waves, universal corruption, entropy, and, of course, Fumiko herself—ground to a state of near-complete immobility. My eyelids began to grow heavier, the rest of my body, on the threshold of sleep, suddenly lighter. I began to retrace my path through Gadbois's apartment, from the entryway to the long, bright hallway that led past the study, past the kitchen and into the dining room. I was coming back for something, but I didn't know what; my mind was trying to reveal itself to itself. Unexpectedly, I remembered that the maid, clearing away the table, had not touched the unused plate. I drifted off with the image of Raoul de Gadbois in his dining room—a dark, shadowlike form beside him. A human shape. Was it Fumiko, come out of her room at last? I couldn't be sure: a curtain made of darkness hovered, obstinately, in front of her head.

I telephoned Gadbois, who invited me to lunch again. Perhaps it was my imagination, but I thought I saw a look of amusement flit across Clarisse's face as she opened the door, before she turned away. I followed her down the hallway. Everything—the heat, the bright glare, the outdated and ageless furniture—was as I remembered it. Gadbois was waiting in the dining room. Solemnly, wearily, he held out his hand, which I shook. And then, taking his lead, I sat down, even as I realized, with a twinge of guilt, that it probably wouldn't have mattered if I had sat down first.

When lunch was brought out, Gadbois once again accused

Clarisse of trying to trick him. Although the fish in front of him really was herring this time, he claimed that Clarisse had bought him carp (which he abhorred). I wondered, almost desperately, if his blindness could have affected his taste buds. I glanced at Clarisse and noticed a slight tremor, of annoyance or anger, run across her face. When Gadbois at last turned to me, I was still asking myself if this was a game he played with all of his guests or a sign of something more serious, like dementia.

"What do you think, Monsieur Blatand?"

"I'm not sure."

"So you agree, then, that it's not herring."

"I can't really say."

"Well, Monsieur Blatand, it's either herring or it's not. Don't you think so?"

"Yes, I suppose."

"Then you agree with me, Monsieur Blatand."

"Yes," I said.

I stared down at my plate (of herring) as Gadbois acknowledged another victory with a nod to his maid.

The meal went by without further incident. The fish (I no longer felt I deserved to call it by its rightful name), though undercooked, was vastly superior to the canned ravioli I heated on a hot plate every night. Gadbois's conversation was less reserved, almost voluble, and his gleaming forehead seemed to catch the light more frequently. Between sips of red wine, he tossed around hundreds of light-years and billions of degrees, and described chimerical landmarks—the Planck length, the Dirac sea, the Einstein-Rosen bridge—as though they were stops along one of the métro lines.

Once we had returned to the study, Gadbois asked me to read through my translation. From time to time, he made me pause so that he might ponder, or pretend to ponder, this or that locution. (I assumed that his knowledge of English was, like the knowledge of dead languages, a mostly passive one.) While I read, the old man never stopped playing with a curious-looking object—a Plexiglas cube made of smaller, identical cubes and able to take on various proportions—and I remembered an episode from an old Greek myth, or the Elder Edda, in which a band of nomads come upon a sumptuous cavern whose enchanted waters have the power to grant eternal life. The nomads realize, at the last possible moment, that the man offering them a chalice to drink is blind: the waters offer immortality—but at a price. Long ago, the first traveler who stumbled into the cavern deceived the next one, who in turn deceived another traveler, and so on. As Gadbois paid me, he announced that he had succeeded in reuniting the multifarious and disparate branches of physics into a cohesive whole, picking up where Poincaré had left off a century ago.

I tried to think of an appropriate response.

"Do you think, Monsieur Blatand, that the Academy is right?" His unseeing eyes seemed to hold my gaze. "Do you think I'm a crackpot? One of those fools who waste their last years trying to square the Euclidean circle or disprove Cantor's diagonal argument?"

"Well," I began, "that is . . ."

"One thing Einstein did not account for was temperature." He let this sink in. "Temperature, in turn, affects light. Light, and its proximity to matter. In other words, *gravitation*. All basic concepts, but S.R."—I realized he meant "special relativity"—"doesn't take into account the effects of gravitation, as though it didn't matter."

I understood, listening to him talk, that he could have given me pure gibberish to translate and it wouldn't have mattered. I wouldn't have been able to tell the difference. Mostly for something to say in response, I asked him when he had started writing his treatise.

"Do you believe in miracles, Monsieur Blatand?"

"I'm not sure."

He nodded, apparently satisfied with my answer. "It all depends," he said, "on how one defines a miracle. For example, it is a miracle that I managed to find a linguistically gifted Danish gentleman with a knowledge of gravitational physics such as yourself. Don't you agree?"

Before I could say anything, Gadbois went on: "When I lost my wife, I found I had too much time to think. When I lost my sight, I found I could think better. My head filled with ideas. Time passes differently. When I'm not working, I let my memories flow or call forth my favorite passages from Tacitus. Or I do nothing—I let myself live. I can remain sitting in an empty room, perfectly still, for three or four hours without discomfort." He paused. "Let us hope, between you and me, that the English will prove themselves to be more open-minded than my countrymen."

He gave me another twenty pages to translate. On my way out, I walked past Clarisse in the kitchen. She was pouring coffee into a small, ornate cup. I saw her—in one swift movement—spit into the coffee. When she glanced up, her face was perfectly blank. She raised a finger to her lips and gave me a half-smile:

"You keep my secret and I'll keep yours."

On my doorstep I found the gray pullover I had given Fumiko for her birthday, which she used to wear when she was in a good mood. (There was a photograph just above my desk

of her wearing it during our trip to Saint-Malo.) Picking up
the crumpled piece of clothing, I brought it to my face to inhale Fumiko's scent. It smelled mostly of wool, but I breathed
in anyway. Clothes washed by her always smelled better than
clothes I had washed myself, in the same machine, using the
same detergent. A strand of black hair was stuck to one of
the sleeves. I walked over to her door. The Franprix bag was
still there, untouched. I backed away from it, as if to take a picture, until I bumped into the wall behind me. I let out a string
of curses in Danish. The one thing I could never really do in
French was swear, in the unthinking, spontaneous, stream-of-
consciousness way of one's native tongue. I sank to a crouch.
In that position, I saw Pascal's head emerge from his doorway,
hair disheveled, skin pale and subterranean—but the circles
under his eyes were gone. His beatific, unfocused expression
abruptly changed when he noticed me sitting on the floor. He
glanced at Fumiko's door and then back at me.

"Are you OK?"

I nodded, trying to smile.

"You look like you're crying."

"No, I'm fine." I wiped at my eyes. "It's the dust. Allergies."

"You should see a specialist. Nine times out of ten, it's the
sinuses."

There was no mockery in his voice. His smile was sincere,
without nuance.

"Is there a disorder," I said, "that affects someone close to
someone with a disorder?"

"What?"

"A sort of 'caretaker's syndrome.'"

Pascal shook his head. "Look, I know what you're doing."

I stared at him.

"If you're going to change the subject, you can at least be

more subtle about it. I may be oblivious, but even I can take a hint once in a while."

As I stood up, still clutching the pullover, I heard Pascal say, "I'm sorry about scaring you with my psychologist talk. I got carried away. I was wrong about Fumiko. And about you. My new outlook has allowed me to make a lot of progress in my research."

I almost told him what was going on, right then and there, but something held me back: the same impulse that had halted my hand in front of the concierge's door.

"By the way," he went on, "how is Fumiko? I haven't seen her around lately."

I focused on a piece of graffiti scrawled on the opposite wall, "*Arrash les ponts*"—"Tear down the bridges"—as I answered, "She's been busy with her drawings."

Pascal's gaze didn't waver. "You can tell me the truth," he said.

For a moment, neither of us spoke, and then Pascal asked, "You guys didn't have a fight, did you?"

A fight. He thought there had been a *fight*. "No," I said, "we didn't have a fight."

"That's a relief," he said. "When you see her, can you ask if she would mind being interviewed again? I have a whole new set of questions." He seemed embarrassed. "She's never home when I knock on her door."

"Sure, no problem."

The latest pages were harder to translate than the first batch. Gadbois's notes and explanations concerning gravity were mostly incomprehensible to my profane mind. Though I did not especially like the sound of my voice, I read passages

aloud; I recited, as dispassionately as I could, "Let x be the path
in space-time between q and t, q incarnating the three coor-
dinates in space and t incarnating time." One by one, I pum-
meled through paragraphs on tachyons and neutrinos. I looked
up "gravitation," in a moment of boredom, and found:

> The phenomenon of attraction between two bod-
> ies, proportional to the product of their masses and
> inversely proportional to the square of the distance
> between them.

In the same entry was a well-known quotation by Einstein: "Gravitation cannot be held responsible for people falling in love." I leaned back in my chair and laughed, and my
gaze fell at that moment on a series of still-lifes pinned to the
wall which Fumiko had done a few months ago, for one of
her ungraded assignments at the École des beaux-arts—studies
of spider and beetle carcasses, long-dead and dusty, dried-out
husks found on windowsills, inside fluorescent-light fixtures
and in hard-to-reach corners. The deceased insects, according
to Fumiko, had been forgotten by the rest of the universe. I
slammed the dictionary shut and went back to work.

At last, the twenty pages were done. They had taken me
almost two weeks.

Lying on my cold, narrow bed that night, I could see Fumiko's cupboard—the eye-of-Jupiter pattern of the woodgrain,
the accumulation of dust in the corners. I could feel, in the
darkness of my room, the relentless deterioration of its contents on an atomic level. I got up and opened my door. Lit only
by the emergency lights, the hallway tiles reflected an eerie,
phosphorescent glow. The Franprix bag in front of Fumiko's
door looked like a tiny white apparition. I stepped out into the

corridor. Underneath the usual smells of the dormitory was the effluvium of decomposing cheese. Still in my nightclothes, I carried the bag to the dumpster, not looking inside to verify whether Fumiko had taken any of the items. If I didn't look, the possibility remained. Back at her door, I sat down next to where the bag had been.

I told Fumiko, in a library whisper, about my new job, the lofty apartment, Clarisse. I described Monsieur de Gadbois, from the wrinkles around his bulldozer mouth to the creases on his moai-like forehead. Fumiko had always been fascinated by the physiognomies of old men. The first time she had visited my room, she had, after examining my meager shelf of books, spent several minutes studying the photo of Samuel Beckett sitting on the terrace of the Closerie des Lilas that I had taped to the wall. She loved the faces of W. H. Auden, Adolfo Bioy Casares, James (Frog-Eyes) Baldwin, even Sir James himself. "Old pears," she called them—for some reason—in her childish French.

"You know what?" I said. "I can't decide if Raoul de Gadbois is deluded or ahead of his time."

Although I always managed to find an English equivalent for each French word I translated, the whole thing seemed to crumble under its own weight when I attempted to reunite its constituent parts.

But, Fumiko's voice in my head protested, you are the one translating it.

"I'm not a theoretical physicist," I answered, as if that settled the matter.

I saw Gadbois again. He invited me to dinner this time, which I took to mean that our working relationship had changed

somehow. The rooms were as brightly lit as ever, and everything had the same unnatural sheen in the evening as it did
during the day. Though I knew I would never ask, I wondered why he insisted on having the lights on at all times if
he couldn't see. Was he able to make out shapes, or at least
perceive, on some level, the difference between night and day?
My father had once told me that some blind men could sense
nearby objects, especially if they posed a danger, through a
sort of acoustic radar situated on the tip of the nose, on the
cheeks and on the forehead: capable, as it were, of seeing with
the whole face instead of just the eyes. I didn't know whether
my father had read this in one of his medical journals (which
he perused the way some people peruse celebrity gossip) or if
he had made the whole thing up, as he was wont to do, simply
because it made sense to him—that men on whom such mis-
fortune had fallen should be compensated with some kind of
special, extra-human ability. Gadbois's blindness, I surmised
from all the paintings and photographs on the walls, must
have come to him late in life. I wondered how it had happened,
whether an accident or some disease had caused it, and what
the old man's days must be like, alone in his study surrounded
by books he could no longer read. Had he dictated his treatise or, given the number of spelling mistakes and off-centered
pages, typed the whole thing himself? The diurnal atmosphere
of the apartment reminded me of summers in Denmark and
Sweden, of days when the sun never seems to set, the annual
celebrations of Sankthansaften and Midsommarafton, when
magic is said to be at its strongest, of bonfires on beaches and
everyone singing "Vi elsker vort land." My parents' apartment
was equipped with something called a "dark room," a fad dat-
ing back to the nineteenth century, which I used not only because of the white nights and my insomnia but also because I

enjoyed the pitch-darkness—just me, my blood flow and my nervous system—like being inside an anechoic chamber. Was this what Fumiko felt in her room? A mixture of invulnerability and indifference?

We had rabbit à la provençale, with slices of aubergine. I savored the overcooked meat, the texture of the burned aubergines. We discussed Scandinavian literature. In Gadbois's voice I could almost see the expanses of exquisite, unblemished snow. He mentioned, with admiration, the names of Hans Christian Andersen and Kierkegaard; Niels Bohr; King Christian X, who had defied the Nazis and donned a yellow star. And then he told me, as though to win me over, that it was a Danish architect—Johan Otto von Spreckelsen—who had designed the Grande Arche de la Défense. My ancestors, according to Gadbois, were an exemplary people, an example for the rest of Europe. I wanted to tell him that my Japanese girlfriend had locked herself in her room for the past three weeks, but I didn't. Dessert was a variety of cheeses—brie, camembert, vacherin, chèvre—each involving a lengthy exchange between Gadbois and Clarisse on its authenticity. As Clarisse cleared the table, she passed over the unused plate, as she always did, without any change in expression.

Later, while reading my translated pages to Gadbois, I had a ludicrous thought: that he gave me more work only because I continued to have lunch—and now dinner—with him, as though that, and not the translations, were the true nature of my services. Had Gadbois wanted, from the start, someone who knew nothing about physics, someone who would be incapable not only of stealing his ideas but of seeing through their inherent fallacy? Perhaps the old man already knew that the British scientific community would react in much the same manner as the French. I envisioned my predecessors, candidates much more qualified than I, giving up on the first day, politely excusing themselves or storming out in disgust. Then again, maybe I was the only one who had bothered to answer his ad. Leaving the apartment with twenty more pages, I walked past Clarisse, who was smoking a cigarette in the kitchen doorway. This time, her smile was slow and deliberate—a knowing, ironic smile, the kind of smile exchanged between two conspirators. Or fellow pretenders.

Instead of going straight home, I wandered around La Défense, the business district, and sat on the steps underneath the Grande Arche, which housed, among other things, the offices of the Ministry of Tourism. I went up the steps to the splendidly illuminated platform. The wind was strong that evening and made the enormous canvas roof, suspended by cables, whip and buckle rhythmically. At that hour, I was the only one walking around the premises. Fifty feet away, an employee in uniform, most likely a security guard, sat inside a glass booth shaped like a giant pill capsule. Peering up at the glittering rows of windows dotting the monument walls, I was suddenly overwhelmed by the sheer size of everything. I told myself that I had every reason to take pride in Spreckelsen's work. H. C. Andersen and Christian X *were* my people. And yet why did I feel as though I had deceived Gadbois?

Stopping only to eat or go to the toilet, I did nothing but translate. A draft was entering my room from somewhere, and in desperation I sealed the window with insulating tape. Yet the feeling of cold persisted. I tried listening to the radio that Fumiko had given me, but the crackling static was ruining my concentration. Reluctantly, I took it out to the dumpster.

I found the newest batch of pages—fewer equations, more text—even harder than the last. My dictionary was now a tattered, sorry mess, its spine broken, its coffee-stained leaves creased and torn. Late one night, unable to sleep, I started thinking about the cupboard again. Had Fumiko eaten anything? The stump of baguette? The chickpeas? Knowing her fondness for apples, she had probably eaten the Fuji, I concluded. Perhaps she had managed to soften the bread with hot water from the faucet . . .

Something about what Gadbois had said tugged at me. "S.R. doesn't take into account the effects of gravitation . . ." Getting up, I turned the light back on and skimmed the pages I had already translated. On a whim, I took down from the bookshelf my abridged edition of Frazer's *Golden Bough* and flipped through the chapters until I found a passage that I had read long ago. It said that magic, in its most primordial form, might be defined as the effect of two independent bodies acting upon one another over a distance, such as voodoo, psychokinesis or telepathy. Two bodies. The distance between them. It was a coincidence, a fortuitous convergence of notions, but as I compared Frazer's definition of magic with the dictionary's definition of gravity, I felt I had discovered Gadbois's secret. In refuting Einstein's theory of relativity, Raoul de Gadbois wanted to prove the existence of magic.

I reached for the remaining stack of sheets, which I'd planned to finish over the next few days. The first glimmer of dawn was squinting over the horizon when, halfway through the last page, in the midst of an interminable paragraph on electromagnetic interferences, I came upon the word "possum." My pen dropped, with a clatter, from my cramped fingers. The word struck me as out of place in a physics treatise. I was tempted to replace it with "positron"—the chapter was on positrons—but reminding myself of my duty as a translator, I started to translate:

> Imagine a possum at point A and at time t, so that,
> at time t', we suspect it to be at point A$'$.

"Have you come to a conclusion about Monsieur de Gadbois?" a familiar voice asked, interrupting the tomblike silence of my room.

I found Fumiko lying on the bed. She was sketching the back of my head and was nearly done.

"If you ask me, I don't think he's all there." She considered what she had just said. "If I was that far gone, I would just eclipse myself."

I watched her fiddle with the radio I had thrown away. When I blinked, her hands, like a prestidigitator's, were empty.

"You know," she said, slowly, "this last time, I nearly did it. I nearly eclipsed myself. Do you know what stopped me?"

"What?" I whispered.

"Your voice. It didn't sound the same. There was a hopeful note in your voice when you came to my door. That's what kept me from eclipsing myself. Your voice."

"Well," I said, going back to my translation, "I'm glad you didn't do it."

A moment later, I turned to say something else, but Fumiko was already gone.

On my way to meet with Gadbois, I stopped at Pascal's door. What if he had been right all along? What if ancestry, in the end, was the only thing that really mattered? There was no answer when I knocked. I tore off part of a page from my translation and wrote on it, "Fumiko hasn't left her room in a month," before adding, "You were right about her. And about me." I thrust the note under the door before I could change my mind.

During the meal, Gadbois hardly spoke, as though our previous meals had worn him out. Only the sounds of utensils scraping against the porcelain punctuated the silence, and it occurred to me, suddenly, that *this* was what the old man's life was like most of the time. A muted, monotonous darkness—like the invisible motion of dark matter around a black hole. Clarisse, hardly disturbing the silence, entered the room bearing a tray. She served Gadbois his coffee first, before coming around to my side. Gadbois had almost touched the steaming cup to his lips when I found myself saying—my voice abnormally loud—"Don't drink the coffee, Monsieur de Gadbois."

Both Gadbois and Clarisse looked at me.

"I don't think," I went on, "that what you have there is coffee."

Gadbois raised an eyebrow. "Oh?"

"It's obviously not coffee."

Gadbois said, uncertainly, "I beg your pardon, Monsieur Blatand?"

"I believe Clarisse is trying to deceive you. I suggest you find someone to replace her, Monsieur de Gadbois. Someone who doesn't have a habit of spitting into the coffee of blind men."

For a brief second, the old man seemed at a loss. Then he cleared his throat, nodded, and, addressing the cup of coffee more than Clarisse, said, "You are free for the rest of the day." He nodded once more. "That will be all."

Without a word, Clarisse gathered up the untouched cups of coffee. As she picked up mine, I heard her murmur, quietly but distinctly, "I've been spitting in yours, too."

Moments later, accompanying Gadbois to his study, I saw him come to a halt, as he always did, in the middle of the hallway. Hesitantly, his hand reached out, and I considered warning him, or even pushing his frail body forward. I watched, instead, as his fingers brushed against nothing, or, rather, the empty wall just to the right of his wife's portrait. To Gadbois, it might as well have been light-years away.

"Clarisse!" he shouted. When she appeared, still holding a dishcloth, he pointed to the wall and said, with icy formality, "Please be so kind as to put the portrait of my wife back in its original position."

I watched as Clarisse, her hand betraying a tremor, adjusted the picture frame until it was within range of Gadbois's outstretched arm.

As if nothing had happened, we continued on our way, leaving Clarisse in the hallway. I almost turned to see if she was still standing there, but I resisted the urge. After all, there must be days when Gadbois made a mistake, started counting his steps too soon, or too late—missing his wife by mere millimeters. It wasn't impossible. In the study, after groping about, he handed me a thick bundle of papers: the remainder of his treatise, whose title page read "On the Persistence of Sorrow in Gravitational Interactions." To my surprise, I said to him, "I'm sorry about your wife."

It was as though he hadn't heard, and for a few torturous heartbeats I wasn't sure if I had spoken the words aloud.

"My wife?" Softly, ever so softly, Raoul de Gadbois said, "My wife passed away thirty-nine years ago, Monsieur Blatand."

Approaching the residence hall, I heard a burst of sirens. At the front entrance, silent blue lights pulsated rhythmically against the brick wall. The parked ambulance was marked I.M.L. VILLE DE PARIS. I closed my eyes, and the pulsations continued against my eyelids. As I stood there, Gadbois's treatise tucked under my arm, I became aware of a flapping noise above me. I opened my eyes. I finally understood what Fumiko had been trying to tell me in her garbled, mispronounced French: not *Ta voix* but *Au revoir.* Gazing up at the rows of windows, I saw the white of bedsheets and Fumiko's silhouette. The illusion held for another second, and then it was gone. Billowing curtains framed the outlines of two men dressed in white. From where I stood, I couldn't tell if they were watching me.

The elevator doors opened at the seventh floor, and before I had time to get out, the two men in white entered with a gurney. I could make out a vague shape underneath the plastic covering held in place with belts. At the far end of the corridor, I saw Pascal, his face undone by shock. I don't know why, but, just before the doors slid shut, I smiled at him. The men barely seemed to register my presence, as I moved back into a corner to make room for them. In order to fit the gurney into the cramped compartment, they were obliged to tilt it vertically—hence the belts—so that the upright litter stood next to me, like a fourth person, as the elevator began its slow descent.

"How long you think she was in there?" one of the men asked, staring straight ahead.

"Hard to say," the other one replied, not looking at his partner. "At least a few weeks?"

"The body hardly smells."

"No kidding. Window was left open the whole time. See the food in the cupboard?"

As we passed the sixth floor, Gadbois's treatise slipped from my fingers and fell with a barely audible thud. I made no move to pick it up. Fifth floor. The one who had spoken first, as if he couldn't bear the silence, spoke again: "I was just thinking . . ."

"Yeah?"

"You think it was windy that day?"

His partner: "What?"

"There was an unfinished cigarette in the ashtray."

"So?"

"Marlboro Lights. Like me."

His partner took this in. "No kidding."

"This is how I see it. A half-burned cigarette means she put it out before she died or that it went out by itself, which means . . ."

"Here we go again."

"But why put out the cigarette before dying? Then again, why leave it unfinished? That's why I think it was windy that day."

In the days following Fumiko's death, Pascal would show me his notes, strewn with one-of-a-kind expressions, Fumiko-isms copied down in a minuscule but legible lycée script. She had told him—an impersonal interviewer, a stranger doing research—what she was incapable of telling me, a Scandinavian who looked too much like one of her own countrymen. "When I am near him, it tugs at me, like a sweet, diabetic longing. A sticky addiction welling up like a blood bubble. And then I want to eclipse myself." Perhaps she didn't want to admit what was happening for the same reason I was unable to admit it to myself. Love makes us do strange things and behave in unimaginable ways. As the elevator light moved from fifth to fourth, I slid my hand underneath the plastic shroud. The men, still talking, didn't notice a thing. I took Fumiko's cold and unyielding hand, firmly, in my own. Fourth moved to third. All the way to the ground floor, I held it like that.

Don't Carry Me Too Far Away

The dissection room is on the fifth floor of the main building, and the thirty-six tables, or "cadaver stations," are arranged in six rows of six. At the far corner, leaning against the walls, are plain wood coffins. For the cadavers, when everyone has finished with them. Unlike all the others, which are stomach-up, yours is lying facedown on the table. This is how you found the body, you and the others in your dissection group. It is the first day of the anatomy course, and the prof is not here yet. The buzz of fluorescent lights is broken occasionally by a muffled cough or a throat being cleared. In the back, the lab monitors look bored, half asleep. A few groups have already started on their cadavers. You don't recognize any faces: the students you knew last year are gone, flunked out.

You and the others have already tried turning the body over. Who would've thought a lifeless body could be so slippery, so elusive? The four of you—Frédéric and Aurélie on one side, you and the art student on the other—barely managed to keep the body from sliding off the table's stainless-steel surface, dangerously slick with fluids. It almost felt as though the body were resisting you, pitting its will against yours. Eyes still smarting from the formaldehyde, you realized, for the first time, that the cadaver is female.

What did Aurélie say earlier? *We got lucky.* She wasn't trying to make a joke, but Frédéric—or Fréd—laughed anyway. You understood that she was referring to the cadaver's overall condition more than anything else. At the nearby tables, the bodies are all visibly older, transformed in unexpected ways by the preservation process, which has robbed them of pubic hair, for example, but left untouched other areas of the body. You wonder if the heads, which are hidden beneath several layers of gauze, to be removed when you get to dissecting them, are also hairless. Yours died more recently, that much is obvious, and the limbs haven't yet completely lost their stiffness—or at least that's what you blamed for your difficulty in turning the body over. But a newer body means better organs with more color to them, easier to tell apart than the uniform gray mess typical of an older specimen. The chemical agents haven't yet had time to dry out muscles into strips of jerky and turn organs into shriveled husks, or, worse, liquify them into a chemical slurry. Normally, only the research surgeons are allowed to have such fresh cadavers. Like Aurélie said, you got lucky.

Your gaze at that moment is drawn to the art student, whose name you've forgotten. The École des beaux-arts is down the street from the medical school, and he's taking the anatomy course as part of some sort of project. That's when you notice that he's not wearing gloves. Did he have any on earlier, when you were all trying to move the body? Strictly speaking, there's no rule about gloves in the lab, but most choose to wear them, for obvious reasons. He is staring down at the cadaver, and you are struck by his pallor, which almost makes him resemble a corpse himself. Despite the refrigerated air of the lab, you can't see his breath, and you continue to watch him from the corner of your eye, waiting for him to exhale.

Suddenly, like a switch turning, the room is filled with sounds and movement. The monitors have come to life, moving briskly between the tables, stopping at each group and verifying names on a clipboard. The prof has arrived at last, unnoticed in the confusion. He strides past you without a glance, leaving in his wake the unmistakable scent of the outside air he's brought in with him. On the whiteboard, he begins to write out a list of the principal nerves and vessels to look for and identify.

"Your first incision," he intones, still writing on the whiteboard, "will be along the medial line of the thorax . . ."

By now, everyone is busy with the cadavers. Fréd asks, "What are we going to do?"

"We'll have to start with the back," Aurélie says, frowning. "Or maybe the legs. There are some structures of the inguinal region that extend into the anterior—"

"What do you think?" Fréd says, turning to you. "Didn't you say that anatomy was your specialty?"

You find it hard to ignore the veiled challenge in his tone. He fixes you with a pointed expression, defying you to prove him right. At the orientation, you said only that you had an interest in anatomy, nothing more. You did not say, for example, that you have dreamt of cutting into a human body since you were a little girl. It has nothing to do with a desire to kill; death is the furthest thing from your thoughts. On the contrary, it is when you really like someone that you want to know what she looks like on the inside. As a child, you sought out the inner workings of things, starting with the alarm clock that you took apart one afternoon when you were seven. It was the sight of the little gears, the coiled springs, all crammed together and yet so perfectly imbricated, that sent a nameless excitement through you. Was it the excitement of looking at something you weren't meant to see? Your parents, initially worried about your lack of interest in normal girl things, then mollified by what they took to be a scientific temperament, were ultimately disappointed when you made no effort to put the clock—or anything else you opened up—back together. They didn't understand what you felt, and you didn't know how to explain it to them. It was, in the end, a drawing of a hand that opened your eyes to what had been around you, all along. The summer before your final year of lycée, you were wandering aimlessly through the streets of Arles on the day of the open-air market. The Grande Fête was a few days away and you could feel the familiar tension, the repressed energy. At one of the bookstalls you picked up a tattered tome at random to flip through the pages. You recall the paving stones beneath your feet tinted pink by the late-afternoon sun. And that's when you saw it. Since then, there have been others— the pelvic cross-section from the *Topographisch-anatomischer Atlas* with its cutaway view of the femur and loops of bowel, like a nineteenth-century CT scan; or the intertwining rivers of blue and red defined by the silhouette of an invisible heart in Jean-Marc Bourgereau's diagram of the left and right coronary arteries—but it was the anonymous drawing you stumbled across, of a hand cut open to reveal a glimpse of muscles, vessels, ligaments, that you always came back to. In bed, at night, you gazed up at your own hand and told yourself that what you couldn't see was far more interesting, and infinitely more complex, full of unseen possibilities, than the bland exterior you knew every day. You found it hard to believe that an arm, a shoulder, or the flayed face of an Albrecht von Haller engraving could contain such structural multitudes. Even now, when you have a spare moment, you like to go to the big university library and leaf through anatomy atlases in the cavernous reading room. There are, of course, Vesalius and Rohen and Gray, but your love has always been toward less-known anatomists, in particular Hortense de Gaulejac, your favorite.

"Someone," Fréd says, "has to make the first cut."

"I'll do it," the art student says.

"Blaise, is it?" Fréd says, and you remember him at the orientation asking, *Pascal or Cendrars?* Blaise, with a felt marker, draws the lines along which the first incision will be made. He is still not wearing gloves. His movements are deliberate, even a little impatient; all the same, there is something practiced and familiar about them—he's done this before, you think. You see him rest his fingers briefly against the cadaver's back, where the spine is, the little gesture at odds with the cold efficiency with which he traced the incision lines. He chooses a scalpel from the drawer under the dissection table and bends down once more over the cadaver. As he starts to press the point of the blade into the skin, you are overcome by a pang of—is it possible?—*jealousy*. It should be you making the first cut. The thought, as brief as a spark, surprises you. A vein at his temple twitches. He puts down the scalpel.

"I can't. I'm sorry."

Abruptly, he turns away from the table. Heads go up as he makes his way between the cadavers. "After all that foreplay with the felt marker," Fréd says, shaking his head, "he's the first to crack."

You look down at the cadaver and see that he didn't even pierce the skin. You pick up the scalpel and place the blade to the line that he drew. The skin is surprisingly resilient, giving way only reluctantly. Liquid seeps out, and for a moment it's as if the blade were cutting into your own flesh. You finish the incision and attempt to peel back the slippery, viscous skin, but it's impossible. Then the prof is there with a pair of scissors, which he uses to snip off a corner from the incision you just made.

"Now the flap can be pulled back more easily," he says.

Aurélie, as if on cue, reaches in with small, dainty hands to loosen the connective tissue and detach the subcutaneous layer from the muscles. The prof commends her on her technique. She has good fingers, he says, and would make an excellent surgeon. He walks away before Aurélie can stammer a reply. You stare at the little triangle of skin that the prof cut out, lying on the table, unnoticed, next to the body it came from.

That night, you have dinner with Bérengère at a Japanese restaurant near Opéra, not the kind of place you had in mind after a dissection lab, but Bérengère loves sushi, and she is usually the one to choose where the two of you eat when you dine together. She is eight years older than you and is no longer a student, but spends her days in the Latin Quarter and Saint-Germain-des-Prés, where she hires herself out to students your age, shopping for groceries and taking lecture notes on their behalf. She works for an agency that liaises with the various faculties in and around Paris. It's a trend that originated out west, in Rennes and Nantes, among the students there, before spreading to other metropolitan centers. It's also how the two of you met, near the end of your first year of medicine.

You've already described to her the dissection room, the stainless-steel tables with their advanced drainage systems, the stench of formaldehyde. (At your place, you took a shower, changed your bra and underwear, but you can still smell it, on your fingers, on your face.) The only thing you leave out is the cadaver itself. You don't tell her it's the first naked body—the first naked *female* body—that you've seen up close, other than your own. Bérengère listens to you while eating, unfazed, and it's one of the things you like about her. You describe to her the other members of your dissection group: Aurélie, who obviously sees herself as the group leader; Fréd, who is everything Aurélie is not; and the art student, Blaise. You don't know what to make of him, you tell Bérengère as you attempt to pick up the piece of eel on your plate with your chopsticks. You're not all that fond of eel, but it's the only cooked fish among the sushi.

"Maybe"—she lays down her chopsticks across her empty plate—"he's a necrophile. Maybe that's why he left the room when he did: to relieve himself in the toilets."

"I remind you that we're eating."

"Speak for yourself." She has a way of wrinkling her nose and her upper lip when she smiles that you've never been able to imitate. "So—this art student, what does he look like?"

She tends to ask this when you express any kind of interest in someone of the male sex, and it bothers you more than you think it should. As a result, you don't do a very good job of describing him, fumbling over details, leaving out others. You are telling her about his strange immobility—like someone looking at an object visible only to himself—when you notice a change in Bérengère's expression. You ask her if she's OK, and she laughs, a funny little sound, then says:

"I was thinking about a student in one of the classes I modeled for."

"Oh?"

"Not that I'm saying it's him or anything, but . . ."

Bérengère, before you met her, was an artists' model at the École des beaux-arts.

"He had this way of staring at me . . . It really gave me the creeps. Like he was seeing something that—how can I put it— that he knew wasn't really there. I can only imagine what his drawings were like. A part of me wanted to take a look; at the same time, I didn't want to know." She motions for another *demi* of Asahi. "It seems silly now, but I had nightmares about it."

"Is that why you quit?"

"I quit because the rooms were never heated, even in winter."
She is rummaging inside her purse for her cigarettes and you
can't see her face. "Besides, I wasn't going to do it forever."

Bérengère doesn't know about your feelings for her, though
you've come close to telling her more than once. Early on,
you gave her an aperçu of your formative years—summers
in the Camargue, the Grande Fête, the crowning of the
Queen of Arles—and recounted, with appropriate flourishes
of irony, the epiphany in the open-air market responsible
for your love of old anatomy manuals, the *changement de cap*
from Literature to Science and the subsequent decision to
study medicine in Paris. You even told her about Hortense
de Gaulejac, a student of Françoise Basseporte like Marie Biheron, another female anatomist. Unlike Biheron and her anatomical wax models, Hortense left nothing behind, nothing
that could be attributed to her by name. She was a woman,
and women were ignored when they were right and ridiculed
when they were wrong. Better to remain anonymous and let
the work speak for itself. It was, after all, a love of the work
that drove her to do what she did—all the scientific texts she
translated or supervised drawings for, which were published
under the sole names of the male surgeons, physiologists and
anatomists who thought of her as an esteemed colleague, if
not their equal. It is not known how many times she did this,
inserting herself into the work of others—the addition of a
paragraph on mercury chloride as a preventive agent against
rot in an essay about bacteria, for example, or the inclu-
sion of a female skeleton among the plates of an anatomical

atlas—which makes the most rudimentary of bibliographies a challenge, if not an altogether impossible task. Nevertheless, you plan to attempt just that for your third-year thesis next year. Hortense de Gaulejac is the reason you came to Paris, you who could have remained in the south, where your parents and friends are. You could have chosen Montpellier or Marseille, where the tables in the dissection room are porcelain rather than stainless steel. Instead, you chose Paris for its medical library, the third largest in the world, and for its manuscript archive, the largest in France.

"All because of a hand you saw in an anatomy book?"

"In a word, yes."

"You really think she used her own hand as a model?"

"If the drawings she made of the clitoris are an indication . . ." You had just told Bérengère about the drawing table, the mirror hidden behind a velvet cloth. "They were never published, and found among her papers after her death. Even when the clitoris was finally allowed in nineteenth-century textbooks, it was cut along the frontal plane like the penis—not transversally, as it should be to show all of the internal organs."

"No kidding."

You had bumped into her at a party in the basement of the Maison du Brésil. A chance encounter. You were there with some med students who lived nearby, in one of the other residence halls of the Cité U. It was she who recognized you first. During a particularly busy week, you'd hired her to do your grocery shopping and water your plants.

"The anatomist. We meet again." You could see that she was a little drunk. With slow, languorous movements, she loosened her scarf, revealing what was hidden underneath. Freshly tattooed along the length of her neck—the skin a little swollen along the edges—was a pair of intertwined serpents, one red and one blue, which made you think immediately of the internal jugular vein and the common carotid artery. The soft, vibrant colors called to mind the drawings of Jean-Marc Bourgereau, who writes in his *Traité de l'anatomie du coeur humain*: "[The] carotid splits into two branches in the thorax, at the fourth cervical vertebra, but until then it runs as a single artery, diverging from the internal jugular on the left side of the body, approaching and often overlapping it on the right side."

You were flattered that she remembered you, among the countless faces she saw on a daily basis, hiring herself out to a student clientele numbering in the hundreds, if not more, though you weren't drunk enough to think it meant anything. In fact, you weren't really drunk at all; you never had more than a beer at these parties, and you rarely finished it by the end of the night. So you were in complete possession of your senses when the two of you, along with others heading home, crossed the street to catch the RER, the last one of the night. You found out she lived in the Goutte d'Or, near the boundary of Barbès, on the other side of the Seine. The train started to slow as it approached Saint-Michel, and you were deciding whether to switch to the métro or walk the rest of the way to your apartment when she leaned towards you and, with a smile, invited you to her place. Before you could stop yourself, you asked her how you would get back home. You saw her nod, as though recognizing the wisdom of your remark, and that was that. You've told yourself since then that nothing would have come of it. For one thing, she wasn't into girls. And yet. In those dead morning hours after emerging from another troubled dream, you can't help but think: If you'd said yes? And: Why didn't you?

The room is filled with the sound of electric saws cutting into bone. The rib cage is being removed today. It's time for the lungs and heart, but your body is still stomach-down on the table. None of you have had the courage to move it after the last, disastrous attempt. The prof has suggested a laminectomy, which involves removing part of the spinal column. "A lot harder than the ribs," Fréd says, half muffled by the face mask, though it is Blaise wielding the saw with its wide, stout blade. Perhaps to make up for his previous failing, he volunteered to do the cutting himself—with one of the manual saws, no less—surprising you all. Before the lab, standing behind a tree, you watched him smoke a cigarette in front of the main building. The dark, bruised-looking skin under his eyes made his face appear even more pale. At one point, bringing the cigarette to his lips, he marked a slight pause, a hesitation, like someone remembering something. What if it really *had* been him in one of the classes Bérengère modeled for at the Beaux-Arts? You weren't sure what you were looking for until you saw it, the familiar red outline through the pocket of his shirt. Chesterfields, Bérengère's brand. You wonder if it means anything. The other night, after the sushi restaurant, Bérengère had stepped into a tobacconist's (she'd misplaced her pack) and returned empty-handed (they didn't have her brand). Now you stare at Blaise's forehead, near the hairline, where the effort of the saw is causing a vein to stand out in relief. Beads of sweat dot his brow. Fréd shouts words of encouragement, no doubt glad to have someone else doing the grunt work. Aurélie is holding a pair of scissors, ready to cut away any stray tissue. Little bits of cartilage, like gnarled roots, fly off the blade as Blaise moves the saw back and forth over the vertebrae. The air is thick with bone dust, and Fréd makes a comment about poisonous aerosols. You imagine the walls of Blaise's room covered with drawings of Bérengère naked as you help Aurélie tear off strips of bone and tissue. The dura mater is the first superficial layer, a protective coating as thick as your finger. Before it can be cut, the spinal ligament along the posterior wall of the spinal canal must be excised, along with the dural sac, whose protective membrane Aurélie carefully slices through with a knife, revealing the arachnoid mater.

"Pouah," Fréd says. "What's that smell?"

Aurélie turns to him with dripping hands.

"No, no. This is different. *You* smell it, don't you?"

You are not sure why you lie to him. Does it have to do with the fact that he put you on the spot the first day of lab? Is that why you do it, why you tell him you coated your nostrils with Vaseline and can't smell a thing?

"Look," Aurélie says, her voice almost a whisper. "The cerebrospinal fluid."

She is pointing to the liquid inside the arachnoid, which rises and falls like a cushion when she presses down on the tissue.

"It's what they drain during a lumbar tap," she says, as though the reason for her enthusiasm should be obvious.

You recognize the arachnoid from woodcuts and engravings depicting the vibrant, pulsing beauty of black tendrils caught in a gossamer film. But the arachnoid, the real one, is beautiful in a way you couldn't have predicted, and you feel the thrill of having something so pristine and perfectly preserved laid bare, something that has never been seen, much less touched, by anyone before you.

The last few incisions are easier, surprisingly enough—the body is no longer resisting the advances of your scalpels, it seems. Cut and pull away the arachnoid mater, uncovering the pia mater beneath, the deepest of the meningeal tissues. Pull away the pia mater, and there it is at last. A slender, fragile mass lined with vessels and nerves. The spinal cord. Every heartbeat, every muscular contraction and skin sensation, an entire life's worth, passed through its depths. You had to break through bone and tissue with a saw and chisel to get at it, but here you are at last.

A moment later, Fréd is holding aloft the stringy bundle like a barbaric trophy, waving it around and repeating a line from a movie you don't know. A peculiar sort of sadness washes through you.

It is Fréd who suggests going out for drinks afterwards. He knows a place not far from the school. The successful dissection has put him in an exalted mood, transformed him into Bernard Kouchner, all of a sudden. Aurélie, too, seems changed, even laughing at one of Fréd's remarks, which she usually ignores. "Are you coming?" she asks you, and then, possibly sensing your hesitation—you saw yourself staying behind to be alone with the body—she adds, "Even Blaise agreed to join us. Come on!" She holds your gaze a second longer than expected, and in that moment you understand that your absence would leave her alone with Blaise and Fréd. Your respective roles within the group have by now established themselves, and there is little doubt, in your mind, that you and Aurélie are the most competent half, the ones most willing to dissect.

This also puts the two of you in competition with each other, to a certain extent, and not only because you and Aurélie are both girls.

The café, it turns out, is one you've been to with Bérengère, and popular with students. Not surprisingly, it is packed at this hour. You spot a couple leaving as you arrive, and you are leading the others to the vacated table when you realize that one of the pair is Bérengère. (She sometimes likes to have a drink before going home.) The guy with her is noticeably younger, stylishly dressed, a thick red scarf wound around his neck. She doesn't seem surprised to see you, greeting you with a kiss on each cheek and introducing her male friend. The others have caught up to you by now and you reluctantly introduce them to Bérengère. When you come to Blaise, you watch for her reaction as you say his name. Her expression doesn't change, but you see her flinch ever so slightly, the hint of a tremor below her right eye. As for Blaise, there is nothing to show that he recognizes her at all—if it was really him. The others are walking past you, and Bérengère leans in and says, "I'll call you," before she, too, moves on with her companion into the night. Even after she's disappeared from view, you can feel the hotness of her smoky breath sweetened by the alcohol.

The mood at the table is boisterous, mostly thanks to Fréd, though the propitious timing of your arrival at the café is not lost on anyone. Your table, carved directly from the trunk of a tree, has a peculiar, vaguely human shape. At the center is a hole, an irregularity in the grain, more like a small crevice, its walls worn smooth over the course of years. Throughout the evening, the four of you—while talking, as an idle gesture, in moments of distraction—take to inserting a hand, or what will fit, into the crevice. You almost succeed, but in the end it's Aurélie who is able to fit her entire fist inside, and from this she conjectures that a human heart might fit as well. A human heart, after all, is about the size of a fist. "More like your fist," Fréd corrects her, laughing, "is the size of a human heart." Aurélie's parents are both psychiatrists in Rouen; at the moment, she is leaning towards cardiology or anesthesiology, and is thinking of doing her third-year thesis on reduced subcutaneous lidocaine efficacy in red-haired patients as a result of their higher-than-average sensitivity to pain. All of this she told you at the orientation, but tonight she goes on to admit that her childhood dream was to be a concert pianist. Alas, her hands were always too small. Like someone who's revealed too much, she interrupts herself and asks the rest of you for your reasons. Immediately, Fréd says that he has no idea what he wants to specialize in. He came to medicine on a whim after failing to get into the École normale supérieure, which he considers a great stroke of luck, as it would only have led him down a path of privilege and complacence. From his tone, he still appears to be mulling over the failure. Somehow, you are not surprised to learn that he is a *normalien raté*. (The Sorbonne is full of them.) You in turn tell them about Arles, about your first months in Paris, when you didn't know anyone. The long solitary walks you took, sometimes until the straps of your sandals dug into the skin around your ankles. You don't mention the flayed hand, Hortense de Gaulejac, or your desire to cut open a human body.

"The ones who hide it the best enjoy it the most." Fréd finishes his beer. "Don't you agree, Blaise?"

Blaise shrugs and mutters into his glass. There is a silence, an awkward break in the rhythm.

Fréd leans forward. "I didn't quite catch that."

"I told you I was working on a project."

Fréd nods, impatient. "Yes, but I'd like to know more about this project of yours. I'm sure the girls here are also curious."

You again imagine Bérengère in that drawing class, exposed to his gaze, week after week. Fréd turns away, already losing interest. That's when Blaise says, "It's about death."

"Pardon?" Aurélie says.

"Love and death. How death changes love. If the person you love dies. Or you're in love with someone who's dead." He stares at Fréd until Fréd looks down at his drink. "Then everything changes. The way you love changes."

Though he hasn't glanced at you once since he started talking, you can't help but feel that, somehow, his words are for you and you alone.

"I wonder," Aurélie says, "is it possible to love someone who's dead?"

Blaise looks up. "What?"

"I mean," she says, slowly, "if your love only flows in one direction—because the dead, obviously, can't love you back—is it still love?"

"If it's not love, then what is it?" You hadn't meant to say this out loud. You hadn't meant to say anything at all.

Aurélie nods. "Good question. I suppose I never gave it much thought before." She smiles brightly. "It's an interesting project, Blaise. I don't quite understand how it relates to the dissection we're practicing in lab, all the same."

"I think he might have feelings for our cadaver," Fréd says. "Maybe he's even given her a name."

"So did the table next to ours," you point out, but Fréd goes on as though you hadn't spoken:

"We've opened up her arachnoid and touched her spinal cord, but we still don't know her name."

"I think," Aurélie says, "it's better that ours doesn't have one."

"She has a name," Blaise says, staring not at Aurélie but at you, across the table. "You just don't know it."

And you do? you want to ask, but Fréd—already drunk—is going on about the advantages and inconveniences of being with a dead person. On the one hand, she won't disappoint you, cheat on you or lie to you; on the other hand, you have to put up with the smell.

"Oh God," Aurélie says. "Not this again."

"Don't tell me you haven't noticed it too. I know I can't be the only one." He looks around the table. "We should be honest with each other. Isn't that why we're here? There's no reason not to speak our minds."

Aurélie looks wary. "Now what are you talking about?"

Blaise is fingering the hole in the middle of the table, and somehow he must have cut himself because you notice blood underneath his fingernail. Seemingly oblivious, he continues to scrape away at whatever he's found. Without thinking, you reach out and stop him by putting your hand over his, and he looks up, surprised, utterly bewildered by your presence.

"We can't keep dissecting the back forever," Fréd says. "Sooner or later, we're going to have to turn the body over."

On the train home, you choose the rear, though there is no shortage of available places. The evening rush is over, and the compartment is almost empty. You are not sure why you touched his hand. You remember thinking, at the time, that the blood under the fingernail wasn't his but—ridiculously enough—from the table itself, as if the latter were alive, wounded by Blaise. You shake your head. Fréd is right about one thing: sooner or later, the body will have to be turned over.

Several rows away, sitting with her back to you, is a woman whose blouse has an oval-shaped opening, closed off by a single button at the nape. From the back, with her long reddish hair, she could be mistaken for Bérengère. Even her skin is pale like Bérengère's, in contrast to your olive complexion and dark-brown hair. But Bérengère has never worn her hair piled up in a precarious, sloppy bun held in place by chopsticks. You stare at the area between the omoplates—the only exposed piece of skin—and imagine yourself making the necessary incisions: short, superficial strokes using the tip of the scalpel . . .

You must have dozed off. Bérengère's pale copy is gone, and you are alone in the wagon. You sniff the back of your fingers: the smell is still there, *her* smell. Suddenly, the wagon seems too small, too empty. You get off a station early. The night air feels nice, and you let it fill your lungs as you inhale, deeply, slowly. In the interior courtyard of your building, walking past a mobylette parked in the passageway, you notice something draped across the seat. A solitary glove. Above you, someone is watching television with the window open. Indistinct voices, a door opening loudly and slamming shut.

At that moment, you are traversed by the idea that the glove was left there for you, and you admonish yourself, *Petite folle va*, as you sense movement out of the corner of your eye: a shadow stepping silently back into the shadows. You take a few steps, then stop. Did you really see something? You tell yourself it must have been a reverberation from the light in the courtyard.

The following week, you are as surprised as you've ever been when you arrive at the dissection room to find the body lying faceup. No one can say how it happened. The body was like that when the others got here, Aurélie informs you after taking you aside. For once, she seems at a loss. She looks around and says, "I think it was Blaise. Two nights ago, I decided to review some structures on my own, and met him on my way up the stairs. I think he spends more time in there than me. But when I open up the cadaver, it's like he didn't touch anything inside. This time, I noticed that, well, the *spinal cord* was missing. I was going to tell the prof, I really was. Then I thought that it might reflect badly on our group. Besides, by that point, we'd already finished with the back." She looks embarrassed. "So I said nothing."

"It could have been one of the monitors," you say, carefully.

"You mean," she says, "as part of a hazing ritual?"

"Possibly."

Back at the table, you avoid looking at Blaise. Instead, you study her body, which you feel you are seeing for the first time. It reminds you of a child's body, though you know she is not a child. *Was*, you correct yourself. Her breasts are not deflated like those of the other female cadavers, with their sunken gray nipples. Her hips are like an adolescent's, though she must have been around your age. Just above the navel is the mark left by an incision where the formaldehyde was injected. You wonder how her body must have once looked, before the chemicals transformed and denatured it, before the blood was drained through the right jugular vein.

"Hey," Fréd says in wonder, pointing. "Pubic hair. Our cadaver has pubic hair."

Beneath the gauze, her face is nothing more than a vague silhouette. No longer turned away, the body seems just as distant and impenetrable.

There is a lot of catching up to do. The other groups have finished with the thoracic region and moved on to the abdomen. Some are even starting on the inguinal region. There is an urgency in the room, like it's a race and you are in last position. The sense of accomplishment enjoyed at the café is a far-off memory. You wonder how you're going to locate all the veins and arteries and nerves written down by the prof. Removing the rib cage requires, once again, the use of a saw. This time you opt for the electric, and grimly take turns with it, all the while trying to ignore the smell, more noticeable than even a week ago—an organic, earthy tang commingling with the chemical sharpness of formaldehyde. The last is Blaise, who backs away from the table.

"We all have to do it," Fréd says.

"I'm sorry," Blaise says, looking away. "I really am."

In the end, the three of you keep going until you are able to pry away the ribs. You've started to take out the right lung when Aurélie stops you. She points to the dark smudges covering most of the lung's mottled surface in dense, overlapping clusters.

"Gross pulmonary lesions," she says. "Symptomatic of acute hypothermia."

"She froze to death?"

Aurélie nods. "It's hard to be sure, though, without examining the subject further. If I could reach the liver, or the gastrointestinal—"

"Isn't it obvious?" Fréd asks. "Do I have to say it? Our cadaver is *rotting*. The smell is only going to get worse."

"So what are you suggesting?" Aurélie says.

"We need to ask for another cadaver."

"Out of the question." She says this as if the decision were hers alone to make.

"If we do that," you say, "we'll lose all the work we've done."

"As it is," Aurélie goes on, "we're behind the other groups."

Fréd turns to Blaise. "Do you have any feelings about this at all?"

"She was a smoker," Blaise says, so quietly you're not sure if the others heard him. That's when you see it, what Blaise all this time has been staring at—what the removal of the right lung has uncovered. Even then, it takes you a moment to take it in—a dense, febrile thing, nestled against the remaining lung. Her heart. Aurélie says something about the phrenic nerve near the hilus, but you're not listening. When she leans down with the scalpel, you grab her arm without thinking.

"Eh oh! Careful!"

It's impossible to say what you're looking for as you half-heartedly push aside the pericardium. The sense of propinquity you felt a moment earlier—like a voice faintly calling your name from another room—is gone. All you can hear is Aurélie next to you, her breathing small and measured: the smell is starting to get to her, too.

"That's it," Fréd says. "I can't take this anymore. I'm going to tell the prof."

"Please," Aurélie says, all authority gone from her voice, "you can't."

"If you go to the prof," you say, "we'll have to tell him what you did."

He's already started to walk away. Now he stops, turns and walks back to the table. "What did you say?"

"I know you took the spinal cord. We all saw you playing around with it. Isn't that right, Aurélie?"

The expression on Aurélie's face is one of incredulousness; but she nods, hesitantly.

Fréd is looking at you with outrage. "What are you talking about? What spinal cord?"

"The one you stole."

Even as you say this, you feel a strange little warmth in the pit of your stomach. Fréd slowly, wonderingly, shakes his head. "What is it with all of you?" He turns to Blaise, then back to you. "You have a thing for our little cadaver too, is that it?"

He laughs, unpleasantly, and walks away without another word. You watch him leave the room.

"Maybe you shouldn't have done that," Aurélie says in a small voice.

"Don't worry," you tell her, trying to forget his laughter, the knowing way he leered at you. "He won't go to the prof."

The rest of the lab passes in a blur of activity. The heart is excised, not without difficulty, and then the other lung. The superior and inferior venae cavae are located, but other structures, like the oblique pericardial sinus, a space below the heart bounded by five vessels, elude you. Fréd doesn't return. As you are passing around the heart, the prof comes over, but it's not to take the body away. As you expected, Fréd didn't say anything.

The prof is a short, wispy man with a burgeoning calvity and nicotine-stained teeth. All of his power and authority emanate from his hands. A practicing anesthetist, he is often late coming from the surgery wing of the university hospital. Like Blaise, he doesn't wear gloves, and you've seen him reach into cadavers with his stumpy fingers, not afraid of what he might dig out. He takes the heart to the sink and runs water through the ventricles to demonstrate the mechanism of the semilunar valves, whose function is to keep the blood flowing in one direction. To you, their geometrical perfection is as beautiful as Vesalius's description in the fifth book of the *Fabrica*.

Afterwards, you are putting the heart back in its place, between the lungs, when you notice what appear to be abrasions near the clavicular line. It's the lack of bruising, and the general discoloration of the skin, that made them hard to see. You look closer and discover other marks, barely visible to the eye. Some of them, you can't help noticing, disappear beneath the gauze enveloping the head.

For the next several days you don't leave your apartment, going through your notes on Hortense de Gaulejac. In the past, you've turned to her when you couldn't sleep at night, or when the pressure of exams threatened to get the better of you. She is also how you avoid things, your way of killing the hours. Sometimes she appears in your dreams, dressed as she is in the portrait by Alexandre Roslin, all dark velours and gilded hemlines. Almost everything you know about her comes from the medical library's manuscript collection and a multi-volume work, *Other Notable Historical Women, 422–1800*, unearthed one solitary afternoon in the archives of the BNF, where the only extant copy is on microfilm.

In addition to anatomy, Hortense conducted studies on the nature of putrefaction, before Pasteur's discovery of microorganisms rendered her work all but irrelevant. Among the substances that she watched putrefy in the course of her experiments are fruits (pears and apples in particular), wet tree leaves, pinecones, various meats, fish, eggs, mushrooms, insects, snakes, birds and even a human body that she was able to procure, on more than one occasion, through a surgeon who admired her work (and her person—alas, it wasn't mutual). You've often pictured her in her modest workshop in Congis-sur-Thérouanne surrounded by dead bodies and rotting flesh.

"Rot is like a contagious skin disease," she writes in one of her notebooks, "caused by humidity and stillness of air. It starts with isolated growths of minuscule, moss-like gray tufts. In time, the skin begins to change; once brilliant and smooth, it becomes dull and starts to shrivel as the vegetation spreads. Soon the entire outer layer is taken over, its original color destroyed, as the vegetation, penetrating deeper, reaches the pedicle. By now the propagation is more rapid, the rot passing from one zone to another, indistinctly, until the whole of the fruit has been devoured . . ."

It is not known what her findings were, exactly—she was not a specialist in the material like Marie d'Arconville—though her unpublished posthumous papers have led you to think that the essay on putrefaction by the Scottish anthropologist Bruce Monro—anonymously translated into French—is entirely her work. You've been compiling a list that you started in Arles, of articles, drawings and books she may have had a part in or authored herself.

One such drawing—you find it, at last, among your notes—comes from Jean-Marc Bourgereau's study on the manipulation of cadaver bodies, *De l'utilisation des noeuds coulants ou desserrés dans la manipulation des corps pour dissection.* (You made a copy of it using the library's scanner.) The woodcut depicts a rope passing underneath the jaw and across the zygomatic arches to the top of the head and knotted in such a way that it functions as a pulley, allowing the cadaver to be raised or lowered, turned over or under, as needed. A version of the method was used by Vesalius himself in his public dissection of the Swiss murderer Karrer von Gebweiler at the University of Basel in 1543.

"You look terrible," Bérengère says when she sees you. Her expression is pitying. Already, you regret letting her in.

"I ran into one of your classmates this afternoon," she goes on. "She said that you weren't at the TD. She really seemed worried about you. Noémie, is it?"

"Aurélie."

"Right, right." Bérengère starts to shoulder off her coat, and you observe her taking in the papers strewn about on the floor, the books scattered everywhere, the abandoned plates of food. "She said that you made one of your classmates quit the class." Bérengère gives you a look, eyebrows raised. "What's going on? Are you avoiding me?"

"As you can see, I've been busy."

"I called you several times."

"I'm sorry," you say, pretending to study the notes in front of you. "I must not have heard the phone." And then, because you can't help yourself, you ask, "How is your friend with the scarf?"

"What? Oh. Him. A former client . . ."

You sense her coming closer and resist the urge to look up from the sentence you've been reading in a loop.

". . . I took notes for him, a cinema-studies course at Censier." Her scent—the familiar harshness, the faint tang of cigarettes—reaches you. "If you're cross with me," she goes on, in a different tone, "I'd appreciate you saying so."

"I'm not cross, but I need to know. About the art student."

Puzzled silence, at first. Then:

"The necrophile? Is *that* what this is about?"

You put down the notes and look directly at her. The hollow between her left and right clavicles, where the skin shines as if polished, is covered with light freckles. Directly above it is the hyoid, connected to the body solely by ligament and muscle without direct articulation to another bone.

"You didn't recognize him at the café."

Bérengère shakes her head. "Should I have? You don't really think . . . ?"

She thinks about it for a moment.

"To be honest, I can't even remember what he looked like. Did *he* recognize me?"

"I don't know," you say, which is the truth, and she looks both relieved and, it seems to you, a little disappointed.

As she's leaving, she looks back at you from the open doorway. She seems about to say something, before finally changing her mind.

The red and blue serpents of her tattoo appear to pulse faintly in the light of the corridor. To you, they always represented blood flowing in both directions, to and from the heart, like love being given and received.

You didn't tell her that you're going to the dissection room tonight. It's not as though you owe her an explanation.

So why do you feel guilty about it?

The lights are on, but there's no one in sight. You walk past the rows of cadavers, your footfalls abnormally loud against the tiles. At a glance, the bodies appear untouched, not yet cut open, but it's an illusion, of course. Closer scrutiny reveals the incision lines, the telltale flaps of skin covering up organs, and muscles stuffed hastily back inside by students eager to leave.

As you approach the table where she lies, you realize that you're holding your breath.

The gauze, when you pull on it, gives way easily, as though it had only hastily been wrapped the last time. You stop and look around the room. You are alone. No one but you and her. You remove the remaining length of gauze, then take a step back.

Her eyes are open. Her mouth is open. Lips. Tongue. Teeth. Small, even rows discolored by the formaldehyde. She appears slightly surprised at finding herself on a stainless-steel table in the fifth-floor dissection room of the main building at René Descartes. A filmy layer covers her gaze like a cataract, a secondary effect of the embalming fluid in her veins, which has replaced the blood that once ran through them. Surprisingly, her hair is intact, as if she died only yesterday. For the first time, you see that the body you are dissecting belongs to a female of Asian extraction. Up to this point, you assumed she was European. Or, more precisely, you didn't think about it at all.

You know nothing about her, though you've held her heart and lungs in your hands, made numerous diagrams in your lab notebook. Her internal organs are almost as familiar to you as the shape of your hands or your reflection in a mirror. You know her heart infinitely better than your own, which you will never see, much less touch. All the same, you have never felt it, this heart of hers, beat even once.

Behind you. You hear something and turn around. The individual lights over the other cadavers are dark, and of the ones at the farthest tables you can make out only a dim outline. You don't immediately notice the human shape, which at first you took for one of the coffins leaning against the wall. He must have been standing there, watching you, all this time.

"The preserving agents weren't applied properly during the embalming," he says. "The absence of formalin in her veins is what gave her body the appearance, if not of life, then of something else altogether. You know what I mean, don't you? It's funny, but after a while I even grew to like the smell that bothered Fréd so much . . ." He starts unhurriedly towards you. "Once the stomach is opened, the odor will become a lot worse. They will have no choice but to take her away."

As you watch him make his way between the tables, you are reminded of the first day of lab when he left the dissection room. You see him again: putting down the scalpel, murmuring, I'm sorry. The words weren't for any of you; he was talking to *her*.

"Sooner or later," Blaise says, "I knew you'd come."

"I only came to look over some things," you say, and he smiles, faintly.

"Thank you. For what you did in lab."

"I didn't do it for you."

"No, you did it"—he nods at the gauze in your hands—"because you've started to have feelings for her."

For some reason, you find yourself thinking about Bérengère, and the way she looked back at you from the doorway before leaving.

"I haven't been able to forgive myself for taking a saw to her," he goes on. "I tell myself that she can't feel it, but . . ."

You remember the marks, as though from knotted ropes used as pulleys, reminiscent of Bourgereau's sliding-knot method.

"It was you. You put her on her stomach the first day of lab, before any of us got to the dissection room, didn't you? You knew her. That's the real reason you're in the anatomy course."

Blaise reaches over and takes the gauze from you. "I didn't want the others to see her yet. I wanted her to myself . . . a little while longer."

He meets your gaze, and for a moment it's as if he has opened you up, taken you apart and put you back together, piece by piece. Then the moment passes. You watch him cover her up again. Afterwards, you stand there with him, contemplating the body, whose face is once again hidden.

"If you want," he says, "I can tell you who she was."

Blaise lives in a garret studio near the Gare du Nord, a busy little street on the edge of the Indian quarter. There is only one window—a small swivel frame giving onto the neighboring rooftops—propped open to let in the night air. You hear the distant roar of a motor, a gust of laughter from the street below. On the floor are plastic cartons filled with hardback sleeves, the kind used to carry sketches. The walls are covered not with anatomical drawings but ideograms—Japanese or Chinese, you can't tell—and in the brushstrokes you almost recognize the curve of a shoulder, a bent elbow, an ear . . . The shriek of a kettle brings you to yourself. Blaise is standing before the stove, his back to the room. You return to the calligraphies, which share the wall with pencil and charcoal drawings of insects, mostly scarabs and moths. All of them appear to be dead, all of them except one. Your gaze is drawn to the insect shaped like a glowing pill capsule.

"Fireflies are one of the few insects not repelled by the solvents in embalming fluid," Blaise says, behind you. He hands you a steaming cup. "Oolong," he murmurs.

You ask him if she was here, in this apartment, and he nods, a faraway look in his eyes.

The thought of standing where she stood, of seeing what she saw, sends a shiver through you. "How did she die?"

It seems like he's not going to answer, but then he looks at you and says, "She killed herself."

You should leave. You have no business here. But you don't leave. To show him you're fine, you take a sip, swallowing the hot, bitter taste, not taking your eyes off him. You are wondering if he might have put something in the tea when he says, "Her name was Fumiko. We were in the same drawing class. One day, she asked me to draw her hands."

On reflex, you look down at his hands, then back up at his face. You feel a queasiness in your chest. "Her hands," you repeat, buying yourself time. "Did you draw them?"

"I drew every part of her body. I got to know her as no one else has, or ever will. Not even her mother. If I close my eyes, I can reconstruct her entire body, every square centimeter of it, from memory."

You are close enough to smell the soap he uses, or his aftershave. A masculine odor. You take a step backwards, and in doing so bump into one of the cartons, knocking it over. Immediately, Blaise is down on his knees, picking up the hardback sleeves scattered at your feet. At the sight of the loose-leaf sheets, your pulse quickens. He selects a portfolio and spreads it open right there on the floor. After a moment, you sit down next to him. He starts to go through the drawings, wordlessly, as though you weren't there. Many are rough sketches, barely begun before they were interrupted, abandoned. One, the silhouette of a hand, looks like it was traced around her real hand. "The hand is typical of the mind," your prof said to the class on the first day. "The material will of the immaterial spirit." Blaise doesn't stop you when you lean over and place your own hand—with a dull slap—over the drawing, obscuring the original outline. You look up, daring him to do something, say something.

Blaise makes as if to reach for your hand—perhaps to lift it off the paper—and, reflexively, you can't help but recoil. In silence, the two of you stare at each other. You are aware of your heart beating inside your chest. Abruptly, he excuses himself. A moment later, you hear him in the bathroom running the tap. This is as good a time as any to make your exit, but you remain sitting where you are, unable to decide if the outline in front of you is really of her hand. You try to imagine the hand of the cadaver in the dissection lab superimposed over it. You are not sure how many drawings you leaf through—of hands, shoulder blades, napes of necks, hollows of hips—before it dawns on you that the bodies you are seeing no longer belong to a single person. The lines are more precisely defined, like anatomy notes, though nothing is labeled. The bodies are from different women of varying ages and builds—only women, no men, as though he never drew them. As though he was practicing. You are not sure if they are all from the same class, or from several classes over multiple semesters. The last drawing you come to makes you cry out. As with all the others, he didn't draw the head, but the pose, the proportions, the curves—you're sure it's Bérengère you're looking at, her nakedness you are seeing. The same nakedness you've thought about but never fully glimpsed outside of your most troubled fantasies. Bérengère, or her headless body anyway, split open down the middle like a book, each layer of fascia and muscle peeled back, revealing the organs, wet and red and alive. That's when you realize that you can no longer hear the water through the bathroom door. You wait, but Blaise doesn't come out, and you are convinced that he is standing on the other side of the door, listening. You finally call out his name, then say, "I know it was you in my courtyard the other night. You followed me home, didn't you?"

No answer.

"Did she really kill herself?"

You hear the lock turn and the door opens slightly. You see him, or his eye, peering at you through the gap. The eye is red, as though from crying. Behind him, you see something floating inside a shallow tray. Something dark and fragile and slender.

"I didn't kill her," he says. "I was in love with her."

"OK," you say.

"If you thought I had something to do with her death, why did you come back here with me?"

"I don't know." Perhaps he was right. Perhaps you really were in love with Fumiko, or with her body, her most secret organs. She let you know her in a way that no one else ever has or ever will, in a way that you will never know yourself.

"What are you doing with that?" he asks, and you look down to find that you are still holding the drawing of Bérengère.

"One of the models you drew, I know her. This is her." Or you think it is. After all, you've never seen her without her clothes.

"Take it," he says. "I have others."

"Hey, wait," you start to say, but he's shut the door again. From the other side, you hear him cough, a small, forlorn sound. For a moment longer you stand there, then go to put the drawing back where you found it, with the other headless corpses. A pair of slippers in the corner, too small to belong to Blaise, catches your eye. Staring at the foot-shaped outline left on the rubbery surface, you try to imagine her in the apartment, the muffled sound of her footfalls as she wanders from room to room in the half-darkness. But like the beat of her imaginary heart, it sounds wrong to you. It is not *your* Fumiko, the one whose body you are dissecting at the moment. Tomorrow, during lab, this is what you will do: Starting at the base of the thorax, you will make a long, clean incision down the midline, then another incision perpendicular to it, through the pubis. Then you will open the abdominal skin, like a book, to reveal a layer of fascia covering the abdominal muscles.

"I'll see you in lab," you call out to him, and, despite yourself, it comes out as a question. You've already turned to leave when you hear his voice through the closed door, coming to you as though from very far away:

"No, you won't. It's just you and her now."

Is It Still You?

Up close, the dead look like the dead; from afar,
they look like themselves.
—Marcel Moiré

I woke in the dark convinced that she was trying to tell me something from the other side. My gaze fell on the clock's glowing red digits at the precise moment they went from 4:59 to 5:00, and it seemed to me a sign, like the oscillations of a swinging door telling me that someone had passed through it only moments earlier. Though she was gone, I couldn't help but think that she hadn't really left; I could still feel her presence in the city. At the Louvre—especially on the first Monday of the month, when admission was free for everyone—I sometimes saw her silhouette among the people standing in the winding queue that disappeared into the Pyramid.

My waking hours were spent asking myself why she had done it, when I wasn't trying to avoid the question altogether. It was only now starting to sink in that I hadn't really known her at all, during the year we had shared at our university residence. She had rarely talked about her life in Japan, and I didn't even know the name of her hometown. I remembered her once telling me that there was nothing worse than having light-colored hair, for a Japanese girl. It was one of the few times she had brought up her past. In high school, a classmate had hair that turned brown in the summer, and the school forced her to dye it black to conform to the dress code. It was after Fumiko noticed that the girl was losing her hair (due, no doubt, to the harsh chemicals of the dye) that she suddenly stopped coming to class, before showing up again, her hair back to normal—thick and full—except that it wasn't her hair but a wig. Years later, Fumiko was still convinced that her classmate had become completely bald and was hiding it to save face.

As the room grew progressively brighter, I watched a bar of light make its way across the wall. I knew it was moving, but no matter how hard I concentrated I couldn't see its movement. It was nearly seven when I finally got up. After the cramped quarters of the Cité U, I hadn't yet adjusted myself to my new living space, and I often found myself reflexively ducking my head or cutting short a gesture in anticipation of a wall that wasn't there. On the other hand, not yet used to the sloped ceiling, I had bumped into it several times already. The room was a garret, with only one window, which opened outwards (like older panes in Denmark) so that I was able to lean over and touch my own roof. I had a view of the nearby buildings with their chimney stacks and parabolas and antennas, and if I craned my neck a little, I could even see part of the street corner.

Just before leaving, I paused at the window and—on an impulse—tried to see what I could of the street below, and my heart almost stopped. There she was, positioned within the sliver of a view, as though she'd known exactly where to stand on the sidewalk. Fumiko. She was just standing there, her face expressionless, wearing a bright-blue corduroy jacket, a yellow scarf wound around her neck. Her short hair looked wet and black, though it could have been the morning light falling on it at a certain angle.

My first impulse was to run outside, but that meant hurrying down four flights of stairs, traversing the hall d'entrée, then the porte cochère . . . Split between keeping her in sight and running after her, I found myself unable to move, unable to decide on a course of action. As the seconds ticked by, I started to sweat. Finally, I tore my gaze away and distanced myself from the window. By the time I reached the ground floor, having nearly tripped and fallen several times, I was in a lamentable state, gasping and cursing. *For helvede, fanden! Satans pis!* In situations like this, it was my Danish that came out, old grammar-school curses, invectives scrawled on lavatory walls . . .

The street corner was empty. I leaned over, hands braced on my knees, and caught my breath. What exactly had I seen? A ghost? An apparition? A remanent image from a dream? I turned and looked up at my garret window, half expecting to find Fumiko gazing down at me, but there was no one there.

A few minutes later, I entered the Gare du Nord through the street-level elevator. As I stepped into the glass cabin, a woman hurried in after me while the doors were closing. Asian, with pale skin and black hair cut so short the follicles stood upward, porcupine-like—she looked nothing like Fumiko, but I found myself stealing glances at her, almost despite myself. She was dressed all in black, with black-painted nails; even her earrings were made of some kind of black stone that gleamed dully in the light. I followed her out of the elevator, then watched her disappear down the stairs that led to the platforms of the RER trains. For several moments, I felt an overwhelming urge to keep following her, if only to find out where she was headed. Around me, some people were in a hurry, and others loitered around for who knows what. Station announcements echoed off the walls, about pickpockets or abandoned baggages (one scenario almost refuting the other). I heard the familiar four notes of the SNCF. Frozen in indecision, I continued to stand there while, below me, I heard the sound of the train pulling in, the brakes squealing and grating. If I ran down the stairs, I could still get on before it was too late, I started to tell myself, before I snapped out of my stupor. What was I doing? I had somewhere to be, important business at the other end of the city. Turning away from the stairs, like someone suddenly coming to a decision (if anyone was watching through the nearby security camera), I headed towards the foot tunnel connecting to La Chapelle and the 2 Line of the métro, a passage so winding and interminable that, each time, it seemed to me that I would come out on the other side to find myself already at my destination.

I joined the stream of morning commuters, dwelling on what I had seen—or thought I had seen—from my window. The clothes she'd had on, the blue corduroy jacket and yellow scarf, puzzled and troubled me. She had never owned a blue corduroy jacket (I was less sure about the yellow scarf); it seemed strange that my subconscious should invent new articles of clothing, an outfit I had never seen her wear, rather than reconstruct something from existing memories. That said, it was certainly an outfit I could imagine her wearing (she had been fond of corduroy). Could I have glimpsed the jacket-and-scarf combination somewhere, at some point, on a faceless mannequin in the display window of one of the clothing shops at the Forum des Halles?

While thinking this, I let my gaze fall on the people walking alongside me. Most were badly and carelessly dressed—cheap-looking clothes, mismatched colors—the usual morning crowd of commuters. I scrutinized everyone, as though I might find the answer to the mystery of Fumiko's blue jacket and yellow scarf in the sea of drab ensembles and low-quality threads. Parts of the tunnel were under construction, and I walked past piles of gravel or bricks that looked like they could have been there for weeks or months. They had stripped the walls, bun-kerlike now, though I seemed to recall the tiles covering them being in perfect condition; at the same time, the ceiling, which had seen better days, was untouched: no sign of a renovation or even a cleaning. I stopped in front of a stretch of temporary siding that had been placed in front of a wall that had been knocked down. Through a gap between two pieces of siding, I was able to make out a dimly lit corridor with bare, unfin-ished walls. Just then, I felt someone bump me as he passed by. Jostled out of my reverie, I turned away from the wall and continued walking. My destination was at the western edge of the city, where the Dauphine campus was located, not far from the Bois de Boulogne. The 2 Line would take me there, no need to change trains. The exam wasn't for an-other two hours, but I liked to be early for things. Lately, I had grown increasingly afraid of arriving late, of missing something, and I always made a point of leaving my place much earlier than necessary, in order to prepare for any and all contingencies.

The morning rush had just ended, and the platform was mostly empty. A few scattered people stood around or were seated on the orange bucket seats. Above their heads, a poster proclaimed, in a pastiche of La Fontaine: "The one who leap-frogs over a turnstile / During a ticket check won't have a smile." On the ground, a copy of the free weekly newspaper, already tattered from being continually trampled, fluttered halfheartedly every now and then. Near the mouth of the tun-nel was a one-legged man on crutches. The empty leg of his pants had been cut halfway off and tied closed. He was standing very close to the edge of the platform and peering around the corner into the tunnel, as if impatient for the train to arrive. I breathed in the hot, dry air of the métro, with its unmistakable "buttery" odor, which had always puzzled me, if only because no one else seemed to understand what I was talking about. (I had first noticed it upon arriving in Paris three years ago.) When the train came slowly, almost reluctantly to a stop, I got on, then stuck my head out to glance at the man with one leg, but he was no longer there, at the far end of the platform. For several seconds I remained like that, thinking . . . Had he boarded the train, or . . . ? I sat down on one of the pull-down seats and tried to forget about the one-legged man. If he hadn't gotten on the train he must have gone back up the stairs, surely. I let my mind wander as we traversed the eighteenth arrondissement: Anvers . . . Pigalle . . . Blanche . . . Place de Clichy . . . I found oddly comforting the sound of the train as it sped through the tunnel, its metal wheels grinding against the rails like a knife blade against a spinning whetstone. Gradually, I became aware of another sound, out of sync and increasingly difficult to ignore. I felt myself start awake. COURCELLES, the large white-on-blue letters read. I heard heavy, labored breathing and glanced around. By then, the compartment was completely empty except for another passenger in the corner sitting with his back to me. I could only see the back of his head, but I was certain it was the man from the platform. The thought of him leaning heavily on his crutches and hopping laboriously from wagon to wagon while I slept, the thought of him pausing in front of me to catch his breath, swaying slowly on his crutches, was enough to make my flesh prickle. Listening to his raspy and guttural respiration, I expected him, any moment now, to turn around in his seat. Then I would know for sure. I waited, with a mixture of dread and longing. There was no way he could see me without turning around, and yet I couldn't help thinking that his gaze was already on me. After a while, the tension in the compartment was such that I had to get off, though there were still two more stations until the terminus, Porte Dauphine.

Once outside, I took several deep breaths. The more I thought about it, the less it made sense to me. What was there to fear from a man with one leg on crutches? The streets here were completely deserted, not a soul in sight, everything immaculately maintained, light-years from the Gare du Nord with its chaos and bustle, its trash-strewn gutters. Many of the residences I passed had service entrances (at the bottom of some somber steps) and a number of them housed embassies, according to the plaques next to the black wrought-iron gates: KAZAKHSTAN . . . POLDAVIA . . . ESTOTILAND . . . CAMBODIA . . . It was impossible to tell if they were open to the public. Their imposing black doors seemed like portals to a world I knew nothing about, a world forever beyond my reach, like a scene in a painting.

That said, even in such a neighborhood I still came across the inevitable dog droppings. They really were everywhere. By now I had become a past-master at avoiding them—guided by an inner radar that warned me of their presence—and in all my years I had never stepped on a single piece of excrement. I turned onto a smaller street lined with tall, ornate buildings in the Haussmannian style. I looked up and saw someone, a housekeeper, draping a large rug over the railing of a balcony. At that moment, the woman paused in her work, and I wondered if she had spotted me. It was impossible, from where I stood, to distinguish her individual features. Perhaps she also felt what I felt, that the very fact of my presence here was something of a spatiotemporal anomaly.

I had no idea where I was going, or if I was walking in

the right direction. The exam wasn't for another hour—still plenty of time. I was continuing to make my way down the street, not thinking about anything in particular, when I noticed someone ahead of me. My attention was drawn to her hair, the top half of which was gray, the bottom half a reddish brown—as though she had colored her hair at some point and then let the roots grow out. The combination of the gray and the reddish brown, one below the other, like colors in a Rothko painting, was eye-catching, I had to admit, especially on this bright spring day. The rest of her appearance was not in any way remarkable. From the back, it was hard to ascertain her exact age, though I would have guessed at least sixty or seventy, judging by the gray of her hair.

I'm not sure how long I had been walking behind her when it occurred to me that I might be following her. Or was I simply walking behind her because she was ahead of me? I could walk faster and overtake her—it wouldn't be too difficult, at the pace she was going—so that *she* would have no choice but to follow *me*. For I was convinced that we were both headed in the same direction. We were both headed towards the Dauphine campus. How did I know this? I didn't, of course. In fact, I thought it rather unlikely that the woman walking in front of me, with her Rothko hair, was, like me, on her way to take the entrance exam for the school of translators and interpreters. But was it any more unlikely than seeing my dead girlfriend on the street corner below my garret window?

I was still lost, though I didn't want to admit it to myself. Thankfully, I had plenty of time to wander around and avoid dog droppings at my leisure. If I was going to waste half an hour or more, this wasn't a bad neighborhood to do it in. I imagined myself calling out to her: the distance between us would have obliged me to raise my voice. It might be unpleasant, even a little frightening, to be shouted at by a complete stranger on a deserted street, despite the sun shining above our heads and the fact that we were in what was considered a "posh" area of the city. I looked at my watch. There was still time. I picked up my pace a little, diminishing the distance between us a bit. Now I could see that the bag she was carrying contained grocery items, a head of lettuce, several carrots, the smooth skin of a tomato. My heart sank. Could she really be headed for the Dauphine campus with that? Far more likely that she was returning home after marketing somewhere nearby. What had possessed me to think otherwise? I looked at my watch again and felt the first glimmerings of panic. I continued to walk behind the woman, but with each step I felt my legs growing heavier. A part of me wanted nothing more than to stop following her, but I was afraid that she might really be headed for the Dauphine campus, in which case any other direction would be the wrong direction. I could run up to her and ask her if she was going to the school for translators and interpreters, but that was the one thing I would never do. Nearing an intersection, I suddenly noticed that the woman was no longer in front of me, and that, at the same time, there was a sign up ahead indicating the direction to the Dauphine campus. All along, I had been on the right path.

The modern-looking buildings, the esplanade, the bicycles— all of it reminded me of my old faculty at Amager, in Copenhagen. The school for translators and interpreters occupied the second floor. I stood in line with the other applicants, French and foreigners alike, and when it was my turn I handed the woman behind the desk my papers. As I did so, it struck me that the last person who had touched my passport was Fumiko.

One day, she had shown me her passport, and I had taken mine out for her to see, remarking to her as I did so that we had come to France from two completely different places, but our passports were the same color. She had come to my room (for some reason, we never went to hers) with a brick of cassis juice and served it in cups so small they could only have been shot glasses. She'd bought the cups by mistake at Auchan not long after arriving in France. I told her to return them, but she refused, saying that she had once tried to return something, a pot holder, and was sent from one part of the store to another by the customer-service personnel; it had taken her two hours to find someone who finally told her that she could exchange the pot holder only for the exact same pot holder. That afternoon, in my room, she pointed out that, in fact, our passports were not quite the same color: mine was slightly lighter, like the color of our hair (hers, she declared, was slightly darker). As the woman behind the desk leafed through the pages of my passport, frowning at my photo, then at the Danish coat of arms on the cover, then at my photo again, as though comparing the two against each other, it was all I could do not to reach over and snatch the thing out of her hands.

The exam was held in the main auditorium, and I chose a seat next to the middle aisle, halfway up the rows—the same spot I would have chosen for myself in a cinema. From my vantage point I could take in everything below me at a glance, and as the minutes went by I watched the rows around me gradually fill up. That was when I noticed, to my left, a familiar head of gray/reddish-brown hair. As soon as I saw her, it seemed to me that the long walk through the sixteenth arrondissement had been a dream. Or rather, all of it had been real—the deserted streets, the service entrances, the embassies—all of it except her. And yet here she was, only a few rows away from

me. There was something in Danish folklore, a spirit capable
of taking on a human appearance and preceding its victim to a
location, but for the life of me I couldn't remember the name.
It was there, on the tip of my tongue . . .

Even if I hadn't run into her earlier, in the street, and
even if her hair had been less bizarre looking, I would
have noticed her, for she was by far the oldest person in the
auditorium.

During the break, I was in line for the toilet when I felt a
presence at my side. I turned to find her, the woman from
earlier, standing next to me. Seeing her up close, I realized
that she must be in her seventies, if not even older. I found
myself staring at her, unable to turn away. Despite her lined,
weathered face, there was something delicate and birdlike
about her.

"On the street earlier," she said, "you called out to me,
didn't you?"

"Pardon?"

She lowered her voice: "There are more lavatories upstairs."

I stared at her.

"Come with me," she said, walking away, and I could
sense from her gait the tacit but full expectation that I would
follow her, which, after glancing at the people ahead of me,
I did. We went up the stairs, the two of us side by side—I
made an effort not to walk behind her—and glancing down
at her bag, I saw that it contained not vegetables but books
and papers, and a yellowed newspaper. Suddenly, she stopped
and looked up at me.

"Well? Don't you need to use the toilet?"

"Yes, yes, of course. Thank you."

Inside, the facilities were very clean. And completely empty. No sign of a graffiti anywhere. When I came back out, she was gazing out the window at the esplanade below. I noticed several ornate rings on her fingers, each ring a different color.

"Few come to the third floor," she said, turning to me. "The library is here. Not much to look at, and the books are outdated, but it's a good place to work. No one will interrupt us. We can talk there."

She started walking, not glancing back to see if I was behind her.

"I didn't call out to you in the street!" I protested, following her down the corridor. As soon as the words were out of my mouth, it seemed to me that I had admitted to something else: that I had been *thinking* about calling out to her. In general, I was loath to approach strangers in the street, even to ask for directions, and in the past I had wandered around, lost, on more than one occasion, rather than seek help from passersby. It was my Danish upbringing, I suppose.

"I was lost, yes, and I saw you in front of me," I went on, not liking the plaintive note in my voice. I was sure I hadn't called out to her. In any case, calling out to someone was not something done unconsciously, like mistyping a letter or worrying a loose thread on a sweater or a blanket. It would have required a concentrated effort, a drawing out of the lungs, a physical exertion—hardly something one could do without being fully aware of it.

We came to the end of the corridor and entered the library. She led me past the shelves and stopped at a table in the corner. A thin layer of dust covered everything. On the opposite wall hung a clock whose hands were stopped at 4:22. We seemed to be the only ones there. "Sit down," she said.

Once we were facing each other across the table, she started talking.

"At first, I thought it was my husband, who's been dead for some time now. When I turned around, there was no one there." She let a silence pass. "And then, earlier today, when I heard you tell the woman at the desk that you were registering as a two-language student, I recognized your voice. It was *you* who had called out to me."

"But I didn't . . ."

"Despite what you may think, I still have all of my mind. Don't be fooled by my age. Even as a child, I heard things. Voices, conversations. Like putting my ear up against a wall. The funny thing is, I hear them less often now than when I was younger. So when someone addresses me, I *listen*."

I thought about Fumiko, and what I had seen this morning. The old woman across from me heard things that hadn't been said and I saw people who weren't there. We were made for each other.

She went on: "You and I are not like the others taking the entrance exam. Most of them are coming from an applied-languages degree. It's much easier to do three languages than two. They simply have to translate *into* French, whereas two-language students have to translate in both directions. We're also graded on a different point system."

"Are we the only ones?" I asked.

"There are also three-language students pursuing an economics specialization who are graded differently."

She had misunderstood me, but I let it go at that.

"Having two languages rather than three," she went on, "is the surest sign that one has fallen into translation rather than chosen, from the outset, to specialize in it. Are you sure you want to do this? Translating into your B language is harder than you imagine. Much harder than translating into your own language."

Little did she suspect that English wasn't my language (though it had, for almost as long as I could remember, existed alongside my Danish).

"It's not a whim for me," I told her.

"No, I didn't think it was."

I was about to ask her why she had brought me here, to the library, when she suddenly stood up.

"Our break is almost over. We should go back downstairs."

"Read the whole thing first, then underline any words you don't know. Cross out what you can't figure out from context. Try to translate the sentence without using those words. They tend to take off fewer points for omissions than for mistranslations."

That was what she had told me before we parted ways in the common lounge, which was shared by the different faculties. Students sat around in scattered groups, talking and smoking, despite the prominent no-smoking sign. I was tempted to point out that an omission was itself a mistranslation, but I said nothing. It was the prospect of dealing, for a change, with someone else's thoughts—and temporarily escaping mine—that had drawn me to translation. My very fate depended on my admission to the school of translators and interpreters. As she walked away, I found myself wondering if she had already taken the entrance exam in the past. She seemed to know her way around a little too well, and yet, at the same time, I couldn't help but feel that she didn't belong here at all, just as a ghost no longer belongs to the place he continues to haunt.

During the exam, I followed her advice, crossing out any words that I couldn't figure out, translating what was around them, and in doing so the meaning, more than a few times, revealed itself to me. (A sentence from a book I'd read, then forgotten, came to me: "*La mort brillait par son absence.*") When it was over, I sought her out among the students outside the auditorium, but she had already finished her exam and left. I went so far as to go up to the third floor, which was no longer empty—there were even a few people sitting at the tables in the library—as though we had been there during a momentary lull in activity. I dreaded returning to my silent apartment, finding everything exactly as I had left it—window open, the rooms plunged in darkness—but it had been a grueling day, and I was exhausted. In any case, I had nowhere else to go. The results would be mailed out in June, which seemed impossibly far away. I wondered if I would ever see her again. I didn't know her name and she hadn't asked for mine.

In the declining light, I walked to the subway station, the one I would have gotten off at if I hadn't lost my sang-froid. It wasn't far from the Dauphine campus. Though the evening rush had started, the platform was completely deserted. I seemed to be the only one waiting for the train. Where was everyone? Then I remembered: I was at the terminus. I had dawdled too long, and my fellow exam takers had all gone home by now. I made my way to the far end of the platform where the tunnel started. Standing near the edge, I leaned forward a little and peered into the shadows, as I had seen the man with one leg do earlier. Sometimes, if the tunnel was straight and short enough, it was possible to make out the distant lights of the next (or previous) station. But this being the end (or beginning) of the line, there was nothing to see, no station glowing in the distance. Beyond a certain point, it was hard to make out anything at all. The darkness stretched away forever, like time itself.

A cramped and cluttered room at the Cité U, across the street from the RER station. At night, when the traffic dies down, I can hear the slow, familiar hiss of the train pulling in. Lying next to me in the dark, she somehow knows to position herself at the outermost edge of my view so that I have to turn my head to see her. But it doesn't matter, I know she's there.

I felt something, a sudden chill. I glanced around, but there was no one else on the platform. Everything looked the same as it had a moment ago. For several long minutes, I remained without moving, overcome by a sort of tremulous longing. Ever since her death, I had been unable to shake the idea that I was waiting for something. Some kind of sign. A message. At the same time, I worried that when she finally sent me one, I wouldn't know how to interpret it. Anything could be a message, but most things weren't. There was a little ritual we had, something she used to say to me in the morning after spending the night in my room. Turning her back to me, she would ask, "Is it still you?" To which I would always answer—like someone giving a code word—"It's still me."

II

BEFORE FUMIKO

Paris Is a Party, Paris Is a Ghost

1. The Mirror

She was the star pupil, extroverted, the teacher's favorite; I was in my third year, unsure of myself, my life and everything in between. I met her in an Ibsen module at Copenhagen University. She always sat in the front row and spent the hour diligently taking notes, or giving answers before anyone else could during the tutorial sessions. I too knew the answers but I didn't say them out loud; instead, I waited for someone else to speak. More often than not, she was that person. When she spoke, her "e," "a" and "æ" vowels were a little too crisp, a little too clean-sounding, like the *rigsdansk* of some bygone TV presenter.

We were the only Asians, two dark spots among the bright blond heads of varying shades, and I wondered if she had also been adopted by Danish parents, as was the case of most Asians in Denmark, brought up to think of themselves as Danish. The only thing Asian about us was our birth and, of course, our appearance. Over the years, I had met a number of others like me: the first when I was fourteen, during a class trip to Paris; the second in my first year of university; another was presented to me at a Friday Bar by a mutual friend; and a fourth, an adoptee from Norway, had been a *kollegium* floormate. Mette Honoré, Helle Nielsen, Mia Kjærsgaard, Unn Fahlstrøm. With each one, things had never

gone beyond the initial conversation, an exchange of back-
grounds. I hadn't given any of them much thought since our
respective encounters, but I didn't forget their names, which
all belonged to Korean-born Scandinavian girls.

At first glance, Ditte seemed to fit the same mold. On the
last day of class, I found her waiting for me in the corridor
outside the auditorium. Up to then, she had behaved as if I
wasn't there, though she must have noticed me the same way
I had noticed her. In the tone of someone who has rehearsed
her words beforehand, she asked me if I wanted to get a beer
at the cafeteria. As we walked in silence, I thought I knew
what was coming. After all, I had been through this before
with other adoptees. Like them, she was surprised when I told
her that I had been born in Japan, not Korea. I wasn't her first
adoptee, but the ones she had met thus far had been girls. I
was, in a manner of speaking, her first boy. I learned that we
had arrived in Denmark at the ages of five and six months, re-
spectively. We were both a year younger than our fellow
students, who had, in the Danish tradition, taken a sabbatical
year to work or travel.

Was she really all that different from the other Korean girls
I had met? That was what I found myself thinking, during our
third outing, as I glanced at her shadowy profile next to me in
the darkness of a cinema at Scala. Now I wonder if it wasn't
so much Ditte herself as how alike I thought we were that
drew me to her. (Or perhaps that is the essence of attraction: a
longing to see something of oneself in another.) Like looking
into an enchanted mirror: when I looked at her, I saw a Dane
who looked like me. I remember, one night, we lay facing each
other and gazed wordlessly into each other's eyes until Ditte
broke the spell by bursting into laughter. In bed, she was very
clear about what she wanted, what she didn't want, how she

felt and how she wanted to feel, with the same thoroughness she had shown in the classroom. Her scent, the consistency of her hair, the color of her nipples—everything about her was at once strange and familiar. When she told me that she had never used deodorant because she didn't have to, I knew exactly what she was talking about. I had never bought a stick of deodorant in my life, though I had carried one around and even pretended to use it, all through my upper-secondary years, so that I wouldn't stand out among the other kids at my boarding school. A look of recognition seemed to dawn in her gaze when I told her about my constant need to prove myself when meeting new people. In retrospect, I'm not sure what these shared moments of understanding and complicity meant to her. Did they mean anything at all?

We were together for almost four months, during which time we explored Copenhagen as if for the first time, with new eyes. Before, I had never noticed all the busts, bas-reliefs and other three-dimensional representations scattered throughout the city, which we baptized "the city of statues" because the statues outnumbered the inhabitants, joked Ditte. She had grown up in Esbjerg, in west Jutland, and spent part of every summer on Fanø where her parents had a summer home overlooking the Wadden Sea. I had grown up in the Whiskey Belt, just north of Copenhagen, my summers punctuated by fishing trips with my father to the Faroe Islands. She loved salted black licorice, the typical Scandinavian kind. Before bed, I would steal mine from the cabinet where my mother kept it in a glass jar shaped like a Swedish Dalecarlian horse. We both loved having *øllebrød* for breakfast; observing the sky on bright summer nights when dusk seems to go on forever; watching old Danish television dramas like *Jeg kan ikke vente til mandag!* and *Olive og Tom.*

Perhaps a part of me already knew it couldn't last, the theory of compatibility that I had constructed like scaffolding around us, and whose fragile symmetry I marveled at in secret. We were too alike, I remember thinking; it wasn't normal to be this close to someone in so short a time, like skipping to the end of a book one has been reading too fast from the start. But the mirror at last reflected someone back at me. Around that time, I had a strange dream. In it, Ditte was my sister, the two of us separated at birth, and though I knew such a thing to be impossible—my blood was Japanese, hers was Korean, after all—I woke in the dark with an erection, my heart beating like a tam-tam. I was alone in my bed; Ditte had gone back to her hall of residence at some point during the night without waking me. When we saw each other again, I made the mistake of telling her about my dream. Though I had left out the part about my erection, bewilderment and disgust clouded her face, as if I had laid bare some unspeakable fantasy. She asked me if that was how I had always seen her. The thought of an incestuous relationship with a long-lost sister had never crossed my mind, I said, but Ditte refused to believe me.

Things were never the same after that. One day, she informed me of her intention to spend the weekend in Esbjerg, where her parents still lived. We had often talked about going together, but the trip had never materialized. The following night, I received a phone call; in the background I heard voices, music, as though she was calling me from a party. She seemed distracted or irritated by something. We ended the conversation without saying goodbye. I eventually learned that she had left me for her thesis supervisor, who also happened to be my thesis supervisor. After that, I couldn't walk past certain places—the statue of Adam Oehlenschläger near the zoo in Norske Allé, the skating rink in Nørrebro Park, even the oil tanks at Prøvestenen—without being reminded of her. The worst was going to see my thesis supervisor. I couldn't be sure, but it seemed that the man had no idea. He was out of shape, dark-haired (for a blond Dane), and his chin receded a bit. Other than his vast and bottomless intelligence, his daggerlike wit, his impressive list of publications, what could she possibly see in him? And that was when I realized that I had never really known her, any more than I had known the adopted Korean girls before her. She had become a name to add to the others. All this time, I had thought of her as a mirror, a strange and beguiling reflection, but it would seem that she had been drawn to me because I was different, a change from all the Danes she had previously dated.

2. An Error of the Deutsche Bahn

My father, who had always wanted me to join him in the textile business, didn't understand why I had to go to France to study Danish literature. I explained to him that it was because I was expanding my research to English literature. To that effect, I had applied for an Erasmus grant. He was still puzzled, I could tell, the morning of my departure. Why not go to England, then? he seemed to want to ask at the station, where he had come to see me off. But England was even farther away, so what was the point in asking? His expression said it all. Nevertheless, he accepted the situation with equanimity and good faith. I think he suspected, on some level, that my departure had nothing to do with English literature or Danish literature. (I had never told him about Ditte. Was it because I thought he wouldn't understand?) He didn't say it, but I knew he was lonely since the death of my mother. At least he still had his business, which designed and manufactured high-end blankets and shawls made from Faroese wool. He was far from helpless, I told myself as my train pulled out of Copenhagen Central and his silhouette grew smaller and smaller.

I had planned to fly to Paris, but my father had insisted that I take the train, though it meant transferring to the Deutsche Bahn, whose trains used a different voltage and, consequently, a different system of fail-safes which my father considered inferior to those used in Denmark. Anything, in his eyes, was better than flying. He had started on about the superiority of electric over diesel, which led to a comparison of cab-signaling and inductive systems, the merits and shortcomings of each . . . until I finally relented and let him buy me a first-class ticket at full price. I had to switch trains in Frankfurt, and the Thalys car I boarded was empty except for a girl, who happened to be in my seat. She was gazing out the window, chin cupped in the palm of her hand and tears streaming down her face. With her short brown hair and olive-complexioned skin, she reminded me of a Velázquez I'd seen at the SMK. I chose a seat at random, a few rows away but facing her so that she remained visible to me through a gap between the seats. In that manner, I watched her as she continued to gaze, unseeing, at the passing scenery and occasionally blinked her wet eyes.

I'm not sure at what point I began to think that she might also be headed for Paris. Once the idea entered my head, it was as if I had always known. I imagined myself getting up from my seat and approaching her, striking up a conversation. The fact that she was sitting where she was took on a bright new meaning: out of all the seats, she had chosen mine. It was as if she had chosen *me*, and I would be a fool not to interpret it as a sign. Even then, I continued to sit there, unmoving. I knew myself well enough to know that I would do nothing; instead,

I would go over the pros and cons until she left the train and out of my life forever. In that manner I was silently berating myself when I felt a presence at my side: the ticket controller. I hadn't heard him enter the compartment. After examining my ticket, he informed me that I couldn't remain where I was. Despite having only a moment earlier contemplated leaving my seat, I tried to argue with him, telling him that there was plenty of room—what harm could it do that I was not in my assigned spot? But he was intractable; he ordered me to move, and waited as I reluctantly stood up and started making my way towards the girl.

Addressing her in French, I showed her my stub, which she studied as though she had never seen a train ticket before. The tears on her cheeks had dried and were impossible to make out if one didn't already know that she had been crying. Her fingernails, I couldn't help noticing, were short and square, as though she bit them regularly, and it seemed oddly appropriate that someone so beautiful should have such ugly fingernails. That was when she replied that she had been issued the same seat as me. Her voice was low and slightly hoarse. An error of the Deutsche Bahn—my father would have been delighted. I told her that if it were up to me she could remain where she was, but the controller had come by and hadn't given me a choice in the matter. As I said this, I turned to point at him, but there was no sign of the man I had just argued with. For a moment I stared at the spot where he'd been standing. Through the sliding door I could see that he wasn't in the next car, or in the car after that. It was beginning to look like I had invented him as an excuse to engage her in conversation. I was about to return to my seat (which wasn't really mine) when I heard her ask me if I planned to stand there like that for much longer: I realized that she was inviting me to join her.

"You're not French," she said as I sat down across from her.

"No," I said. On her lap was a copy of Blaise Cendrars's *Prose du Transsibérien*.

"How did you know I was French?"

"Your book?" I said, pointing, and she laughed, though of course it hadn't been the book, which until now I hadn't noticed. I wanted to tell her that I had seen her crying earlier, that I had seen the tears streaming down her cheeks as I watched like a Peeping Tom through a gap in the seats.

"The truth is," she said at last, "I don't have a ticket."

I stared at her.

"I don't usually do this kind of thing," she went on. "I had my ticket when I left for the station. Somehow I lost it, and I had no money to buy another seat. But then I told myself the controllers don't always pass through all the cars . . ."

Maybe in France they didn't. In Denmark, they went from one end of the train to the other with the ineluctability of a law of nature, even on regional trains.

"Are you German, by any chance?" she suddenly asked.

"No. Why?"

"Something about the way you talk. You remind me of someone." Then: "She was German."

I told her I was coming from Copenhagen, she told me that she had just left Amsterdam ("'Dam," she called it), and I gathered that she had experienced some kind of heartbreak of her own there—hence the tears. She told me her name and I told her mine. We talked some more. Any moment I expected Luce to return to her book, but that moment never came. She had just informed me that she was originally from the south of France and starting her first year of medicine at René Descartes, when I saw a railway employee coming from the opposite direction, and as the door slid open I saw that it was the same man I had argued with earlier. How had he managed to reach the other end of the train without walking through our compartment? Without thinking, I took out my ticket and passed it to Luce, shooting her an *appuyé* regard and nodding, as though to say, He's behind you. The controller, who had by now reached us, asked to see our tickets. There was no inflection in his voice, nothing to indicate that he remembered our earlier exchange. I saw the hesitation in Luce's eyes, but she couldn't give me back my ticket, not in front of the controller. When the latter turned to me, I stood up and told him I had gotten on without a ticket. At that moment a female voice over the speaker announced the next station (Mannheim), and we started to slow down. Conversely, everything else sped up, as in a dream, and before I knew it I was following the controller out of the compartment. Only afterwards, sitting in another Thalys headed for Paris, did I think to myself that I should have asked her for a phone number, at the very least. I didn't even know her last name. All I knew was that we were both headed in the same direction.

3. Two Korean Girls

They could have been twins, dressed in identical black peacoats, long black hair tied back in a ponytail, mismatched only in height. Their presence in Paris on this cold autumn afternoon seemed to me an aberration, an enigma. Neither spoke a word of French or even English, and it was mostly with gestures and pantomimes that I attempted to express the idea of not being Korean. (I knew better than to attempt to express the idea of being Danish.) In the end, I wasn't sure if they had understood me. It was impossible to know what they wanted. Were they in the habit of accosting random Asian-looking persons on the streets of Paris? When the shorter girl had called out to me, she had reached out a hand, and her cold fingers had brushed against mine for a brief moment. I barely knew anyone in Paris, but my first thought was to ask myself if she could be someone I had already met.

I was coming from the Sorbonne, where I had gone to pay my university fees. A woman at the secrétariat had allowed me to defer (for several weeks) the 251 euros required for tuition. In Denmark, there wouldn't have been any fees at all, and the added expense had caught me off guard. Afterwards, I had stopped at my thesis supervisor's office—as it was in the same building—but of course she wasn't there, her door closed. I had spent a few minutes on a bench outside one of the auditoriums doing nothing in particular, thinking about the empty hours ahead and how best to fill them. In front of the Sorbonne, I had watched students from the conservatoire perform something by Bach or possibly Handel, then made my way down the rue Victor-Cousin until I reached the rue Saint-Jacques. Near the entrances of Gibert Joseph and spilling out onto the sidewalk were the usual discounted books, packed so tightly in their bins that it was all but impossible to browse through them. I'd been halfheartedly walking among the tables when I noticed the girls coming towards me.

In truth, I wasn't entirely sure they were Korean—I had only the vaguest notion of what the language sounded like, and it was mostly through a process of elimination that I had ruled out Japanese and Chinese. The shorter one did all the talking while the other girl stared wordlessly at me, fixing me so intently that I wondered if she saw me at all. Unlike her partner, she was tall for an Asian girl, almost my height, and—despite what appeared to be a cold sore near her upper lip—unexpectedly beautiful. The other girl's plainness only accentuated her own lack thereof, which her shabby clothes, ragged-looking hair and cold sore couldn't fully mitigate. It might have been a combination of being stared at relent-lessly by her while the other talked at me in a language I didn't know—all of a sudden I wanted nothing more than to get away from them. As though remembering an urgent appointment, I blurted an apology in Danish and walked quickly away, all the while resisting the urge to look back, as I pictured them stand-ing there, watching me go. Only after ducking into a Paul did I finally let myself peer out the window, but from my angle I could no longer see the sidewalk. Rather than going back outside, I decided to treat myself to a *formule étudiant*—a sand-wich, a flan, a drink of my choice—which I ate at a table over-looking the street, all the while watching for a pair of black peacoats among the passersby. My meal finished, I doubled back to Gibert via an adjoining street, entering the bookstore through one of its other entrances and taking the escalator to the third level, my favorite ("French and foreign literature"). I spent the next hour happily going through first the used, then the new sections, looking for titles that weren't available at the municipal library. After a while, I started to think about the two girls and the way I had just left them in the middle of the sidewalk. What had possessed me to storm off like that? (As if I might be in some kind of danger!) Surely, they must be long gone by now. I tried to concentrate on the books, but it was no use. Finally, I gave in and made my way down the escalators to the ground floor. I walked out to the sidewalk and retraced my steps. There they were, exactly as I had left them; it was as though they hadn't moved at all. They hardly seemed surprised to see me. Breathlessly, I pointed to myself

and said my name. After some false starts and quiproquos, the
shorter girl communicated to me that she was Yun-su and her
friend—sister?—was Min-ha. Then she said something else,
another set of foreign syllables, which I realized must be the
place they were from. I hesitated, not wanting to complicate
matters further, but then I went and did it anyway: I pointed
to myself and said, "Denmark." I could only hope the name
sounded similar in their language. I said it several more times.

"Hello, Dan Mark," the shorter girl said, and I started to
correct her, but, seeing her smile falter, I quickly accepted the
hand she held out in greeting. It felt as cold as when her finger-
tips had brushed against me earlier, and I was the first to let go.
Her mismatched twin, to my surprise, also offered me her hand,
mutely, and hers was even colder, as though the two of them
had been out walking since the smallest hours of the morning. I could feel the hardness of her callused palms. The shorter
girl was holding something out to me, and I saw that it was a
slip of paper, so worn and frayed that it looked like a piece of
cloth. On it was an address, written in a typically French hand
with European-style "1"s. My classes at the Sorbonne hadn't yet
started; the only thing waiting for me was an unmade bed and a
stack of paperbacks with reinforced slipcovers from the municipal library. Suddenly, another uneventful evening seemed to me
a burden rather than a gift. Until a few days ago, I had reveled in
my solitude: eating alone at the canteen; long, exhausting walks
through the city; the pleasure of thoroughly picking my nose in
the tranquillity of my room. Other than my weekly visits to the
Crous to buy a booklet of meal tickets ("*Un carnet, s'il vous plaît*"),
I could go for days without talking to anyone. It was a change
from Copenhagen—my first time living in such a densely pop-
ulated place, and yet I had never been so alone in my life.

We left the rue Saint-Jacques and then the Latin Quarter.

Several times, I stopped to consult a map as the two girls, behind me, talked urgently amongst themselves. In the end, I was
able to find the address indicated on the paper, a nondescript
building in the Marais. Had they come here to meet someone?
Or was this where they were staying? I wondered if this was
the moment to take my leave of them. After all, I had done
my duty. Yun-su punched in the entry code and pushed open
the large door. Min-ha turned to me then, and her expression
was like an invitation. Why not? I figured. The ascending steps
looked very steep and narrow. "A gentleman never goes up the
stairs behind a woman," I had read in a novel by Hubert Mon-
teilhet, "even when she is wearing pants." The girls led me up at
least five or six flights, and didn't stop until we'd reached the
last floor, which had only one apartment. Yun-su unlocked
the door. Inside, the place was as dark as a cave: all of the shutters were lowered and the curtains drawn. As I followed them
through the unlit rooms, I had the thought that I could be
walking into a trap of some kind. They led me up a further set
of stairs, this one narrower still, and through a door so low I
nearly hit my head. The room it opened onto was smaller than
my living quarters at the Maison de Belgique. There was only
one window, about the size of an A4 sheet of paper, and a cord
dangled from the ceiling next to a bare bulb. In the corner, a
cheap-looking blanket—the kind displayed on the sidewalk
along the rue Vieille-du-Temple—had been rolled up like a
carpet. A small black crucifix hung on the wall. Other than
a valise on wheels, there was nothing else. How had they found
this wretched place? Why was the apartment below so dark,
and who was living down there if the girls lived up here? How
had they ended up in Paris in the first place? I wondered for the
nth time, and it occurred to me that I would probably never
find out.

Yun-su started to speak in a soft, droning voice, and I thought she was reading something until I saw that her eyes were closed and I understood that she was praying. Min-ha had also closed her eyes; I could make out the whiteness of their breaths. As if they were two paintings in a museum, I continued to stare at them. First Yun-su: the uneven part of her hair, her chapped lips. Then Min-ha: the skin of her eyelids, her flushed cheeks, the cold sore above her upper lip. I felt foolish, not to mention a little stupid, for not having grasped what should have been obvious from the start: they had brought me here to convert me, though neither of us spoke a common language. Finally, Min-ha opened her eyes, and I looked away. The utter hopelessness of their task made me feel sorry for them. Yun-su was leafing through a book with a black leather cover and thin, gossamer pages. She handed it to Min-ha, who started to read a passage. The intensity of her concentration was such that I could almost hear the blood pulsing at her temples. Abruptly, she stopped reading. They both turned to me as one person, and I found myself wondering if they had invited me up here or if I had invited myself, taking advantage of the language barrier to follow them up the stairs, driven by a familiar mixture of boredom and curiosity and despair.

4. The Bridge

The first person I befriended in Paris was a Swede named Joakim. He was completing his doctoral thesis on logic design (his domain, which he tried explaining to me, had something to do with "two-dimensional iterative logic"). It was his second year at the Maison de Belgique, where we were both residents. We had met in our floor's communal kitchen—he had guessed that I was Danish from the way I pronounced my "t"s—and after discovering that we liked to eat at around the same time, we began to prepare our meals together, a Dano-Swedish (or Swedo-Danish) collaboration not unlike the bridge that connected Copenhagen to the Skåne region of southern Sweden (which had once belonged to Denmark). Back home, it might have been harder to ignore the mild but omnipresent aura of competition originating from centuries of rivalry, not to mention a long and prolific succession of wars waged, most of the time, for no particular reason; but here, as the only Scandinavians among the Belgians and the French in our residence hall, one might say that we felt something like a bond between us.

Or so I thought.

Right off the bat, there was the question of how we would address each other. With Norwegians, it was customary for me to Norwegify my Danish, bending my accent and favoring cognates whenever possible, the understanding being that my interlocutor would do the same—i.e., Danify his Norwegian, as a matter of politeness more than anything else, given that Norwegian and Danish were practically the same language. (One of my father's friends had been in Denmark for forty years and continued to speak Norwegian to everyone.) With Swedes—especially if it was a superior—I sometimes spoke Swedish, which I happened to know better than most Danes, thanks to my school years in Sweden. Otherwise, I spoke Danish—Swedifying it, of course. This was what I did with Joakim, who in turn Danified his Swedish.

Every night in the communal kitchen, we continued to cook our meals together. For a while, we got along well, chatting late into the night, about the typical things one talks about in the first weeks in a new city: school, home, France, the differences and similitudes between the three. To be honest, I'm not entirely sure what we were discussing when Joakim made his remark about the lakes in Sweden. Thinking back on it, I wonder if he might have taken exception to my observation that Sweden boasted the highest number of unsolved crimes in Scandinavia (never mind that the figure was almost certain to be lower than the murder rate in Paris alone). In any case, what he said was: "It's what happens when you let everyone in." Then: "All the same, I shouldn't forget how much smaller Denmark is." Before adding: "And to think that there are lakes in Sweden larger than your country . . ."

And that was how it started. Back in Denmark, I had never been much interested in football and found the very practice of watching a sport puzzling at best. Now, for the first time in my life, my show of nationalism was, I realized, entirely sincere. It felt strange not to have to pretend for once; I finally understood the fervor of my classmates each time the national team faced off against Sweden. The possibility that Joakim might consider me less Danish than he considered himself Swedish—that he might allow himself to say things he would not have said to a blond-haired Dane—had the effect of making me feel *more* Danish, which of course made him seem, in turn, even more Swedish. Was this what every football fan went through during a match?

Sometimes, residents from our floor would walk in on us arguing, Joakim in his Danified Swedish and me in my Swedified Danish. We had by then moved on to other subjects: Danish vacationers buying up property in Skåne (because it was cheaper), Swedes stocking up on alcohol in Copenhagen to take back to Sweden, Danes going to Stockholm for prostitutes, Swedes going to Christiania for drugs, Danes being unwilling to take in refugees, Swedes taking in refugees for the wrong reasons (i.e., a guilty conscience). One evening, I found a feast for two set out on the table and Joakim waiting with what I thought was a tight Swedish smile of satisfaction. He told me, as I sat down, that it was silly to go on the way we had. He added that he had always been against the Sweden Democrats and people like Jimmie Åkesson. There were cabbage rolls, beef patties à la Lindström, slices of jellied veal, even some *surströmming*, which he informed me was a Norrland specialty. That night, we talked politics, each of us trying to outdo the other in progressiveness. I went so far as to posit myself as the product of my parents' "progressive" decision to adopt from outside of Denmark, adding, for good measure, that Carl Th. Dreyer had been adopted. Things might have gone on in that manner, with each of us trying to outdo the other, if a Korean named Guang-ho hadn't come over to our table during one of the "kitchen parties" that our floor began to be known for as the year progressed, and which could last all weekend as partygoers ran to the nearby Franprix for two-euro bottles of merlot, six-packs of Desperados and other vital provisions. Guang-ho must have been intrigued by the sight of two guys—an Asian and an Aryan—sitting across from each other like chess players at the eleventh hour. I had already noticed him a few times in the kitchen—making instant ramen or smoking a cigarette on the window ledge, the lone Korean among the Europeans. He was slight of build but had the coiled grace of a dancer, or someone on the qui vive, always dressed in the same black jeans and worn leather jacket, his thatchy hair falling past his shoulders. It was difficult to guess his age, though something told me he was a bit older than the rest of us.

In all this time, he was the first person to approach us

wanting to know what we were arguing about. Without missing a beat, Joakim turned and asked him which term he preferred, Öresundsbron or Øresundsbroen? Shouting to be heard above Manu Chao's "Bongo Bong" blasting from the speakers, I explained to Guang-ho that they were the Swedish and Danish names of the bridge between Malmö and Copenhagen. Then I repeated the question, Øresundsbroen or Öresundsbron? We continued, drunkenly, to repeat the name of the bridge to him, each of us in our own language, louder and louder, until Guang-ho finally silenced us with a gesture, like the conductor of an orchestra at the end of a movement. He lit himself a cigarette—striking the match against the thick heel of his boot—then told us, in his Korean-accented French, about a long-standing dispute between Korea and Japan over a group of little islands. The Koreans called it Dokdo and the Japanese Takeshima; everyone else called it the Liancourt Rocks. Even the name of the surrounding waters was disputed by both countries. Then he crossed his arms and leaned back in his chair, as though suddenly exhausted by his story. In Joakim's face, I thought I saw something flicker and go out. Without another word, he downed the rest of his Desperados and slowly put the bottle back down on the table between us. Then he got up and staggered out of the kitchen. I spent the rest of the night talking to Guang-ho—who, it turned out, wasn't a resident of the Maison de Belgique at all. (He'd started coming here for the French newspapers in the ground-floor reading room.) After that night, Joakim and I stopped preparing our meals together. I still ran into him in the kitchen, but things had cooled between us. Nevertheless, when I spoke to him—to ask how much longer he needed the stove, for example—I made an effort to Swedify my Danish.

5. The Errand

Guang-ho's not-quite-ground-floor room (through the window one saw mostly headless passersby) was a few minutes' walk from the Sorbonne Nouvelle, where he was a student. "Student" might've been an exaggeration—I had no idea when he had last spoken to his thesis director. (He'd told me they saw each other exactly once a year, when he brought over his annual offering of a bottle of wine in return for a signature on the matriculation form.) On his desk, a dark layer of dust covered a stack of papers—his thesis on Descartes—surrounded by old Styrofoam instant-noodle bowls filled with cigarette ash. For some reason or other, he could no longer receive the housing grants he'd been subsisting on, and now washed dishes at a Korean restaurant and freelanced as a tour guide for Korean tourists.

I went to see him when I had nothing better to do. He always welcomed me with the same bemused smile, as though my reasons for wanting to visit him in his hovel were beyond him. I suppose, in some ways, it was beyond me too. At first, I was simply curious: all of the Asians I'd met up to now had been girls, Scandinavian Korean girls, and Guang-ho was neither Scandinavian nor a girl. He was the first Asian I got to know who hadn't been adopted. That he had grown up in South Korea, surrounded by people who looked like him, with parents who were Korean like him, was a source of endless reverie for me.

He'd left his country five years ago to finish his degree here in Paris, and, clearly, things had not gone as planned. Somewhere along the way, he had started to veer off course, and now it was too late, he'd gone too far to retrace his steps. To return home was to admit defeat, but to stay was to be reminded of it every day: he chose to stay. Every time I entered the squalor of his living quarters, he seemed that much closer to giving up the struggle once and for all. But then I would run into him in the street—more often than not, he was running an errand for his boss at the Korean restaurant—and he seemed a different person entirely, as though the cold, bracing air had made him temporarily forget his troubles. Or that was my theory: an hour or two spent wandering aimlessly through the streets of Paris was usually enough to cheer me up, especially after being locked up in my room all day. (There was always the possibility that I might run into Luce, the girl from the train. When I went out, it was often with the thought in the back of my mind, though I had read somewhere that one rarely meets the person one is hoping to meet—no more than three or four times in the course of a life.)

Sometimes I would accompany Guang-ho on his errands, which consisted of bringing an item to a supplier in the *quartier chinois* or getting a few last-minute, ready-made items like dumpling skins from the big Asian supermarket in Lognes. But they could also be of a more personal nature, such as standing in the little alley behind the restaurant while his boss had his afternoon cigarette (I pictured Guang-ho leaning forward with the lighter), or sitting with him at the counter of the bar for a drink after everyone else had left, at the end of the night. I knew about these moments because Guang-ho told me about them, always with the same ironic smile, as though he wanted me to know every detail, making me a witness to his life in Paris. After a while, the errands no longer had anything to do with the restaurant, becoming progressively more random and sundry in nature (dropping off a bottle of rosé late at night, going out to buy a pair of nail cutters). Though he hadn't told me in so many words, I had gathered that in addition to what he earned from his job at the restaurant, the man that he called "*mon patron*" had also helped him out of a few tight spots in the past. Over time, Guang-ho couldn't help but feel more and more indebted to him as a result.

One night in late November, there was a knock at my door and there he was, Guang-ho, standing in the hallway, his leather jacket splattered with blood. How had he managed to get past the concierge in such a state? I was so surprised that I merely stepped aside and let him into my room. Immediately he went to the window, as though to see if anyone was in the street below. As I observed him, it dawned on me that the blood on his jacket must be someone else's. He took out the pouch of tobacco, and his hands shook slightly as he rolled the paper for a cigarette.

The story he told me that night was difficult to believe. His boss had asked him to buy a pack of cigarettes at the nearby tobacconist. The restaurant had closed for the night, and Guang-ho and the other workers had just finished cleaning up the kitchen. By then, it was ten-thirty, and he knew that the tobacconist closed at eleven. When he returned with the cigarettes, he found the lights still on at the front of the restaurant. Something felt off. Then he heard a noise from the back, the sound of voices. He walked into the office to find three boys, two Arab and one black, standing around his boss, who was on the ground. He didn't appear to be moving. Without another thought, Guang-ho ran at them, and one of them pushed him away, kicking him in the sternum so that he stumbled backwards, nearly falling. At some point, he managed to grab the fire extinguisher off the wall and started spraying it at them. That was when the three ran off—the same way they had come, presumably. It wasn't until he was alone with his boss, who was barely moving but still alive, that Guang-ho realized he'd been screaming profanities in Korean the whole time.

They must have waited for the employees to leave before entering the restaurant through the back door, which often remained open while everyone was cleaning up, taking things out to the dumpster. Later, I came across an article in *Libé* about gangs whose specialty was robbing Chinese, or anyone who looked Chinese, on the assumption that they always carried large sums of money on them. Being illegals who didn't know any French, they wouldn't go to the police. And being Asian, they would be weak, unlikely to fight back. For what it was worth, Guang-ho's boss didn't fit any of these stereotypes. He had been in France for almost thirty years and had gone so far as to take a French name when he was naturalized (giving up his Korean citizenship in the process). But he knew that, no matter what, he would never be seen as a French citizen—that to most he was little more than a *métèque*, no matter how conscientiously he learned the language, no matter how thoroughly he assimilated to the culture. Not one to wallow in helplessness and self-pity, he found it easier to turn against those whose skin was darker than his, and after a while, he even came to derive a certain kind of pleasure, a certain kind of pride. He voted FN, he said, because the enemy of his enemies was his friend.

As Guang-ho fell silent, I suddenly realized who the blood on his jacket must belong to. He ran a hand through his hair and said, with his customary flair for the litote, "It hasn't been a very good day."

"What are you going to do?"

He smiled at me, shrugged. "What else is there to do? I'll go back to the hospital and see if he needs anything."

Of course. "Why did you come tonight? I mean, that is to say . . ." He had a number of Korean friends in the city, other people he could have gone to see.

"Are you asking me why I told you all that?"

I hesitated, then nodded.

"I'm not sure." He looked down at the cigarette between his fingers. I noticed a small cut on his hand, the only visible injury from the scuffle. "Your place was on the way home."

He rummaged around inside his jacket for something, then took out a crushed pack of cigarettes: the Marlboro Lights (or *Liktts*, as some kiosquiers in Copenhagen pronounced it) his boss had sent him out to get.

"And you," he said, "why do you listen to me?"

I looked at Guang-ho, and we both laughed. I walked him down to the street, and then to the RER station on the opposite side. It was past midnight, but I saw that the kébab place at the end of the block was still lit up, a bright little square in the night. As we were taking leave of each other in front of the station, a rowdy group of kids came out, laughing and shouting amongst themselves. One of them suddenly turned to Guang-ho and, an unlit cigarette between his lips, demanded loudly, "Got a—" He made a flicking motion, his thumb centimeters from my friend's face. Guang-ho, maintaining his affable smile, said calmly, "*Désolé, mais je ne fume pas.*"

The kid, with an audible snort of contempt, turned back to his friends.

For a moment after they left, we stood there in silence; then Guang-ho said, "I know why I tell you all this."

I waited for him to go on.

"I tell you," he said, "because I know that you will listen."

6. Empire of the Dead

I met Sang-hoon through Guang-ho. The two of them free-lanced as guides for Korean tourists to Paris. It was a part-time

job, and they were called in by an agency whenever a tour
group arrived. They drove everyone around the city in a van,
helped them take photos in front of the Eiffel Tower, accompanied them to Versailles ("the palace of camera flashbulbs,"
Guang-ho called it). Sang-hoon, in many ways, was the opposite of Guang-ho. Heavyset, taller than most French people,
he had a family who had come with him to France. He was
also working on his thesis and needed the extra income. At
his spacious apartment in Antony, just outside of Paris, where
I had been invited along with Guang-ho and a few others for
the end-of-the-year *réveillon*, he told us that he liked to show
his countrymen a side of Paris they otherwise would never
see. Of course, he did the usual—the Sacré-Coeur, the Arc de
Triomphe, and so on—but he made sure to approach the latter, for example, not via the Champs-Élysées but by one of
the other avenues—the Grande Armée, for example—where
all the high-end motorcycle dealerships were. He took genuine pleasure in clearing up misconceptions. In his group, there
was always someone who thought that the French drank only
wine, and who was amazed to discover that one could buy beer
in Paris. After spending the day driving a group of strangers
from one location to another, he could return home to his family, satisfied and reinvigorated. By that point in the evening it
was just me, Sang-hoon, Guang-ho, a guy named Ji-sook and
two girls, Ji-hae and Na-min. (Sang-hoon's wife and two kids
had already gone to bed.) The talk moved to other subjects,
and soon there were several conversations going on in tandem.
Guang-ho put on Serge Gainsbourg's "Bonnie and Clyde," and
Sang-hoon told him to lower the volume. I was chatting with
Ji-hae and Na-min, who were going to visit the catacombs
the next day. No doubt Sang-hoon had convinced them to
go—he often saved the catacombs for last, as there were fewer

people towards the end of the day, and also because, he said, it was a fitting way to finish a tour. Ji-hae, beside herself with excitement, seemed constantly on the verge of bursting into laughter or tears, or both. She and Na-min made an unlikely pair. Ji-hae was flamboyant, pretty in a childish way, quick to laugh, whereas Na-min was moody and at least ten years older. She was the only one among us who wasn't a student; instead, she had a real job—at L'Oréal, no less—something to do with marketing and sales. Ji-hae had come to Paris to study at the École des beaux-arts but had dropped out after a month; now she was taking remedial French-language classes at the Sorbonne. Despite all this, the two seemed to be best friends, their friendship the kind only possible abroad, where the fact of their being Korean overrode all other considerations. It was Ji-hae who invited me to accompany them to the catacombs, throwing out the invitation in her characteristically impulsive manner, and I had the impression that Na-min wasn't pleased. Moreover, I'm not sure why I accepted. It was true that I had never been to the catacombs, only one RER stop from the Cité U. The idea of making my way along dimly lit corridors and emerging somewhere else, somewhere completely different, sent a shiver of excitement through me. Ji-sook must have overheard our conversation, because after the girls went off together to the toilet, he approached me to say that I should be careful around them. From his tone he seemed entirely serious, and I was surprised enough by the warning to ask him what he meant by it. Were the two of them more than just friends? At this, Ji-sook started to laugh. All evening, he had barely opened his mouth, silently nursing his glass of Orangina (he never drank alcohol) and keeping his distance. He had been in France the longest of them all, at least seven or eight years, Guang-ho had told me. He lived frugally, never went out, and his place, located in one of the seedier areas of Château Rouge, was supposedly even more of a hovel than Guang-ho's. With government aid and student restaurants, it was possible to get by. He was working on some kind of thesis (most of the Koreans were), and, unlike Guang-ho, he really seemed to be working on it. Instead of answering my question, he went on to say that the catacombs—the *real* catacombs—were far larger than what the public was allowed to see. Most of the tunnels were inaccessible, the openings walled off or blocked by grills. They stretched farther than anyone suspected, miles and miles of nothing but emptiness and silence (*"rien que le vide et le silence"* were his words). In the areas forbidden to the public, there was no light at all, and over the centuries a number of unfortunate souls had died trying to find their way back. He then asked me to imagine being surrounded by darkness like a solid wall that went on forever in every direction: what must it be like (he wondered aloud) to realize that there was nothing beyond this darkness? After a while, it would no longer be possible to know if one was still alive or already dead.

The next day, I woke in my room at the Cité U still wearing my clothes from the night before, my scarf tangled around my ankles. Glancing at the digital clock, I realized that I was going to be late for my rendezvous with the girls. I felt horrible from all the vodka and wine I had spent the evening drinking and considered not going, except that I didn't have their numbers. At least I was already dressed; all I had to do was get up and walk out the door. I had agreed to meet them at the corner facing the statue of the Lion of Belfort, but they weren't there when I arrived, forty-five minutes late. The day was overcast, and I didn't see a single person waiting in line for the catacombs. Stranded in the middle of the intersection, the Lion looked forlorn and sad amidst the passing cars and the

holiday guirlands suspended above the streets like giant cob-
webs against the paleness of the morning sky. I wondered if
they had gone ahead on their own, and was thinking about
going in after them when I heard someone shouting my name.
A moment later Ji-hae ran up to me, out of breath, her cheeks
flushed from the cold. She was wearing a puffy jacket and her
hair was tied back in a neat little bun. Na-min wasn't with her.
We hurriedly kissed each other on the cheek, and Ji-hae told
me that her friend wasn't feeling well. They too had overslept,
she confessed, laughing, and I had a brief image of the two
of them waking up in the same bed. We bought our tickets
and then started making our way down the steps. I could feel
the air growing less humid as I stared at the back of Ji-hae's
head, breathing in her hair, which smelled as though she had
just washed it. The interminable steps finally debouched onto
a gallery of sorts, and on the walls were illustrated panels
detailing the history of the catacombs, along with an expo-
sition on various personalities of the French Revolution—
Madame Élisabeth, Fouquier-Tinville, Robespierre, Lucile
Desmoulins—whose remains had ended up in the catacombs.
There was a portrait of each, and when I came to the one of
Desmoulins, I couldn't help but stare: the resemblance with
the girl I had met on the train to Paris was undeniable. The
description mentioned that the portrait was a presumed likeness; it was thought to have been painted when she was eigh-
teen or nineteen—the same age, more or less, as Luce, the girl
from the train. Next to me, I heard Ji-hae yawn loudly. I reluctantly left the room behind and followed her down several
narrow, low-ceilinged corridors. According to a sign on the
wall, we were walking beneath the parc Montsouris where
it juxtaposed the reservoir of the fourteenth arrondissement.
We seemed to be descending gradually deeper underground.

The last corridor opened onto a series of quarries, and I
saw that several adjoining galleries had been closed off. We
reached the ossuary, whose entrance was marked by a plaque
near the ceiling with the admonitory words: *"C'est ici l'empire
de la mort."* Inside, there were galleries of different sizes, all of
them decorated with bones and plaques with quotations from
famous nineteenth-century authors in French or in Latin. Ji-
hae let out a cry of delight, running around and marveling at
a fountain made entirely of tibias. I wondered if I might still
be drunk from the night before. Everywhere I looked there
were bones—skulls, femurs, tibias—all neatly aligned in an
impeccable pattern, though on closer inspection I discovered
that, beyond the first layer, disorder reigned, a chaos of skeletal
remains. All the while, we were the only ones in the galleries. I began to lose all sense of time: I felt that several hours
had gone by, though it probably hadn't been more than half an
hour since we had entered the catacombs. The gravel underneath our feet sounded too loud in my ears. I strived to keep
up with Ji-hae, whose breath I could make out in the gloom.
We came to a large room dedicated to the pre-Romantic poet
Nicolas Gilbert, whose verses were engraved on the walls
(*"Au banquet de la vie, infortuné convive, / J'apparus un jour, et je
meurs . . ."*). There was a gravestone—the only gravestone in
the catacombs—belonging to Françoise Gellain, who devoted
her life to freeing an inmate from Bicêtre after coming across
a letter he had written and thrown from one of the prison
windows. She didn't even know what he looked like until
he was released, twenty years later . . . I saw Ji-hae disappear
through an opening at the other end of the ossuary. Hurrying
after her, I glanced back at the light coming from the chamber
we'd just left, and for a moment I stood there, like someone
given a glimpse into his past. Seeing the light grow fainter

with each new step, I sensed myself making a terrible mistake, but what else was I to do? By the time I caught up with Ji-hae, the light from the ossuary no longer reached us, and I told her we should turn back, but she only laughed and said that we couldn't turn back, we had already paid for our tickets. It had grown much darker, and I could barely see where I was going. The air felt different; I noticed that the corridors were no longer illuminated, though the vague shapes of things remained visible, which meant that light still reached us from another source. Had we taken a wrong turn somewhere? Impossible, of course: there were no bifurcations in the catacombs, at least in the part open to the public. I remembered what Ji-sook had told me, and began to wonder if I might have died without realizing it. And if I was dead, then what about Ji-hae? I could no longer see her silhouette ahead of me. Strangely enough, I felt no alarm and found myself thinking once again about the girl I had met on the train. Was she really the reincarnation of Lucile Desmoulins? At that moment, it seemed to me that the darkness surrounding me had changed. I saw before me the outline of an immense wall composed of countless vertical and horizontal lines—like a sheet of grid paper whose squares suddenly began to break down into complex geometric motifs, right before my eyes. Perhaps my brain, unable to cope with such unrelenting nothingness, had filled the void with symbols and signs—the way one is tempted to see shapes in the clouds or patterns in the ceiling—or so I later reasoned to myself. Something told me not to continue staring at the grids, and, despite not being able to make out anything in front of me, I started running as though for my life. I saw a faint light up ahead, and without warning I emerged into the blinding late-afternoon sun shining down on the sidewalk, a nondescript street with parked cars and two bicycles—one missing a seat, the other a wheel—chained to a barrier. Ji-hae was, once again, next to me. I looked back at the door we had just walked through, and there was nothing to indicate that behind it was the underworld, Hades, purgatory, death. For a moment I considered trying the door, then thought better of it. I looked over at Ji-hae, and she silently returned my gaze. Her face was pale, and I wondered what the past half hour had been like for her. We went to a café-tabac nearby and tried to talk about it, but we didn't get very far. There was nothing to talk about, really. I ran into her again a few more times after that, mostly at Sang-hoon's. At some point she and Na-min had a fight about something and stopped seeing each other, though that's another story altogether.

7. Little Pyongyang

Guang-ho claimed to have found a North Korean restaurant in Paris; Sang-hoon, who prided himself on knowing the city like the inside of his pocket, said that such a thing was impossible. And that was how it began, with neither wanting to be proven wrong. After all, in Amsterdam there was one, the first on European soil. It had appeared rather inconspicuously, like mushrooms after a rainfall, then closed its doors a few months later, only to reopen them, in a new location, under a different name. Then again, that was Amsterdam, where it was known to rain a lot. In the end, Guang-ho grudgingly agreed to take us there so that we could see for ourselves. He had his pride, after all. I knew that he was doing it mainly for Sang-hoon; I accompanied them because I had nothing better to do. It was a bright spring morning and the streets had already started to come to life. The people who passed us had straw baskets slung over their shoulders; others pushed strollers, and I could only surmise that there was an open-air market nearby. Their obliviousness to our unlikely mission—finding a North Korean restaurant in Montmartre—made them seem unreal to me, like figurants in a movie. During the train ride, Guang-ho had recounted in detail what had happened: he had stumbled across the restaurant by accident while on his way to see someone. ("A girl," Sang-hoon said, half asking. "A girl," Guang-ho said, half answering.) He was already running late, and on top of that it had started to rain, but he found himself stopping in front of the restaurant for a second glance. Even then, it wasn't immediately clear to him what he was seeing. Most Korean restaurants—including the one Guang-ho himself worked at—were in the fifth and sixth arrondissements; he'd never heard of one in the eighteenth, where he rarely ventured, though that wasn't why he had stopped. Here he paused in his story to roll himself a cigarette so that it would be ready once we got off. Inside the restaurant, Guang-ho went on, spitting out a shard of tobacco stuck to his tongue, the servers were all women, dressed in traditional *hanbok*. There was something off about the colors, the reds and greens and yellows a bit too garish, verging on neon. At the end of the room was a small stage, with a keyboard and several microphone stands—the typical setup for karaoke (or "*noraebang*" in Korean, Sang-hoon informed me). The customers facing the stage with their backs to Guang-ho were all Westerners. And then it finally hit him. The *feeling*.

It was similar to what he'd experienced, years earlier, during a visit to Germany. There had been a period, shortly after he arrived in France, when his papers weren't in order, and this required him to leave the country temporarily every three months before his tourist visa ran out. He usually spent a weekend in London, and on his return, the counter back to zero again, he had another three months of peace of mind. In any case, the little subterfuge seemed to work; he never had any trouble at the border. Sometimes—finances permitting—he would even make a little detour along the way. On one such trip, he had stayed at a youth hostel in what had once been East Berlin. It was the off season, and he'd had a dormitory room all to himself. Sometime during the night he had woken from a dream to notice that, across the room, there was someone sitting up in one of the upper bunk beds. For a long time, he lay there in the dark, staring at the silhouette, terrified but unable to move. At some point, exhaustion overcame him and he fell back asleep. When he woke the next morning—much later than he had planned—he was alone in the room. Later, after his situation was regularized, he met someone at the Cité U, an Irish student and resident of the Collège franco-britannique, who had spent several months at the same hostel as Guang-ho in Berlin. He told Guang-ho that, even if the staff was German, the building itself was owned by the North Koreans, and that it had once been a residence for diplomats from Pyongyang. All of this was apparently something of an open secret among the people of the neighborhood. The memory of the hostel—he hadn't thought about it in years—came back to him as he stood in front of the restaurant, the rain starting to come down harder and harder.

"Did you go in?" Sang-hoon asked.

"Would *you* have gone in?" Guang-ho made as if to light his cigarette, then seemed to remember where he was.

Instead of answering, Sang-hoon turned to me and explained that, under the National Security Law, it was illegal for a South Korean to enter into contact with North Koreans.

Knowingly walking into a North Korean restaurant would fall into the aforementioned category.

"Like I said," Guang-ho muttered, "I was in a hurry that night."

My Korean companions were unusually quiet as we made our way down the street in the morning light. By then, we were in the Goutte d'Or; to our left was the boulevard Barbès. It was, I thought, an unlikely place for a restaurant, amid the noise and the odors, far from the areas frequented by tourists. Sang-hoon insisted that Guang-ho had been mistaken, but Guang-ho didn't reply, drawing pensively on his cigarette. Nearby, he informed us, was a tobacconist, one of the few in Paris that sold Chesterfields, though he'd gone back to rolling his own paper because it was cheaper. Every few hundred feet, Sang-hoon declared us lost, all the while commenting like a tour guide on the graffiti-covered façades, the trash strewn everywhere, a streak of canine excrement that seemed to go on for several blocks. Guang-ho made us double back and retrace our steps. For the first time, he seemed unsure of himself.

"It was here, I'm telling you . . ."

"Admit it. You have no idea where you're going!"

"Just shut up and let me think!"

I wondered why Sang-hoon was so eager to prove Guang-ho wrong. Was it his professional pride at stake here? Granted, a segment of his Paris tour included what he called North Korean sites of interest, another hidden facet of the city that he enjoyed sharing with his clients, Korean tourists who came to Paris looking for a different experience, something off the beaten path. Many of them didn't even want to see the Eiffel Tower and had no interest in climbing the crowded steps of the Sacré-Coeur while fighting off African street vendors trying to palm off bracelets and other trinkets. They were younger, more savvy and disillusioned: they'd read accounts of Japanese tourists coming home traumatized after discovering that their beloved City of Light—the backdrop of so many mangas and TV series—was in reality a City of Darkness; they'd heard stories of Chinese tourists being mugged in front of their hotels by thugs from the suburbs who came into the city by RER with the express intention of targeting Chinese—or anyone who looked Chinese—because, q.e.d., all Chinese were rich and defenseless, easy targets. They had found out about Sang-hoon's tour from outraged clients who had complained that, instead of going up the Champs-Élysées, Sang-hoon had taken them up a "side street" with nothing but motorcycle dealerships. Others had written reviews on the Internet, as detailed as they were scathing, and that was how word had spread about "Little Pyongyang."

Typically, it started in the fifth arrondissement, at the hotel where the daughter of Chang Sung-taek, Kim Jong-il's brother-in-law, had committed suicide. After bringing his tour group to the street where the hotel was located—a cul-de-sac—he would launch into the story of how Chang Kum-song, a film student at the Sorbonne Nouvelle, had become romantically involved with a dark and brooding French class-mate (whose name was Sébastien on some days, Stéphane on other days). Then the fatidic order to return to Pyongyang had come . . . If there was nobody behind the desk, Sang-hoon would sneak everyone upstairs and point out the door of the very room where the lovesick student had, after failing to overdose on sleeping pills, hanged herself with the curtains. The tour continued at Censier, where, during happier days, she had attended lectures on the art of cinema. Afterwards, Sang-hoon would take his group down to the thirteenth arrondissement, first to the Tolbiac center, where Kim Sul-song, Kim Jong-il's daughter, had studied for a time, then to the Institut d'études politiques, where several of North Korea's elite were discreetly enrolled. If he could convince the guard at the entrance to let them in, there would be a tour of the grounds, including the English garden with its brick-laned walkways. Other sites of interest included the Salpêtrière hospital, where Ko Yong-hui, Kim Jong-il's consort, had died (breast cancer), and the hideout house where Yi Han-yong had stayed before defecting to South Korea. (His mother had been the nanny to one of Kim Jong-il's illegitimate children and was also a defector, whose whereabouts were currently unknown, though she had lived for a time in Geneva with a Japanese assistant, kept a diary and read Chekhov in Russian.) Sang-hoon would also make a stop at the house of Amélie Nothomb, for no other reason than because it was nearby and he knew how to get there. The last stop of the tour was the architecture school at Paris–La Villette, up in the nineteenth arrondissement, where more of the Dear Leader's elite were studying to build the new Pyongyang (the real one back home). Sang-hoon would have his group stand with him in front of one of the impersonal residence halls and point out a row of windows chosen by him at random. The effect of the setting sun against the glass was a nice little bonus. Depending on his mood, he might take them to the architecture school at Paris-Belleville, also nearby, instead. The North Korean segment had become so popular that he was thinking of turning it into a stand-alone tour.

"This is it," Guang-ho said at last. "It's just around this corner . . ."

I'm not sure how long we stood in front of the storefront's iron curtain covered with graffiti. There were pylons, an empty

wine bottle, temporary fencing plastered with old posters for
bygone municipal elections (22 AVRIL, VOTEZ ARLETTE LAGU-
ILLER). Was this really it? Or something else altogether? It
looked like no one had been by in months, maybe even years.

Was it me, or did Sang-hoon seem relieved? Guang-ho too
seemed mollified, despite all of his efforts to find the restaurant,
and I saw him mechanically start rolling another cigarette. It
was a habit he'd acquired in France (no one rolled cigarettes in
Seoul); he'd gotten so proficient that, walking down the street
on a rainy day, he could do it with one hand while holding an
umbrella in the other. We started moving again. It was almost
noon, and I suggested a kébab followed by a cheap beer at the
nearby McDonald's.

On our way back to the métro station we came across the
Passe-muraille, a statue of a man emerging from a brick wall,
only his head, an arm and part of a leg visible. Someone had
painted his nails red. It depicted a scene from a short story
by Marcel Aymé, about a functionary named Dutilleul who
is able to pass unimpeded through walls. One night, as he's
leaving the abode of a woman he's secretly seeing (a married
woman, an unhappily married woman), his powers abandon
him, and he finds himself trapped in the wall forever.

Guang-ho put out the cigarette he'd been smoking while
Sang-hoon continued to stare at the stone wall where the
Passe-muraille was eternally trapped.

"I got it," he said at last. "A secret monument erected by
the North Koreans."

It took me a moment to understand that he was referring
to the statue.

"Just think about the beauty and horror of it. Everyone
thinks it's an homage to a dead French writer, but in reality

it was commissioned by the North Koreans, a little reminder to all the comrades residing in Paris, lest they think about defecting. Fitting, isn't it? But the *real* mark of genius, of course, is that the memorial to our fallen hero is only a stone's throw from the two architecture schools."

8. A Ghost in Paris

For some time now, I had been trying to see my thesis supervisor. It was true that, at first, I hadn't been trying all that hard. In Denmark, there was a get-to-know-one-another cocktail, a chance to meet professors outside of the auditorium and in a more casual setting. Here, in France, one had to flush them out, hunt them down. It was like a game of cat-and-mouse, in which I was the mouse hunting the cat. Each time I came by, I found her door shut. On one occasion, there was a sheet of paper taped to the door: "*Mme Tousez est souffrante.*" She was ill, indisposed, and all of her courses had been canceled. I couldn't have said why, but suddenly I was convinced that it was a lie, a subterfuge, and that in reality she was standing behind the door, ready to pounce. I placed a hand against the hard, unyielding wood and tried to imagine her on the other side. We'd started out communicating exclusively by post, then electronically, and for the first several months she had been little more than a name, words on paper, lines on a page. Even now—after a handful of visits to her office—a vague mental image, partially obscured by the stacks of papers on her bureau, was the best I could muster.

Several weeks into the second semester, I encountered yet another obstacle, this one of an administrative nature: I was asked to provide proof that I had indeed failed to finish my thesis in Copenhagen. Frankly, I couldn't imagine why they wanted proof, given that I had already been admitted as a student. Why would anyone lie about failing something? I could understand them asking for proof that I had finished my thesis, but that I *hadn't* finished it? As if proof of past failure were a necessary condition for studying at the Sorbonne . . . I was tempted to point out this absurdity to the woman at the secrétariat, but in the end I said nothing. I left the building and walked out to the square, weighed down by a growing sense of futility. At a nearby kébab place, I ordered a *grec-frites* and sat down at the counter, next to a tiny little sink jutting out of a corner of the wall. As I ate, I thought about my dilemma. The conclusion I arrived at was that proving one's success was always easier than proving one's failure. Success, completion, admission all resulted in some document or other: a diploma, a letter of acceptance. How does one prove that one failed an exam? How does one prove that one took it in the first place? One wasn't given anything in the event of failure: there was nothing to give. That said, was failure any less real than success? Wasn't the unhappiness associated with something lost always greater, in one's mind, than the happiness associated with something gained?

The days went by. In the connecting corridor at Montparnasse-Bienvenüe, I noticed someone on the moving walkway going the other way. All I caught was the back of a head, the cover of a book, but I became convinced that it had been her, Luce, the girl from the train. By now, I told myself, she had probably established a routine, formed new habits, a daily schedule. As the weeks passed without another sighting, I found myself imagining her life at René Descartes, where she was starting her first year of medicine. I imagined her in a crowded auditorium or bent over a book, alone, at the library. Or bent over a dissection table with other students in an anatomy class. In Denmark, dissections of cadavers didn't begin until the second or third year of medical school. Was it the same in France? One day, I went so far as to visit the rue des Saints-Pères—not far from the École des beaux-arts—and loiter for several hours at the front entrance, watching people come and go. The only other things I knew about her was that she was from the south of France and that she had suffered a heartbreak in Amsterdam. "You remind me of someone," she had told me on the train. It seemed foolish to place so much importance on a chance encounter with a stranger, and yet I couldn't help but feel a connection between us, as though, even now, we were leading parallel lives intersected, at some point, by a third and unknown line.

In the meantime, I continued to attend my classes, often in a sort of daze, and on one occasion my fading attention resurfaced in time to hear the professor say that "perchance to dream" could be translated as *peut-être rêver.* For lunch, I usually bought a sandwich from the student café and ate it sitting on the bench across from the (closed) door of my thesis supervisor, Madame Tousez. I spent a lot of time in the Beaubourg library. If I got there late enough in the day, the line at the entrance wasn't too long, the reading room not quite as crowded. After the BNF, it was the least depressing place to study (especially compared to the library at the Sorbonne), though the toilets were atrocious, the raised urinals blocked up and on the point of overflowing, impossible to flush. Among them was a urinal perpetually wrapped with black tarp, which made me think of something monstrous and alive, an excrescence growing out of the wall itself. I avoided using the facilities when I could help it. Most evenings, I dined at the student canteen at Port-Royal, down the street from the municipal library. On my way out of the dining hall, I overheard a girl telling her friend, "*Toi, tu es mince. Elle, elle est maigre.*" (Small but not tiny, slim but not skinny.) The form of the sentence in French—more than its meaning—resonated inside me, within me, and all the way home on the train I repeated it to myself, over and over again, like a mantra.

That same night, I wrote a letter to my former thesis supervisor in Copenhagen, asking him to confirm that I had failed to finish my thesis. In the letter, I asked about Ditte, how she was doing, whether she had finished her thesis, as if she were simply one of his students and nothing more. She had been studying the different manifestations of magic in the Elder Edda when we knew each other. My thesis, at the time, was a rereading of *Oedipus Rex* in light of Frazer's *The Golden Bough*. After Ditte had left me for my supervisor, I hadn't been able to go back to it. We had often argued about the paternity of the poems of the Codex Regius, or about the authenticity of the myths in the Younger Edda (I was pro-Snorri, Ditte was anti-Snorri). I didn't mention any of this, of course. Perhaps he already knew, perhaps she had already told him. Instead of sending my letter, I continued to revise what I had written, sometimes in my head while out walking or waiting for a train. I was no longer sure who I was addressing—him or her, or the two of them—in these messages that I didn't end up sending.

Two-thirds into April, there was a student-wide strike at the Sorbonne. I arrived to find a large crowd assembled in front of the main entrance. I hadn't seen the square filled with so many people since the Fête de la musique last year. They stood around in groups, smoking, as if at the theater during an intermission. I made my way past all of them and walked up the cold marble steps to the secrétariat, whose doors were, obviously, closed. The corridors were deserted. Moments later, I found myself standing, once again, in front of my supervisor's door. I leaned forward and pressed my ear against the wood. I didn't expect to hear anything—there was surely no one on the other side—and yet I remained like that for a long time, listening. When I had sent out inquiries to various professors in Paris (one at the Sorbonne, another at the Sorbonne Nouvelle, a third at Nanterre), asking whether they might want to oversee my thesis on Samuel Beckett, I had gone out of my way to choose only women. I went back down the stairs, and with some difficulty traversed the courtyard, where the ambience had turned almost festive. Someone was cutting through the crowd from the opposite direction. As he passed me, he held out a piece of paper, which I took, mechanically. It wasn't a tract but a flyer for, of all things, a gallery opening. "A light shines in the darkness and the darkness doesn't understand it," the show was called. Below the title was a photograph of a girl standing on a bridge. I could make out a canal in the background, bicycles attached to a guardrail. Was it really her, the girl I had met on the train coming to Paris? I studied the black-and-white image, which had been shrunk to fit the flyer. The girl photographed was Luce, and at the same time someone else—a twin, a lookalike. She seemed to be staring directly at her photographer, and as a result, staring directly at me.

On the D-day, I showed up at the gallery not knowing what to expect. No one gave me a second glance. I helped myself to a glass of white wine from a table and walked around the room. There were photographs and paintings by an artist whose Germanic name struck a familiar note in my mind, though I couldn't have said why. The photographs consisted of desolate resort towns, sinister vistas, ruins lost in the crepuscular gloom. As for the paintings, they were done in an almost impressionistic style reminiscent of Spilliaert, whose works I had seen at the Louisiana, near Copenhagen. I guessed them to be self-portraits, though no one in the gallery looked anything like the tall, brooding woman depicted in the paintings, with her mane of red hair and her dark, androgynous nineteenth-century suit. I was so taken by them that I had half forgotten my reason for being there by the time I came across the photos. Placed near the exit, almost as an afterthought or an epilogue, they were different in style from both the landscapes and the self-portraits. I downed the rest of my wine and stared at the black-and-white images. In one of them, I could make out the words—LUX IN TENEBRIS LUCET—tattooed across the back of a neck I had never seen in real life. In another, she was sitting on the floor in front of a carton of pizza and using a pair of scissors to cut herself a slice. There was also the photo from the flyer, and, seeing it full-size, I realized that she wasn't staring at me but at a spot slightly to the right of the photographer.

I had at last found her, yet I was no closer to discovering who she was. The following day, the courtyard of the Sorbonne was empty once more. People were walking in and out of the secrétariat, business as usual, as if the strike had never happened. In front of my supervisor's office, I put my ear against the door and strained to hear something, anything. This time, though, I didn't turn away. Instead, I took a small step back and knocked several times on the door. A moment passed. Then another. As I stood there, waiting, it occurred to me that I still didn't have proof of my failure.

9. Shroomsterdam

It was raining when I arrived in Amsterdam, and the first thing I did was walk into a café and order a beer, four euros a pint, cheaper than in Paris. From my table, I gazed out the window at the canal, though I ended up focusing on the rivulets making their way down the glass instead. There was a television mounted near the ceiling, a football match in progress (Netherlands–Czech Republic, I later learned, the last match before the quarter-finals), and everyone in the café was watching. Everyone, that is, except me and three guys sitting at a table near the door. If not for them, I might have felt that I was completely alone. Almost despite myself, I found myself glancing at them, which amounted to observing their hunched backs from across the room. They appeared to be deep in discussion, like three co-conspirators. I wondered what could possibly be more interesting than the game, only to remember that I myself wasn't interested. At last they got up and left, and not long after that, I finished my beer and left as well. Out in the street, I expected to see her, Luce, at every corner. I had reserved a room at a hotel, in reality a converted boat docked near the port. It was nicer than I had expected, with cable and two porn channels. I left the "botel" (as it was called) and, mostly to get out of the rain, went to the Van Gogh Museum, an ultramodern building near the canals. I spent a long time looking at the paintings of his room in Arles, which made me think of my own room at the Cité U. I then lingered in front of the Paul Signac landscapes, which had always reminded me of patterns used for detecting Daltonism. It was starting to grow dark when I left the museum, and I walked around aimlessly for a few hours, only to find myself in the red-light district. I walked past the windows, lit up like department-store displays, though the lighting—pink-and-blue neons—was more gaudy and the "mannequins" were human (I was startled the first time I saw one of them move). That night, I dreamt about the trio from the café; they were poring over something on the table between them, but even in my dream I couldn't see what it was.

The next morning, I visited the Anne Frank House. Like the Van Gogh Museum, it was a sleek and modern structure, all slate-gray panels and mortar, built squarely around and over the original house, though all of the original furniture, disappointingly, had not survived. There was a replica of the house—faithful to the smallest detail, according to the accompanying card—as well as various items that had once belonged to Anne Frank, everything displayed inside transparent cubes. Her journal was opened to a page where she had copied down passages from her favorite books ("The rich perfume of roses embalmed the atelier, and when the light summer breeze disturbed the trees in the garden, there came through the open door a heavy odor of lilacs . . ."). Afterwards, outside, I sat on one of the banks and ate a sandwich. A man walking past called out to me, in English: "Have a good appetite!" Amsterdam seemed strangely quiet, almost deserted, like a city under curfew. I considered renting a bicycle but it was too windy, too cold. In the end, I took a ride on a bateau-mouche while sipping a Heineken. I also visited a café that sold weed (not as numerous as one might expect) and examined the selection of chichas, narghilas, bongs, maslocs, lighters and old-fashioned tobacco boxes. The items were displayed under glass, like at the Anne Frank Museum. There was even "instant" weed that could be applied to a cigarette: three drops were enough to turn one into a joint, according to the man behind the counter. I didn't buy anything. Instead, I walked into a bar, the first establishment I came across (they weren't as numerous as one might expect, either), and once again there was a football match playing on the television. I thought about the three friends again and their hunched, conspiratorial postures—like three anarchists in a Paris café—though my memory of them might already have been tainted by my dream of the night before. I looked around, but there was no one who wasn't watching the game (Czech Republic had made a surprise comeback to beat Netherlands during yesterday's match, I later learned), and after finishing my beer I decided against having another. What was I doing here? What had I expected to find, exactly? I was heading back to the botel with the intention of taking a nap when I came across three Danes in the reception area. They were arguing in Danish about whether the Van Gogh Museum only had works by Van Gogh or works by other painters as well—a rather heated discussion, as though their decision to visit the museum was riding on it. Perhaps because the one claiming the museum had works by other painters was outnumbered by his two (misguided) friends, perhaps because I was feeling a bit lonely, I couldn't help interjecting. For a second, they all stared at me, and then one of them, the one whom I had spoken up for, asked if I was from Copenhagen. His name was Mads, and his friends were Nikolaj and Ulrich. They were from Aarhus, first-year students at the university, and they didn't ask me about my ethnic background, the way most Danes back in Denmark would have. At that point, Mads asked me to settle another argument for them. He took out a plastic baggie filled with several rather pitiful-looking stalks. They had come up with three possibilities: the Van Gogh Museum, the Anne Frank House, the Vondelpark (the city's largest and most popular green space). In retrospect, the best place to take the mushrooms would have been here at the botel, relatively familiar and sheltered from unpredictable elements, but

since they deemed me an authority, I opted for the Vondelpark, if only because I had already been to the Van Gogh Museum (and because the Anne Frank House just seemed like a
bad idea). One thing led to another, and I found myself walking with them to a pizzeria ("New York Pizza," the sign read),
and it was only after the four of us were seated at a table that I
thought to wonder if I had accepted their invitation because
they reminded me of the three conspirators from the café. Ulrich solemnly sprinkled the shriveled little stalks on the pizza
that he'd ordered for us. The mood at the table was subdued,
almost grim. It didn't help that we were the only ones in the
restaurant. I noticed that the tip of one of the mushrooms on
my slice of pizza was blue, a blue such as I'd never seen before,
and I remembered someone telling me that it was impossible
to overdose on shrooms. The others finished the remaining
slices, though there was nothing on them (i.e., only normal
toppings), and then the four of us started walking around, not
saying much, waiting for the effects to kick in. We paused
to watch a street performer—a contortionist—performing a
routine with two chairs. Suddenly, I felt something, though it
was much too soon, barely a quarter of an hour had gone by. I
glanced at my companions, but they seemed oblivious; they
were watching the contortionist and didn't seem to notice that
the cobblestones had come to life, slowly moving up and
down like piano keys. My center of gravity descended several notches. I thought of letting the others know that it might
be time to head to the park, but before I knew it we were
moving again, though I didn't recall any words having been
exchanged. On the sidewalk, complex geometric patterns appeared without my having to concentrate on them. At times I
was walking behind Mads or Nikolaj, and other times Ulrich
was beside me and all of our movements were synchronized,

our shadows playing against the sidewalk in perfect harmony. It seemed to me that we would never reach the park, but I didn't mind; I could have walked alongside them like this forever. Of course, nothing lasts forever, not even sadness. I wasn't sure who had started the argument; I became aware of voices, distant at first, then overwhelmingly close, so close that it felt like they were inside my head. They were arguing about the capital city of Germany: Nikolaj was convinced that it wasn't Berlin but Bonn, and Mads and Ulrich were trying to convince him that he was mistaken. But Nikolaj wouldn't budge from his position, insisting that it was a misconception, one of those received ideas like humans using only ten percent of their brains or the King of Denmark wearing a yellow star during the war. Then he started going on about Denmark during the German occupation, saying that the real war had been between the Danish resistants and the Nazi collaborators. I wanted to tell him to stop talking, but I realized that I no longer knew the words in Danish (though, somehow, I could still understand everything). As though I had no other choice, I addressed my companions in French, which none of them understood, obviously. Little by little, the world around me began to change, color seeping progressively away, until it became something else entirely. Cold and reptilian. Everyone I passed on the street appeared to fix me with suspicion and contempt. Their whispers reached me as though funneled through a tube, hitting my left or right ear but never both ears at the same time, in a sort of pseudo-stereo, and several times I heard what sounded like Luce's name among the half-intelligible jumble of words. We finally arrived in front of the Vondelpark, but the street we had to cross loomed impossibly wide, twenty-five lanes of traffic at least. I was wondering how we would ever get to the other side when someone whispered what sounded like the words "*lux in tenebris lucet*" in my ear. I immediately turned towards the voice, but there was only the four of us on the roundabout. Suddenly, as if by magic, the cars waiting at the intersection were gone and the sun was shining (where moments earlier, the sky had been overcast). As I walked through the park entrance, I noticed two individuals next to their bikes, and one of them smiled at me—a knowing, conspiratorial smile—as though we both knew something the rest of the world didn't. Once inside, the four of us found a place to sit, and that was when things really started to get weird. I lost all idea of who I was; it was like seeing myself struck with amnesia, but in the third person. Like being locked out of my own mind. I had been exiled, and Mads, Nikolaj, Ulrich were my fellow exiles. With some reluctance, I came to accept the loss of my Danish identity. What was done was done, I told myself. How many years had I been sitting there, in the park? At one point I seemed to be in Copenhagen, then at the parc Montsouris, and I realized that I had been repeating over and over to myself, "Time is a slope, not a curve . . ." In Danish, no less—my Danish had returned! I turned to the others, I wanted to tell them the good news, but they weren't there. I was alone. For a long time (or so it seemed), I watched two people throwing a Frisbee back and forth. Then it started to rain, and I finally stopped peaking. As I walked back in the direction of the port, I felt strangely, inexplicably happy, and also relieved to have recovered my mind, which I thought I had lost. The city seemed even emptier, a house after all the partygoers have gone home, but as the sun began to set, everything looked very calm and beautiful. At an intersection, I stopped to stare at the sky, the movement of the clouds, and at some point I noticed that the rain had stopped. The light made everything around me seem unreal, sharpened to perfection. It felt like summer. All the way to the botel I couldn't stop smiling, while another part of my mind kept wondering, kept asking itself: What happened, what just happened? What in the world *was* that?

10. Paris Is a Party

> Q are there ghosts in this room
> A most of the objects here are ghosts
> Q really
> A have you been to Paris
> Q no
> A Paris is a ghost
>
> —Anne Carson, "Ghost Q & A"

At a party for first-year medical students of René Descartes, I told a number of people that I was going away for a while. I told them I was going up north, to Kiruna, above the Arctic Circle in Swedish Lapland. Why Kiruna? Was it because I had spent part of a summer there when I was eight? This was just before I started at the Stockholm International School, where, for the first time in my life, I wasn't the only black-haired kid in my class. Afterwards, I had returned to Denmark to finish my upper-secondary. Of my time in Kiruna, I remembered the way the sky looked at midnight as the sun was setting; the lake whose waters were clear enough that I could see to the bottom; the leaves of the katsura trees behind the cabin; the rapeseed field that I had to traverse on my way to the moraine, which overlooked the whole town.

I said that I was leaving to escape the heat growing worse

with each passing day. Even in the early-morning hours, with
the windows open, I found little relief. Several deaths had already been reported among the elderly. Fans were becoming a
scarce commodity, entire inventories disappearing from stores
(I had bought one of the last at Darty). I don't know how many
people I talked to in the course of the night; people told me
their names and I forgot them immediately. Not that this kept
me from swearing oaths of eternal camaraderie and everlast-
ing friendship. Most of the parties I went to were hosted by
people I didn't know, and I would have been incapable of recognizing anyone in the sober light of day. On one occasion,
I had crashed a birthday bash in a bowling alley off the place
d'Italie, where the beer was served in tall cylindrical containers called "giraffes" and I got so drunk that I sent a bowling
ball rolling backwards into the seating area behind me. At another soirée, because others around me were giving speeches, I
got up on a chair and recited, in Danish, a piece of doggerel by
Halfdan Rasmussen:

> When the reserves shall mobilize
> to tear the world apart
> I will write with curly parsley
> the world's shortest epic.

Everyone I knew had left for the summer, but I had chosen
to stay in Paris and work on my thesis, because without my
supervisor's signature on the inscription form I wouldn't be
able to renew my student card, provider of sundry benefits like
meal tickets at university restaurants, health insurance, a room
at the Cité U—in short, nothing to scoff at for a person of
modest means like myself. I watched a lot of movies alone, up
to three or four some days, thanks to my UGC Illimité pass.

The dark, air-conditioned projection room was a welcome re-spite from the heat. And yet. I began to feel the same creeping boredom that had plagued me on my arrival in France a year ago. Those first months had been among the loneliest of my life, and things I would never have noticed or paid attention to began to acquire an ineffable significance of their own. Every evening, walking back to the métro from the Beaubourg library, I would pass a *traiteur asiatique* and glimpse through the window a girl working in the kitchen. It was hard to tell her age; I only ever saw her from the back. For several months I walked past her, like clockwork; and then, one day, she wasn't there anymore. In all that time, I never once saw her face. Her disappearance had a disproportionate effect on me, left me in-consolable for a week, and after that I took another path to the station, though it meant a more circuitous walk. Then I grew busy with my classes at the Sorbonne, I got to know my fellow residents at the Cité U. My life, all of a sudden, seemed a little less humdrum. But I was sometimes overcome by an unfath-omable sadness, an almost exhilarating loneliness, as though I were the last of my kind.

Towards the end of August, I decided to take a break be-tween two chapters of my thesis and crash a housewarming party. The place was hard to find, and reluctantly I stopped to ask passersby, who turned out to be tourists. (It was August, after all.) When I at last found the building, it turned out to be located along a cramped little street ending in a cul-de-sac. There was a porte cochère (no code, thankfully), an interior courtyard with a small fountain. At the door, I stood for a mo-ment, listening to the sounds coming from the other side, like a ghost needing to be invited in by someone from the world of the living. The apartment itself was peculiarly laid out, with no hallway, one room leading directly into the next like

adjoining hotel chambers. Another particularity: there were
two entrances, at opposite ends of the apartment, and in the
center, sandwiched between the rooms, a kitchen with a bathtub. All in all, a strange layout. Perhaps it was the heat, but the
air seemed faintly charged with electricity. I had been there
for less than an hour when I spotted her near the doorway. She
wasn't talking to anyone, and for a moment her gaze seemed
to meet mine. Then she turned away, and I saw her disappear
into the next room. She had shaved her head, close enough to
the skin for me to distinguish the contours of her scalp. A bit
thinner too, olive skin a bit paler, as though only recently it
had been tan. But it was *her*, Luce, the girl from the train.

I started to make my way through the crowd, fighting
against a sea of bodies determined to keep me from her. The
music, a frantic techno beat, seemed to be getting louder and
louder. In my eagerness, I shoved someone a little too vig-
orously, a girl, and she shoved me back. Her angry face was
framed by an impressive *crinière* of frizzy brown hair, and she
stared at me with hostile contempt. On another night, I might
have shrugged it off, or even apologized, but tonight I told
the girl in no uncertain terms what she could do with herself.
Her response was to fling the contents of her drink in my face,
and the gesture was such a cliché that I started laughing and
couldn't stop. It was only after the girl had turned away from
me in disgust that I realized I was crying, and also laughing, at
the same time. Tears were streaming down my face.

In the kitchen, standing over the bathtub, I rinsed the beer
off my face. Floating forlornly in the water were a few tall cans
of Kronenbourg, all the ice having melted long ago. On the
wall was an old poster for a Guy Debord symposium (*Agent der
Kritik gegen ihre Anerkennung*). The lukewarm water felt good,
and I leaned down to soak my hair, which was too long and

always poking me in the eyes. Normally, I got it cut with my father, a ritual between us. He was the type to get his hair cut like clockwork five times a year, but he didn't mind being a little late and waiting for me so that we could go together. After my graduation from gymnasium, I had gone with him not to our usual coiffeur but to a fancier one in Vesterbro, where they tried to charge a supplement for my cut, citing my stiff black "*kinamand*" hair, apparently more difficult to sculpt than my father's blond Scandinavian follicles. In the end, he had paid the higher price, but for both haircuts, placing the extra money on the counter like he was leaving a tip. That was the kind of person he was. On the phone, I'd told him I still had my thesis to finish, which was only partly true. I didn't want to admit that I couldn't afford the train ticket; I didn't want to turn down his inevitable offer to pay for it.

No sign of Luce in the next room. Had it really been her? Every few steps I raised myself up on tiptoe to look over people's heads. What were the chances of running into her like this, a year later, at a stranger's housewarming party? I had dreamt about her, dreamt of just such an encounter, from which I always woke up with the impression that the real dream was now starting, so that all I wanted was to return to that other world, the one I had just left, more or less unwillingly, right in the middle of things, right when it had started to become interesting. Countless times, I had imagined her life in Paris, her first year of medicine at René Descartes . . .

I reached the last door without finding her. Beyond it there were no more rooms; I knew this, but I turned the lever anyway, like a dead man. In my mind, I could already see my empty room at the Cité U: the towel draped over the radiator, the photo of Samuel Beckett (a postcard, really) on the wall, the desk with its mess of papers, the pile of books from the municipal library, one of them lying facedown on the unmade bed . . . And then, suddenly, there she was, standing with her back to me, waiting for the toilet, a stand-alone cabinet located on a landing outside the apartment proper. The party, muffled by the door, called out to me like the lights of a distant town at night. After all the cigarette and hashish smoke, emerging onto the landing was like a breath of pure air. There were two people in front of her. She shifted her weight but didn't turn around when I got in line behind her. Leaning forward, I closed my eyes and breathed in deeply. For a long time, I remained like that—not exhaling, not moving a muscle. When I opened my eyes again, there was no one in front of her: the two of us were alone (in a manner of speaking) for the time being, and I realized that, one, I was more drunk than I had thought, and, two, I needed to pee rather urgently.

I focused on the nape of her neck, and on the words tattooed there.

"The light shines in the darkness," I said to her, slowly, as if reading the words, "and the darkness doesn't understand it."

She didn't react right away, as though thinking about what I had just said. At last, she turned around. Now that all of her hair was gone, there was nothing to focus on but her face. Despite her paleness, she seemed more beautiful, more *herself*, the Luce whose memory I had been carrying around in my wallet all this time like a worn ticket from a concert long past. I hesitated. And her? Did she still remember me?

At that moment, the door to the toilet opened, and she glanced back at me one last time before going inside. She hadn't said a word. I couldn't decide whether to interpret that as a sign or not. I tried not to picture her in there doing her business. And that was when it hit me: all those parties I had gone to, all the strangers I had talked to . . . I hadn't wanted to admit it to myself, but I was looking for *her*. I heard the water going down, and she emerged at last. With her newfound paleness, she resembled more than ever the (presumed) portrait of Lucile Desmoulins that I had seen in the catacombs. As I opened my mouth to speak, the thought of making a fool of myself, of saying the wrong thing, once again brought me up short. Would she, after all this time, still remember our encounter on the train if I brought it up now? Or would she shake her head in incomprehension, as though it had never happened? Better, perhaps, not to ask at all; better to pretend I already knew the answer, I told myself, trying to ignore the throbbing of my bladder. One thing was sure: if I continued to stand there any longer, I was going to wet myself in front of her. *That* would give her something to remember. In the end, I was the first to look away, brushing past her and ducking into the cabinet, though not before blurting out that I would be back, I'm ashamed to admit.

The cabinet was remarkably small, the size of a telephone booth—or a coffin—and as I lowered my zipper, I breathed in the air around me, but there was no trace of her odor, to my disappointment. My urine came out as clear as drinking water, and before the stream weakened I attempted distractedly—an automatism more than anything else—to dislodge a pubic hair stuck stubbornly to the edge of the bowl. There was a door at the bottom of the stairs, through which the two of us could slip out, unseen. Except that I had nowhere to take her. The roof? No, it was probably crammed with people. A bunker deep beneath the ground? A swimming pool filled with ice cubes? If only I wasn't so drunk. The answer I wanted, it was there, in front of me. If I could only . . . And then it came to me: *Kiruna*. In the winter, the sun hardly came up, and for a few weeks it came up not at all. A perpetual dusk reigned, the *blå time*, which was nothing more than a reflection of the sun against the surrounding snow. Of course, I had been there during the summer, when the sun never went down and I had to sleep in a room with blacked-out windows. The Kiruna I had known was full of light, blinding and pure, the light of a camera flash frozen in time . . . My mind continued to race over recollections, images, fantasies, all of them useless to me, all of them beyond my grasp, as I stood there, sweating and peeing. Evacuating urine was one of those things that felt so much better when one was drunk, and I almost wished I could stay here, in this cabinet, forever. It was turning into the longest pee of my life; I had no idea if anyone would be waiting for me when I came out.

III

AFTER FUMIKO

Crow the Aesthète

1. Maryvonne

I became a student at the school for translators and interpreters in Paris because I thought it would be easier than the doctoral thesis I had abandoned. My languages were English and French; neither Danish, my native language, nor Swedish, which I also knew, was part of the school's curriculum. Had my German been better, I might have had an easier time as one of the three-language students, translating into my native tongue but never out of it. (Those who only had two viable languages had to translate in both directions.) To an outsider, working with two languages might seem easier than working with three, but it's always easier to translate towards the language one knows best than away from it.

There were two others like me: Maryvonne, a Frenchwoman in her seventies—by far the oldest student at the school—and René, who had grown up in Switzerland on the shores of Lake Léman and in the French commuter town of Annemasse. (His father was a career diplomat.) He spoke French and English with equal proficiency, his English devoid of the telltale French inflections, the English of a French-speaker educated at an international lycée. He would have been at home among the Anglophones or among the Francophones, though I saw him with neither group. Mostly, he kept to himself, and my few attempts at conversation had met with such blank unresponsiveness that I had soon given up. Maryvonne, on the other hand, I ended up befriending—if such a word could be used to describe what happened—during those first weeks, when it seemed to me that we were always running into each other. Otherwise, we had nothing in common, or so I thought. From the start, she addressed me in English, and though it was clear to me that my French was better, I went along and answered her in kind. Her English was nothing like René's—an English learned in France, with frequent cognates and the occasional false friend. Every morning, I would see her walking ahead of me as I emerged from the subway; every evening I would spot her at the other end of the platform, and after some hesitation, I slowly made my way over to her. That was how we came to be study partners. In the train, we often had to stand because all the seats were taken, her face so close to mine in the crowded car that I was able to make out the little hairs above her upper lip as I tried not to press up against her. She always got off before me, at Étoile, where four subway lines intersected, which meant that she could be going to any part of the city. I could have asked her where she lived, but I never did.

I had no idea what had made Maryvonne decide to become a translator at this point in her life, but I had only to observe her, matter-of-fact and businesslike in Fauchier-Delavigne's class (where we translated from English to French) but timid and hesitant in Michaels's (where we translated from French to English), as a rule deferring to the Anglophones in matters of grammar, to see that I was much the same, albeit the other way around: faltering in front of Fauchier-Delavigne, more at my ease with Michaels. It was perhaps only logical, and inevitable, that a partnership should form between us. We spent a lot of time in the school's bibliothèque, modest even by French-university standards and usually empty, especially since the computer posts were in another room. Sometimes an entire afternoon could go by without another student coming in. At a table in the corner, we would work on our assignments together, articles from *Le Monde* or *The Times* that we translated from French to English and from English to French in preparation for the next exam, where we wouldn't be able to use the dictionaries we had lying open around us. I once tried asking Maryvonne about her reasons for studying translation at the school of translators and interpreters. Right away, I sensed her ready to change the subject, as she leafed slowly through the dictionary in front of her, first in one direction, then in the other, like someone unable to decide what word to look up.

There are ghosts everywhere, she finally said. The city is filled with them. It's become a giant cemetery. When I asked her what she meant, she looked around at the nearby shelves as though we might not be the only ones in the bibliothèque. A few days earlier, on the train, she had nodded silently at an empty corner of the otherwise packed car. It could have been a puddle of vomit or a dog dropping, but Maryvonne had said, A ghost. After that, whenever I noticed an inexplicable gap in a crowd or a mysteriously vacant seat on a bus, her words came back to me. She was a little like a ghost herself, carrying around an invisible burden, it seemed to me. I sensed a distant trauma from her youth responsible, somehow, for her presence here. Watching her make her way through a crowd of students less than half her age, I couldn't help but notice how everyone in the corridor moved aside without a glance in her direction—like tightening the collar of a coat without bothering to verify the provenance of a chilly breeze.

Most of the time, we didn't make small talk, concentrating

on the work at hand, though once she asked me if everyone in
Denmark spoke the way I did. And what way is that? I replied.
My English, according to her, wasn't like *theirs*. (She meant the
Anglophones.) I seldom used slang and my pronunciation was
very clean, very easy to understand. There was something rigid
about my grammar, she concluded, and I wasn't sure from her
tone if she meant it as a compliment or not. For many Danes,
English was like a second mother tongue, a faithful shadow, a
watermark: I read in English more than in Danish, I watched
more films in English, but on a daily basis it was Danish I spoke,
not English. In the end, I told her that it was because English
wasn't really my language; it's easier to be rigorous with a language that isn't one's own. I wasn't sure if Maryvonne took my
answer seriously. She wasn't one to laugh at a joke, and I found
it impossible to guess what she was thinking at a given moment.
Nevertheless, I would commiserate with her when we received
our exam results: in general, my French-to-English was as high
as her English-to-French, her French-to-English as low as my
English-to-French. It occurred to me that if we could somehow become a single person, we would be a force to be reck-
oned with. I told her this, smiling to let her know that it was
meant in jest. She gave me one of her nameless looks, as though
she felt sorry for me, and I immediately regretted my remark.

Of course, there was already someone like that: René,
the diplomat's son. He alone held his own in the company of
both Michaels and Fauchier-Delavigne. Every bilingual has a
language he favors, the way an ambidextrous person always
has a weaker hand. But it was hard to tell with René. As one
might expect, he did well on his exams, which two- and three-
language students took together in the big auditorium. I would
glance up from my paper to see him walking serenely past the
rows of heads bent over desks, and I had the impression that,

for him, the exams were a mere formality. They consisted of
two 250-word articles, extracted from newspapers and reviews
of recent date; we had just under an hour. A monitor stood behind a lectern and, in a show of vigilance, occasionally walked
up and down the rows. But it was obvious to me that keeping watch over an auditorium full of students was difficult, if
not impossible. Individual seating was left to our discretion,
the rows of seats sharply graduated in concentric semicircles
around a "stage" where the monitor stood. Such an arrangement also gave me a view of the students in the rows below
me. Each seat—bolted to the floor—did not quite line up with
the seat in front, one level lower, due to the way the rows
curved around each other, and I found that I could look down
and glimpse an eraser, a hand gripping a pencil, an exam sheet
partially obscured by a shoulder, and that, by leaning forward
a little, ever so discreetly, I gained a better view. If I squinted a
little, I could even make out some of the handwriting. How
many others, through the years, had realized the same thing?

I have Maryvonne, or her presence in front of me, to thank
for my little discovery. It was customary for the two of us to
walk into the auditorium together, coming as we did from
the bibliothèque where we did our last-minute revising before
an exam. Naturally, we ended up choosing seats near one another. Sometimes Maryvonne sat behind me, other times I sat
behind her. (We never sat in the same row, because she found
it distracting.) I did not set out to cheat; I simply wanted to see
where she was on her copy. Any moment, I expected her to
turn around in her seat but she never so much as looked up from
her exam. The idea of cheating did not enter my thoughts, or
at least not right away. This wasn't a mathematics or chemis-
try exam, with correct and incorrect answers; we were being
tested on the quality of our translations, and cribbing another

student's sentences would have been stupid, an admission of guilt. Nevertheless, I let myself glance at Maryvonne's paper when I was stuck on a word (the French formulation of "dandy roll," "chives," "fair trade")—i.e., a small and easily definable unit of meaning, something that a glance inside a dictionary would have resolved in other circumstances, that is to say, anywhere outside the auditorium. I did well—better than on any of my previous exams, where, all too often, not knowing a word or the full meaning of an expression had undermined and compromised the rest of my translation. Not being hampered by vocabulary allowed me to concentrate on the text itself as a whole. Practicing translators—unlike, say, interpreters—would always have their dictionaries at hand, and to forbid their use during an exam was to emphasize unrealistic working conditions. Or that was how I justified it to myself. After all, no one else at the school had to work in two languages not his own; I was simply re-establishing the balance.

Maryvonne congratulated me. I didn't ask what she had scored on her French-to-English. It seemed more and more likely that she would not have her first year. I considered telling her about my discovery, but at the same time I feared her reaction. (I remembered her glaring disapprovingly at a group of students smoking in the common lounge, underneath the no-smoking sign.) She might very well forbid me from sitting behind her after that. In the end, I decided to keep it to myself. At the next exam, we entered the auditorium together as usual, and ever so subtly I let her fall ahead of me so that she would sit down first. Earlier, in the bibliothèque, she had been unusually subdued—even for her—but I chalked it up to nerves: this was, after all, the mid-semester exam. I stared at the back of her head, her silvery gray hair which she didn't bother coloring like most women her age, and I experienced in that moment a flash of tenderness for her. If she only knew! That was when I saw René: he was sitting at the edge of one of the rows, and looked up as we approached. Our eyes met, but there was no change in his gaze: no way to tell if he had recognized me at all. In front of me, Maryvonne suddenly paused, then took the only empty seat in the row directly behind his. All of the nearby seats were taken. It had been so unexpected that I just stood there for a full second, staring down at Maryvonne, who was already busying herself with her little zippered case, the kind used by French schoolchildren for carrying pencils and erasers. Had she figured it out? But how? And why hadn't she said anything? There was nothing else to do; with leaden steps, I continued up the aisle.

The next day, when it became clear that she wasn't going to bring up what had happened, I tried to broach the matter as delicately as possible. But confronted with her blank, unwavering gaze, I found myself hemming and hawing, fumbling for words, and it dawned on me that what she had done—at least on a basic level—was choose a seat because it was available. To dig any deeper was to risk exposing my own motives for bringing up the subject and open myself up to other questions that I wasn't in any position to answer. A few days later, we were given our exam results, and Maryvonne received her highest score ever on her French-to-English. I, on the other hand, had done even worse than usual, on both my English-to-French and my French-to-English. I did my best to pretend I was happy for her, but the more I thought about it, the angrier I became: at her, at myself, at the school. I caught up with Maryvonne after Michaels's class—where, for once, she had been rather sure of herself—and I asked her, right there in the hallway. Or rather, I accused her. In any case, that was how it came out. I told her that I knew she had cheated on her last exam. Anyone walking past could have heard me, but she didn't seem bothered in the least. Her face, calm as a mirror, betrayed nothing. She gazed steadily at me and asked why I thought that. I crossed my arms and replied that it wasn't a matter of thinking it but of knowing it. She had fooled the others but not me. I went into detail about obliquely angled seats, the discretion involved, until the pitying expression on her face made me falter. Finally, I stopped talking altogether and walked away, leaving her standing there—a solitary figure in the corridor that a moment earlier had been full of students—not daring to look behind me before I had turned the corner and was safely out of sight.

I could have apologized, of course. She was pragmatic, if nothing else, and I like to think that she got as much out of our relationship as I did. Had we been more than classmates or study partners, I might have seen things differently, perhaps. I might have given more thought to her feelings. But there was no getting around the fact that I had just admitted my own guilt to her. In accusing her, I had only managed to accuse myself. What if she went to Michaels or Fauchier-Delavigne? What if she denounced me at the secrétariat? When she did neither, I began to avoid her. She seemed to take the hint and didn't insist. We ignored each other in class and in the corridors. She didn't sit behind René again, and he didn't sit in front of her, either. As for me, I made a point of sitting behind one of the Chinese students, to show her that I wasn't cheating. My exam scores suffered, and the thought occurred to me that, all along, it should have been her and me sitting together. Not one of us behind the other but, rather, side by side, glancing at each other's tests when necessary, she at my French-to-English and I at her English-to-French. She was my dictionary as much as I was her grammar, and vice versa. It would have been the logical arrangement, a happy marriage of convenience. But things could never go back to what they had been. I had sought her out at the start of the year because I felt that it made sense, given our respective weaknesses. Deep inside, I had never liked the silent judgments, the reticence, the general lack of feeling. A part of me began to suspect that she hadn't cheated on the exam at all, and in some ways that made it worse: she had managed, without cheating, to get a good score on her French-to-English.

Alone, I studied more assiduously than ever before. Each new expression or word in French I noted diligently in a large Clairefontaine notebook. I read as much as I could, and always with a pencil in hand: a book I didn't take notes on was a book I hadn't really read, I told myself. My marks improved, though I feared it wasn't enough to save me. One afternoon, in the bibliothèque—I tried to use it when I knew Maryvonne wouldn't be there—René walked in and sat down at one of the tables. The entire time, he did nothing but stare blankly at the wall. Or so it seemed to me. Then, just as suddenly, he stood up and walked out. In the auditorium, observing him from several rows away, I grew familiar with his exam-taking habits. He always took off his watch before he started, and every so often he liked to pick his nose discreetly with the eraser end of his pencil. There was also a steady supply of sweets— gummy bears, usually, or a chocolate bar of some kind. He worked unhurriedly, methodically, rarely changing what he'd written. It was almost as though he wasn't taking the same exam as the rest of us. Sometimes, on my way to hand in my copy, I would walk past his empty seat. The only trace of his presence was one or two crumpled candy wrappers on the desk.

2. Crow the Aesthète

Edward Michaels was, to say the least, one of the more eccentric professors at the school for translators and interpreters. He owned a vintage motorcycle—a beautifully restored Triumph Bonneville—and there was a chair in his name at the Collège de France. Rumor had it that he had missed being elected to the Académie française by a single vote not once but twice, and was waiting for another *académicien* to croak and vacate a seat so that he could try again. (Victor Hugo had also made it on his third attempt.) If elected, he would be the first Englishman to join the ranks of the Immortals.

The day he gave us Marcel Moiré's poem to translate, one of the Anglophones questioned the choice of material. This being a technical school, literary translation was relegated to the background, when not ignored altogether. Michaels—who considered himself the last bastion of the old guard, its self-declared defender, a role he seemed to take both seriously and as an obscure joke he was playing on himself—replied that anyone could translate a technical document with the right vocabulary, because there was nothing hidden beneath the surface. (He made a joke about juridical language being the exception, and a few people laughed.) On the other hand, the number of poems defying translation were legion. A poem was, by definition, untranslatable. And that was where, from time to time, every translator worthy of his profession should test his mettle.

We were given a week to translate Moiré's poem into English, which to me seemed excessive. An entire week to translate six small lines? I couldn't help but wonder if there was something else, something more, that Michaels wanted us to discover; if, perhaps, the poem might be a litmus test, a shibboleth for translators, his way of asking us a question, though I wasn't sure what the question might be.

My initial effort was a word-for-word translation:

> *A crow / landed on an island / in the middle of a river. /*
> *The discerning bird / equally pedantic and clever / did it for*
> *the rhyme.*

With my next, less-than-literal translation, I attempted to reproduce the rhymes of the original:

> *A black-jet / alighted on an islet / there amidst a rivulet. /*
> *The corvo / clever little thing, did so / for the archipelago.*

I had maintained the poem's principal elements—the bird, the piece of land, the body of water—but Moiré's plain vocabulary had been swallowed up by my baroque language. Over and over I retranslated the poem, toying with different registers and styles, as I tried to replicate in English Moiré's elusive voice. For most of the week, I worked on the poem and little else. The more I pored over the words, the more I became convinced that a week wasn't enough. A lifetime wouldn't be enough. I gave up on meter and then on meaning as well:

> *A crow / took roost atop a château / near a mound of snow*
> *A crow / perched on a garrot / in the shade of a chestnut*
> *A weasel / stood on an easel / within a patch of teasel*
> *A lizard / shook its gizzard / amidst a blizzard*
> *A mink / sipped a drink / on a kitchen sink*

By the end of the week, the original crow had become every animal under the sun and performed, for the sake of the rhyme, all manner of aleatory acts. The words themselves were not important; Moiré's doggerel was not dependent on meaning at all. Was that, I wondered, the answer to Michaels's unspoken question?

> *Crow the aesthète / smartest bird I ever met / did it for the couplet.*

I don't know what methods my classmates opted for, what conclusions they arrived at. No doubt, some chose to translate the poem literally and were done in a few minutes, while others took longer to find a suitable compromise between the literal and the idiomatic. The purpose of the exercise, I imagine, was to demonstrate the difficulties of translation, in the face of which a good translator must always find an adequate solution. You are not translating a language, you are translating a text. That was what Edward Michaels had told us at the start of the semester. A good translator is neither faithful nor unfaithful. A good translator goes beyond content and form to reveal the impossibility of defining a language.

On the day we were to discuss our translations, I noticed right away that René was absent. Michaels had yet to arrive. (He was often late.) The Anglophones, as usual, were chattering amongst themselves. At that moment, my gaze fell on Maryvonne. She was sitting in her usual spot, and I realized with a start that she was staring at me. Her gaze felt strange after so many weeks of ignoring each other. How long had she been watching me? I continued to return her stare.

Only the other night, I had dreamt that Maryvonne was waiting for me, as usual, at the far end of the platform. As I approached her, she said, "If you want, I can put you in contact with her." When I said nothing, she went on: "I know that you've lost someone. At the translation school, from the moment I first saw you, I could tell." Unexpectedly, she smiled. "You needn't be afraid."

"Who says I'm afraid?"

"You blame yourself for her death. But it wasn't your fault; you didn't kill her. She killed herself." Then: "It's important that you continue to translate in both directions, as you've been doing. From English to French and from French to English. It's the only way."

Before I could question her further—the only way for what, exactly?—the dream ended and I woke up.

Lying there in the darkness, I wanted nothing more than to ask my former study partner how she had translated Moiré's poem. What had she come up with? Had she decided in favor of meaning or rhyme, or both? I saw myself going over to her and apologizing, suggesting that we study together again. But then I saw her eyes narrow, knowingly, and I realized that the loneliness I saw reflected there was none other than my own. I remembered my father once telling me that in a dream, I was everything and everyone (and everything and everyone was me). We had argued about it for a long time. Perhaps he had been right, all along. I got up and left the room; I made my way down the deserted hallway until I came to the biblio, where I found René, alone, in the corner. He didn't look up when I approached the table—the same table where Maryvonne and I had spent many long, studious hours. To my surprise, he was still working on Moiré's poem. It's hard to say how many translations there were. I counted at least forty or fifty—I myself had not gotten past thirty—by the time his pencil stopped moving and he acknowledged my

presence. I deduced, from the scattered bits of paper, that he
was translating his own translations, going back and forth between his two languages.

Forgot the time, he muttered, and I told him not to worry,
Michaels was late again. No doubt practicing the elbow lift in
his office, René said, mimicking someone raising an invisible
drink to his lips, and we both smiled as though at an old joke.
Hastily gathering up his papers, he asked me why I had sought
him out. How had I known he would be here? I pretended to
study the dusty shelves, the rows of outdated dictionaries in a
dozen languages that didn't include Danish. A sort of restless-
ness, or should I say loneliness, or sadness, had led me to the
bibliothèque. How do you know I came here for you? I said
to him. It was a challenge, the way I said it, and he laughed,
suddenly no longer in a hurry. He slowly, lazily, threw himself
backwards in his chair, like someone who has made a decision.
I don't feel like class today, he said. Let's go downstairs.

In the student canteen, we stood at one of the cannabis-
and-merguez-smelling tables with our thimbles of coffee from
the automatic dispenser and discussed cinema, literature, music.
All the while, I felt that we were skirting around the subject of
school, of grades and exams, as though some tacit understanding influenced the course of our thoughts. I waited for him to
say that he had noticed me staring at him in the auditorium,
watching him from afar; instead, he said that students cheated
during exams all the time, especially if one of their languages
wasn't strong enough. Without looking up from my empty
cup, I asked him what he was suggesting. As long as you
don't get caught, it's not a big deal, I heard him say. Everyone
here does it, or practically everyone. Listening to him talk, I
couldn't help questioning my own obliviousness to something
that had been going on all around me, right under my nose.

And what about you? I asked. *You* don't need anyone's help. What's in it for you? He seemed to think about my words before answering. I could use an ally, a like mind. A friend, he meant, though he didn't say it. For a moment we were both silent, as though an angel had passed by. I asked him what he'd ended up with, after translating Moiré's poem back and forth so many times. René smiled, then recited:

> *A crow / flew across a meadow / chasing its own shadow. / The bird was fine / it hadn't lost its mind / it did it for the rhyme.*

A week after the end-of-semester exam—or "passage exam," in the school's jargon—I came back to the school and there it was, my name among the students *reçus en deuxième année*. Just above it was René's. Our names, on the bulletin board where exam results were posted, had never been so close together. I didn't see Maryvonne's name anywhere. I remembered the way she had stared at me from across the room, and suddenly I was convinced that it hadn't been contempt but despair in her eyes that day. What would have happened if I had asked to see her translation of Marcel Moiré's poem? I imagined her admitting—after some hesitation—that she had given up after failing to come up with a satisfactory English version on her own. Would she have been grateful if, at that moment, I had shown her mine? Now I would never know.

It was strange; though I must have continued, until the end of the first year, to catch glimpses of her—in the corridors, emerging from the elevator, seated at her desk—I have no memory of it at all, as though she ceased to exist in the waking world after appearing before me in my dream. More likely, it was I who had become increasingly preoccupied with my immediate future. I would do whatever it took to become a translator. By then, I had started sitting next to René during exams, the two of us in the same row, side by side. After all, what is so strange about two friends choosing to sit in proximity to one another? Absolutely nothing, of course.

The Impossibility of Crows

1. Henrik and Gém

I'm not sure at what point I first noticed the woman following us. Gém and I were at the big Monoprix in Saint-Germain-des-Prés, and we'd just left the wine-and-beer shelf where I had picked out a six-pack of Grimbergen. Now I was pushing my little caddy towards the frozen foods and casting discreet glances behind me. She was pretending to look at the artisanal ciders. Mid-thirties perhaps, the cut of her blond hair fashionably asymmetrical. Could she be a social worker? An undercover cop? She was too well dressed for a cop. Or a social worker, for that matter.

It was a typical outing for Gém and me. Taking my god-daughter shopping for her favorite foods gave me a reason—an excuse—to spend time with her. I had only chosen this particular Monoprix because we'd been to see a puppet play across the street at the Crous, which I had frequented in my student days for the odd workshop. It told the story of a girl who, upon learning that her brothers were transformed into ravens when she was an infant, sets out to find them. There weren't many fairy tales about little girls embarking on adventures, and I thought that an adaptation of "The Seven Ravens" might appeal to Gém. Since leaving the center, she hadn't stopped talking about the play, walking alongside me with one delicate hand on the cart like a supermarket shepherdess. Suddenly, I noticed that the woman was no longer behind us. Had I imagined the whole thing? I stared at the spot where she had been just a moment ago. I should have been relieved, but I wasn't. Once again I looked around. And that was when I realized that Gém had also disappeared.

After scouring the entire store, I finally spotted her near the cash registers. With her was the woman I had noticed earlier. Seeing them together, I was struck by how alike they looked, with their similar blond hair, their similar skin. Like mother and daughter. My first impulse was to go to them, but I didn't move. Instead, I imagined myself turning my back and walking away. I would leave the Monoprix, cross the intersection, descend the steps of the métro, and melt into the crowd of commuters. Gém would never hear from me again. I would move to another arrondissement, change my phone number, disappear from her life. I would become a ghost in this city. The seven brothers, after they were turned into ravens, retired to a mountain made of glass, far from everything and everyone. That was what I would do. They had lived like that, all those years, until the little girl came looking for them . . .

I heard my name being called. Gém was calling out to me. When I approached them, the woman said pleasantly, "I found her wandering around and thought she was lost."

"I wasn't *really* lost," Gém said in a patronizing tone. "My father and I like to play hide-and-seek when we go to the store."

"And where is your father?"

"He's right there."

The woman looked at me, like someone unsure of a joke. "So she's your . . . ?"

"Yes," I made myself say. Thanking her, I started to turn away when she held out a card, which informed me that she was a scout for an agency in Paris, recruiting children for a publicity campaign.

"She's very talented, your . . . daughter."

I looked up from the card, which had only her forename, as if she were a movie star or a variety singer. "Talented in what way?"

"Well, she's very, shall we say, convincing. She convinced me, for example."

"And what did she convince you of, exactly?"

"That you're her father."

When I was out with Gémanuelle, we would sometimes play a game. It was Gém herself who had been the initiator. One day, I had taken her to an exhibition on Samuel Beckett at the Beaubourg center, and we were in line when she pointed to a sign stating that parents didn't have to pay admission for children under ten. She told me that she could be my daughter; then I wouldn't have to pay for her. I told her I didn't mind paying, but she was insistent, as if it were her money. (In passing, I always refused René's offers to reimburse me for an outing: I wasn't a babysitter; if I chose to spend time with my goddaughter, it was because I wanted to.) That day, as I was buying our tickets, Gém declared loudly that I was her father, but the woman behind the glass only smiled at her, as if she didn't see me at all, and for the rest of the afternoon, while Gém continued to call me "Papa," obviously enjoying the attention, I kept thinking: if I really were her father, would she feel the need to announce it to the world?

I had planned to tell René about the incident when I gave him the highlights of my day with his daughter, but for whatever reason I never got the chance. He might have come home later than usual and found me asleep on his couch, or perhaps I had been awake that night and he started talking to me, as he often did, about some problem at his work. In any case, the moment passed, and it became our secret, between Gém and me. For a child, she was very good at keeping secrets. If I told her not to say something, I knew that she wouldn't tell René. Once, I had tested her: After we saw a dead pigeon on the Terrasse Lautréamont, I told her we should keep it between us. (This was at the height of her pigeon obsession.) A week later, I asked René if he knew anything about a dead pigeon on the Terrasse Lautréamont, and he had looked at me like I was crazy.

Maybe I was a little crazy. To be perfectly honest, I'm not sure which one of us turned the daughter-father thing into a game. I saw how much fun she'd had at the Samuel Beckett exhibit (did she notice that it brought me pleasure too?), and I suppose it made a certain kind of sense to play make-believe again when we went to the park or to the supermarket, even if it resulted in calling undue attention to ourselves. I could never say no to Gém. She was used to René being at work, or away on a business trip, or, when he was home, shut up in his room working on his newest project (at the moment, a film script). I, on the other hand, always had time for her. Was it any surprise that she should want to pretend that I was her father? Or that I might want to keep this little detail from my friend, at least for the time being?

In public, I tried not to notice the heads turning, the second glances we were the object of—even without the "Papa" routine. It wasn't hard to see why. She was a strikingly beautiful six-year-old, tall for her age, with long blond hair, and I was her supposed father: of unremarkable height, shabbily dressed, unmistakably Asian. At a commercial center, seeing the two of us in one of the wall-to-wall mirrors, I had the thought that we didn't belong to the same species. The oddest of odd pairings, we were like Charles and Cordelia, Léon and Mathilda, Alain and Joséphine . . . That said, why *couldn't* she be my daughter? My own Danish parents, after all, looked nothing like me. In fact, Gém could have easily passed for their child—or grandchild, as though certain family traits had simply skipped a generation. But it went deeper than mere appearances. For the space of a few moments, she really *was* my daughter, or something more than a daughter, although what that "something" was I couldn't have put into words or given a name to.

On the way home, there was an incident in one of the subway tunnels. "Incident" meaning someone had tried to throw himself onto the rails, the degree of success or failure reflected by the duration of the delay. We could remain where we were or take one of the RER lines, whose trains stopped less frequently than those of the métro. On the other hand, it involved braving the jungle of Châtelet–Les Halles, something I tried to avoid whenever possible.

I let Gém choose, knowing already what she would answer. She loved the long passageway with its moving walkway that led to the station. She seemed more animated than usual, glancing behind us like we were being followed and giggling to herself. I asked her what she found so funny, but she only shook her head, hiding her smile with her hand, as I struggled with my many shopping bags. We came to a stop on the "rolling carpet," as Gém called it. On the walls was the same poster—repeated over and over—for an upcoming concert at the Zénith, showing a man with long greasy hair and a bloody nose and mouth, which was stretched upwards in a rictus. I reached into my pocket to make sure I had our tickets for the métro and felt something else against my fingers. I thought I had tossed it, but here it was, at the bottom of my pocket. I carefully set down the shopping bags between my feet and took out the card while Gém, with her back to me, stared up at the passing posters, one for a Danish film starring Paprika Steen alternating with another for Bonduelle salads. When I brought the card up to my nose, I detected a faint whiff of what might've been perfume. Back at the Monoprix, after asking me to call her if I changed my mind, she had placed a hand, briefly, on my wrist. I could still feel the weight of her fingers against my skin.

"Gaëtane said that I could become famous," I heard Gém say.

"Who?"

By then, we were standing on the platform waiting for the RER. "*Gaëtane*. From the *shop*. You weren't there when she told me." She seemed to think about it for a moment, then looked up at me, almost shyly. "Do you think I could become famous, Papa?"

There was no one within earshot on the platform. And yet she had addressed me as "Papa." I told her—stammering my words a bit—that fame wasn't necessarily a good thing, or something to that effect.

"Really?"

Her expression was more curious than petulant. "She said that my face would be on posters." Gém glanced around her, as though looking for someone. "But I don't really want that," she said, soberly.

I looked down at her. "You don't?"

"What I want," she went on, her voice suddenly very loud,

"is to be in *movies*. I think that would be far better and far more interesting."

The train pulled in. As usual, a number of people started to board as soon as the doors opened, instead of making way for those getting off, and a general tohu-bohu ensued. There were no available seats left in the compartment. I tried to shield Gém with my body as more people got on. For a while, the platforms had been decorated with couplets in the style of La Fontaine ("The one who, getting on, shoves another / Will not make the train leave any faster"), but it would seem that the slogans hadn't had much of an impact on the general population.

Near the doors, an argument had broken out between two men. One seemed to be the aggressor, taking advantage of the other's unwillingness to escalate the confrontation.

"We can talk about it later," I said. "In the meantime, let's not tell your . . . René about any of this just yet. OK?"

"But why?"

I thought about the dead pigeon on the Terrasse Lautréamont. "You know how busy he is. Promise me you'll keep it between us for now?"

At that moment, the man itching for a fight decided to take things to the next level, and this time several heads—including Gém's—turned at the unmistakable sound of a fist making contact with someone's face.

We got back to René's place and were greeted by a burnt odor noticeable even from the landing. In the kitchen sink I found several broken dishes and a blackened casserole encrusted with charred, embryonic remains that looked almost extraterrestrial in origin. I'm not entirely sure why, but the idea came to me that I was staring at my soul laid bare in all its somber and gruesome splendor, like a portrait of Dorian Gray or the image of a smoker's lungs as seen in an anti-smoking poster. I heard René whistling Charles Trenet's "La Mer" in the bathroom. With some difficulty, I tore my gaze away from the burnt remains of the casserole and went in search of my friend. He was hunched over a piece of plywood balanced across the tub. Atop it was an old Hermes typewriter and a mess of papers. For several long moments I watched him at his makeshift desk, pecking laboriously away, one letter at a time. He didn't notice me standing in the doorway until I cleared my throat.

"Ideas," he said, continuing to type, "they're like dreams: you forget them if you don't write them down at once . . ."

I realized that he was drunk. Only then did I notice a bottle of Tullamore Dew that had been partially hidden by the typewriter.

"Go on to your room," I told Gém, who was still beside me, staring at René.

"No, no, it's fine. She can stay. It's not like she hasn't seen me like this before."

Gém turned from me to René, then back to me.

"Don't look at *him*," René said. "I said you can stay."

"But I want to go to my room," she said.

When Gém was gone and it was just the two of us, René sighed. "See that? She already listens to you more than she listens to me."

I asked him what he was doing home so early, and he made a vague gesture, as though the question was too complicated to address.

"Did something happen at work?"

"Is that what you think?" He shuffled distractedly through

the papers in front of him. "You know, sometimes, I think *you're* her real father."

It wasn't the first time I had heard him say this, and each time, a part of me wanted to believe he was being sincere.

He started typing again. "It's a funny thing, the idea of a godparent . . ."

"What do you mean?"

"My point exactly. It can mean something, or nothing at all."

Without waiting for an answer, he turned his attention back to the Hermes, typing so slowly and with such long pauses between key strikes that each letter could have been a word, an entire sentence. I stood watching him for a few moments longer, then went out to the kitchen. After all, someone had to make dinner.

When was the last time the three of us had sat down together for a meal? It was either Gém and me, or—if she was already in bed—me and René. Out of the corner of my eye, I noticed Gém fidgeting in her seat, and before I could say anything she announced to the table, "We saw a real fight today!"

René looked at her, then at me. "A fight? Really?"

"It was nothing," I said, relieved that she hadn't mentioned the woman. "Two idiots. Or rather, one idiot, who picked a fight with someone who didn't want to fight. Typical, right? Then the one who didn't want to fight suddenly knocked him out with one punch."

"It was just like in a movie!" Gém said.

René leaned over to her. "Which one?"

She looked at him, uncertain.

"Who are you in the movie, Gém?"

"Um, I don't know."

"Are you OK?" René turned to me. "Is she OK?" Then, before I could answer, "Why didn't you say something earlier?"

"It slipped my mind."

"Is there anything else you haven't told me?"

I forced myself to return his stare. When the moment was right, I would tell Gém that she wasn't to call me "Papa" unless it was part of the game. As for the game itself, I didn't know if I was capable of putting an end to it just yet. The thought that she might for a little while see me as her father left me feeling happy and despondent at the same time.

René shook his head. "This city gets worse each year. When they're not overturning cars and setting fire to them . . ."

Only last week, he'd gone on about the Forum des Halles under construction, the black tarp covering one of the towers in Montparnasse, another Starbucks that had just opened near Opéra. He had even misquoted Baudelaire ("*le coeur d'une ville change plus vite que la forme d'un mortel*") while mourning the end of an era, a Paris that had become unrecognizable, the shadow of its own shadow.

". . . and I started thinking about what a bad father I've been lately."

He was still staring at Gém, and as if on cue, the two of them started pumping their fists in the air for a game of pebble-leaf-scissors.

"That's why," René went on, distracted, "I took . . . a leave . . . of absence . . ."

I watched them play. Real father and real daughter. This was their little thing: each was the other's mirror. Pebble for pebble, leaf for leaf, scissors for scissors. The two of them could keep it up for far longer than should have been possible. I had once attempted the same thing with her, but it amounted to me guessing what hand she was going to play, and nothing more. Perhaps, in the end, that was all it was.

The next day, sitting on the steps of the BNF, I reached into my pocket and took out Gaëtane's card. Below her name she had written down a phone number—her personal line, no doubt. When was the last time a woman had given me her number? Next to me, my lunch, a *formule* from Paul, lay mostly untouched. Even if it didn't mean what I might want it to mean, I couldn't help but let my thoughts wander. Down below, on the sidewalk, people walked past—locals, tourists, students—a continuous stream. Every day I took my lunch here because it was easy to find a secluded spot, and it wasn't far from the pharmaceutical firm where I worked, in the translation department.

I turned the card over, but there was no additional message on the back. Danish visiting cards were often printed on both sides, so that if dropped they would land right side up. I let the card slip from my fingers and watched it flutter to the ground near my feet. Bending down, I saw that it had landed right side up. On an impulse, I picked up the card and dropped it again. Right side up again. I dropped it a third time, and a third time it landed right side up. My neck prickled. I looked up, half expecting to find Gaëtane standing there, but there was only a group of students at the far end of the steps, taking a break from a study session in the library's rez-de-jardin. Their voices, the sound of their laughter, reached me as if from an impossible distance.

All of a sudden I felt utterly alone, condemned to nothingness, like the last of the Mohicans. Back in Denmark I used to watch a show called *Sporløs* every Sunday. Each episode featured a guest whose close one had disappeared, and who, with the host, passed most of the hour communicating via satellite with a reporter in some far-off country (because Denmark was too small for anyone to disappear within its borders). By the end of the episode, they were able to locate whoever was missing—as if anyone could be found when one made the effort—and it was obvious that only the success stories became episodes, which made me wonder about all the failures, the relatives who remained missing.

Seeing people reunited after being apart for many years left me with a strange feeling of emptiness. I remember an episode in which they tracked a Swede to a small Japanese town where he was the owner of a French restaurant. He had mostly kept to himself and never married—no dutiful Japanese wife for him. The townspeople thought he was French. The episode concluded with a shot of two Swedes embracing at the French restaurant. The Japanese staff could be seen at attention in the background, and I remember thinking that tracking down a blond-haired Swede in Japan couldn't be all that difficult, a much simpler task than looking for my biological parents, which would be like looking for a piece of hay in a haystack.

In the past, my thoughts had turned to them at odd moments. Though I didn't even know what my biological parents looked like, I would wonder if they were happy where they were. Assuming they were still alive, of course. When asked—often by those who didn't know me—if I wanted to find my "real" parents, I would answer that my parents—that is, my Danish parents—had found me first. *They* were my real parents. What did it matter that I didn't share their genes? If anything, I considered myself lucky not to have my father's unreliable metabolism and absurdly bad memory. Or my mother's hereditary cancer. I took after them in other ways: a certain Danish shyness and pedantism, a fondness for rainy days, *Olsen Gang* references and the poetry of Halfdan Rasmussen. As if I had, simply by being near them, absorbed their habits and values like so much discarded genetic material floating around their bodies in the form of dead skin cells and other motes of dust.

I ripped the card into tiny pieces and let the wind scatter them over the steps. In no time at all, there was nothing left. It was for the best, I told myself. In the end, I was doing Gém a service. She needed, more than anything else, a normal childhood; things were already hard enough for her, having someone like René as a father. (Her mother had left when Gém was less than a year old. I had often thought: If Gém had a mother, would she still need me? Then I would think: Does she really need me? Or am I the one who needs her?) Gathering up my uneaten lunch, I noticed that a stray piece from the card had fallen into my jambon-gruyère. I carefully picked it out and saw that it was part of Gaëtane's phone number—one digit, half of another. A dozen steps farther down, I found another little white speck, but there was no writing on it. I couldn't even be sure it had come from her card. Though it was already late, I started scouring the ground for other bits of paper. I promised myself that if I came across one more digit from her phone number, or a letter from her name, I would tell René everything. I continued to make my way along the sidewalk, pausing every time I saw something small and white. The shadows had grown much longer by the time I gave up. No point in going back to work now.

I had combed the entire length of the promenade and was now standing in the quadrangle of the nearby MK2. Without a second thought, I walked in and got a ticket for the film whose poster I had seen in the underground tunnels. Paprika Steen plays an alien who takes over the body of a Danish woman and becomes a teacher at a high school in Viborg. Her character has come to Earth as part of an intergalactic expedition to learn about human behavior and bring back a few specimens to the mother planet for cloning. Perhaps it was the effect of my native tongue; perhaps I wouldn't have been so moved if the film had been in French. When the lights came back on, I realized that I had wept through the entire thing. My friend trusted me with his daughter. And why shouldn't he? I was good for Gém and he knew it. Why should that change now? I asked myself this, for the nth time, as I left the cinema. At one of the brasseries along the promenade, I stood at the counter with my half-pint of beer and stared at the scraps of paper laid out like confetti on the zinc. (There was even a chickpea that had somehow gotten mixed in among them.) I would tell him anyway, come what may. I would empty my rucksack, show him everything I'd been carrying around—the woman, the game, all of it.

I was a little drunk when I reached René's building and tottered up the stairs to his floor. Standing in front of his door, I tried to make out the voices coming from the other side. Music, a woman's laughter. I continued to stand there, not moving at all. A man and a woman of a certain age from one of the upper floors came down the steps. They nodded and said "*Bonsoir.*" I nodded and said "*Bonsoir.*" Then I was alone on the landing again. Did it ever bother me, growing up, not to look like my parents? René had once asked me. The truth was that, most of the time, I forgot that I didn't look like them. Was it a conscious effort on their part not to put mirrors in the house? I had never asked them about it; the answer had never interested me. The only mirror—that I recall, anyway—was in our bathroom, and it wasn't until my sixth or seventh year that I was tall enough to look into it without standing atop the footstool that my father had built when he lived in the City during the seventies. I turned back to the door. My secret fear had always been that any child of mine wouldn't resemble me at all. It was also, strangely enough, my secret hope, my unspoken fantasy.

René had made me a key when I first started picking Gém up from school, but I reached out and pressed the bell.

2. The Farewell Party

A month later, I couldn't help but feel a sensation of déjà vu, of déjà vécu, standing in front of his door again. From within, I heard voices, music, laughter. I still had the key, my key, which René hadn't asked for, or even brought up, since finding out about "the game" I'd been playing with Gém—most likely, he didn't realize that I still had it. Gaëtane was now her agent, manager, whatever you cared to call it. Over the past few weeks, when no one was there, I had taken to letting myself into my friend's apartment, for no other purpose than to prowl around the rooms like an amnesiac burglar, observing all the little changes that had taken place since my banishment (a new magnet on the refrigerator, a cushion that had changed position, René's sempiternal bottle of Tullamore Dew next to a pack of Gaëtane's Muratti cigarettes). I knew that Gaëtane hadn't forgiven me for lying to her about Gém and—in her words—making a fool out of her. I continued to stand there, staring at the door, a typical French-style door, with the knob at the center that didn't turn. And in my hand, the key that no

one knew I had. An image came to me then, a fragment of a
dream from a few nights ago. In my dream, I had found myself
in the crawlspace under one of the métro grates. Above my
head, I could see people walking past, across the grate. Once
in a while, a cigarette butt would land at my feet, like a stray
flake of snow. It didn't occur to me to wonder why I was down
there, or why no one ever questioned my presence under the
sidewalk, but—thinking about it now—I had probably been
watching the passersby for months, if not years.

"What the hell are you doing?"

I looked up to find René staring at me from the open
doorway.

"I almost thought you weren't coming." Did he seem disappointed, or simply surprised?

"Have I ever missed my godchild's birthday before?"

"Come on," he said, ushering me in, "let me show you
something."

On the kitchen counter, next to the sink, was an enormous
white cake.

"Beautiful, no?"

I glanced over at René, who wore the faintly satisfied smile
of an artist contemplating his handiwork. It was to all appearances a painstakingly detailed likeness of an Haussmann-style
building, one I might expect to see in the eighth or ninth
arrondissement.

"Are you and Gaëtane getting married?"

"Very funny. Our relationship is strictly professional." He
returned my gaze, and I wasn't sure whether to believe him or
not. "She's Gém's manager, nothing more, nothing less. The
cake was her idea." From the fridge, René took out two bottles of Grimbergen and passed one to me. "Look closer. Go on.
Look."

I did as he asked, and it was only with my nose practically touching the frosting that I was able to make out the minuscule writing above each of the doorways. L'ORÉAL, it read. Suddenly light-headed, I straightened up and took a long swallow of my beer.

"It's an exact replica of the main headquarters, right down to the sidewalks. Don't ask me how much it cost because it cost a fortune."

I didn't know what to say.

"Of course, we could also have gone with the international division in Clichy, but a larger L'Oréal logo seemed, I don't know, tacky. I think, of the two, this was the better choice . . ."

She doesn't want this, I wanted to tell him, but I held myself back. There had been a moment to say such things, when it wasn't too late.

"These past few weeks," René said, sipping his beer, "so much has changed. Thanks to Gaëtane. *She* did all this!"

I knew that Gaëtane would have preferred that I not be present to celebrate her new job at the Ambrosio Group, a talent agency in Rome where she would have her own office overlooking the Tiber. This was her party as much as it was Gém's. My friend, bottle halfway to his lips, nodded at me. "I told her that you would come no matter what, that you had never missed one of Gém's birthdays. Frankly, I think she's a little jealous of what the two of you have. Can you blame her? *I'm* jealous. She wants what's best for Gém, the same as you."

That day, in the subway, Gém had said what she wanted. She had pointed at the movie posters and said, That's what I want. What I hadn't realized, at the time, was that she was addressing not me but Gaëtane, who had followed us and was standing nearby, just beyond my line of sight.

René went on: "I know you still don't trust her. But that's

because you don't know her like I do. It's true that she can be a bit . . ." He made a vague gesture with his hand. "At least be happy for Gém. Her face is going to be on billboards all over town!"

I had told myself that I wouldn't make any trouble. If it had been me, no one would have known I was leaving; I would never have given a going-away party, which was like a celebration of sorrow. I put aside my misgivings and helped René carry the birthday cake into the living room, where everyone was waiting. They were all there, René's guests and their kids. It was quite a turnout. Gaëtane had brought her new Italian assistant, Nunzio, a curly-haired young man with the broadshouldered physique of a footballer. They stood on either side of Gém like bodyguards. Gém was the only one sitting. As René and I set the cake down in front of her, I tried to catch her eye. Her hair had been done up in a strange fashion, intricately braided, and she had what looked like sparkles at her temples and on her cheeks, multicolored accents that caught the light in the room.

"I'd like to thank everyone for coming tonight to celebrate this momentous occasion," Gaëtane began, as I tuned out the rest of her speech, which wasn't meant for me anyway— I had the impression that she was addressing everyone in the room but me.

Nearby, two small boys sniggered. I saw them eyeing Gém in a none-too-friendly way, and it occurred to me that having her face plastered all across the city was not going to help her popularity any, among her classmates. Behind her, a homemade banner proclaimed BONNE ANNIVERSAIRE. The mistake in the gender—it should have read BON ANNIVERSAIRE— was René being his usual inattentive self: I had already seen him make the same slip on more than one occasion, possibly owing to a conflation with BONNE ANNÉE. (Even when we were students at the translation school, his work—however brilliant—had often contained elementary spelling errors that I attributed to the privilege of a native speaker in his own language.)

René had his hands full, laughing at jokes, kissing people's cheeks. I didn't know anyone; most of the guests were either colleagues or former colleagues of René's in one capacity or another. From afar, I tried to keep an eye on Gém, waiting for an occasion to speak to her, all the while talking to René's colleagues, or former colleagues, fielding questions about translation, sushi and Denmark. Were the Danish really as happy as they claimed to be? I told my interlocutor that it was hard enough answering that question for myself without having to worry about five million other human beings as well. At one point, I noticed Gém at the other end of the room. She was sitting on the floor, sprawled there idly, sluggishly, as though she found her own body a nuisance. The people near her behaved as though they didn't see her at all. Where was Gaëtane? When I looked again in Gém's direction a moment later, she was no longer there, as though what I had seen had been nothing more than a vision of her. Not even bothering to excuse myself, I walked away from the person I was talking to and headed towards the kitchen. Intending to get myself another beer (or something stronger), I started to push open the swinging door when I saw them: Gaëtane and her assistant. They were breathing hard, and Gaëtane gasped, "You're an octopus!" I let the door close silently on them.

Of course. I might have guessed. Resisting the urge to leave the party right there and then, I continued wandering around like someone with nowhere to go. Like a ghost haunting the remains of his old life. In the hallway, I found René waiting in line for the toilet. Something in his expression irritated me, and I asked him, point-blank:

"Do you really think she wants what's best for Gém?"

"Henrik, we've been over this."

"Have you seen her card? All it has is her first name!"

"That's her thing," René said. "To differentiate herself from the other scouts."

"And following people home? Is that also to differentiate herself?"

René ran a hand through his hair. "You have to stop this." He glanced around. "If Gaëtane hears you . . . This is why she didn't want you here tonight. You can't keep accusing her of things you have no proof of. You know what she told me? That *you're* the bad influence on Gém."

I knew why she didn't want me here: I was her only real competition for Gém's affection. Suddenly, the party, the cake—it all became clear.

"Are you going with her?" I asked him.

"Huh?"

"To Rome. Tell me you're not going."

René didn't answer. He looked uncomfortable, but it could have just been his increasing need for the bathroom.

"Deep inside, you know she doesn't want this. The modeling, the billboards, the fancy hairdo with all the little tresses . . ."

"Henrik, let it go." He sighed. "Gaëtane has worked with a lot of—"

"Gém isn't like other kids! If you spent more time with her, you would understand this."

"Like *you* understand, right? The thing is, Henrik, you can take her to supermarkets and puppet shows and pretend all you want—you're never going to be her father. You need to get that through your head." He raised his eyebrows—a bit condescendingly, I thought. "It's fun to pretend sometimes, but sooner or later you're going to have to face the truth."

In the end, I didn't tell him what I had seen in the kitchen. I talked to some more people—I couldn't tell if they were colleagues or former colleagues of René's, and, frankly, I no longer really cared. I realized that I had never gotten myself that drink, which I needed rather desperately. Then disaster struck: the toilet—which had never been very robust to begin with—got clogged up. Too much toilet paper, a sanitary napkin, who knows what had caused it. The floor was a swamp, brown water everywhere. I wondered, distractedly, if René had been able to use the bathroom—unless this was *his* doing. In the hallway, I watched with the other guests as Nunzio jabbed at the opening of the bowl with the cleaning brush. A plunger might have been better suited to the task, but there wasn't one to be found, and the shops were all closed at this hour. Standing behind him, Gaëtane urged her assistant on, all the while chastising him for his ineffectiveness; Nunzio didn't reply, though his thrusts became more and more violent, sending up little splashes each time. Every once in a while, he tried pulling the lever. It was no use; the water refused to go down. Finally, Gaëtane said, "Stop, stop! You're getting that filth on me! What's wrong with you? It's obviously not working. You're going to have to pull it out manually."

"What do you mean, 'manually'?"

"I mean with your hands."

"I know what the word means, thank you."

"If you can't do it, just say so."

"I didn't say that . . ."

As I listened to their exchange, it dawned on me that Gém wasn't with them. No one was watching her. Moments later,

I found my godchild asleep, fully dressed, in her room. Her ridiculous hairdo had come undone at some point, but there remained a few sparkles on her flushed cheeks. I noticed that her soles were black from walking around barefoot all evening. On the wall above her was an old poster of *Corto Maltese en Sibérie*. For a moment I stood watching her sleep. An outcast at her own party, I thought to myself. In the past, I had watched her sleep countless times, but for some reason I felt a wave of sadness wash over me, as though I had come to say goodbye. When I roused her, she was awake instantly, like a cat.

"We're moving to Rome," she said as she sat up in bed. Her voice was deprived of emotion, but when I met her eyes I saw the sorrow written there, visible in the slight tremor of her pupils. She went on, "It was Gaëtane's idea. Is she Papa's new girlfriend now?"

"I don't know," I said softly.

She stared down at her toenails, which were painted to match the sparkles on her cheeks. "Will you come see me in Rome?"

"Of course. Now follow me," I said, and she complied without asking me where we were going.

The only way to leave the apartment was in plain view of everyone, but it didn't matter: the important thing was to act like everything was normal. With Gém beside me, we made our way down the hallway, past Gaëtane and her boy Friday, who was still struggling with the toilet before an audience of fascinated and disgusted guests. There were kids running around chasing each other, and one person was trying to rouse the others into starting a conga line. As I made my way through the living room, temporarily empty as if everyone had already left, I lifted Gém up and put her on my shoulders. It was hard to believe, but there had never been a reason for me to carry her on my shoulders, though I had seen René do so more than a few times. In that manner, we strode out of there and onto the landing.

"Elevator or stairway?" I asked her.

"Stairs!" she said, and so stairs it was. We made our way down the two flights, and the night air greeted us like a warm friend, a soothing hand. There was a small park nearby, only a few streets away; sometimes the gate wasn't locked at night. I had just stepped out onto the sidewalk when I heard something, a movement, in the alley next to the building. I lowered Gém to the ground and quieted her with a gesture. Then, slowly, I peered around the corner and that was when I saw René. On reflex, I took a step back, though it was unlikely that he had seen me. He was squatting, his pants around his ankles, and underneath his pale, hairy thighs I could make out the semi-transparent shape of a grocery bag dully reflecting the light from across the street. Only then did it dawn on me what he was doing. I heard him let out something between a grunt and a sigh.

"Henrik?" Gém, behind me, was tugging at my sleeve. I couldn't let her see her father defecating into a grocery bag. René had told me that when Gém was three he had once surprised her behind their vacation home in Bourgogne. She had called out and waved, a gleeful expression on her face, as though she'd been waiting for him to notice her, crouched in the shade of a tree.

This was different, of course. Parents can watch their child defecate, but not the other way around. Never let your child see you naked, as Danish wisdom goes.

"What is it? What'd you see?" By then, we were halfway to the park. Summer wasn't far off; I could feel it in the air.

"I didn't see anything," I told her, affecting a nonchalant tone. "There was nothing to see."

3. The Loneliness of the Augur

> The crows claim that a single one of them could
> destroy the heavens. This is no doubt true, though
> it proves nothing against the heavens, for heaven
> simply means: the impossibility of crows.
> —Franz Kafka, *The Zürau Aphorisms*

I saw her before she saw me. She was standing next to a self-service booth in the waiting area of Roma Termini station and looking the other way, as though oblivious to the movement around her. She let fall to the ground her cigarette, then crushed it with the toe of her shoe. Gaëtane, my friend René's new wife. Gém's new stepmother. It had all happened so fast that her marriage to René hadn't quite sunk in yet. She was wearing a sleek little astrakhan coat over her anthracite-blue tailleur. It wasn't for me that she had dressed up; this was how she looked every day as a manager of young talents. She was no longer a scout, at least not in any active sense, delegating the field work to those below her, though she might still swoop down from Mount Olympus if some young promising thing caught her eye. Even now, she blended effortlessly into the background—like any good scout—though it was no effort for her to materialize, card in hand, should the occasion call for it. I watched her, draped in my own, second-rate brand of invisibility: as long as she didn't see me, it was as though I wasn't there. On any other morning, she would be going over the day's schedule in her office, returning calls to casting agents, following up on appointments with clients. But instead, here she was, waiting for me.

The previous night, she had called from Rome to say that René had lost the plot, had really gone off the deep end this time. All she would say on the phone was that he had suffered some sort of breakdown. Offering to pay for my ticket (which I made a show of turning down at first), she had begged me to come and talk some sense into my friend. If anyone was going to break the spell, it would be me, she said. Apparently, he wanted to put Gém in a film he was trying to get made with several collaborators "of dubious standing" (her words), among them Renato Amorese, a.k.a. the Prince of Cannibals, as the Italian press had christened him in the late seventies, during his fifteen months of fame. As her first acting role, a début in something questionable, low-budget and no doubt violent could, according to Gaëtane, not only be "fatal" for Gém's budding public image, but also traumatize her young and vulnerable mind. The veneer of concern for Gém's welfare was only a façade: above all else, Gaëtane was concerned about her own career (which she owed to Gém, her biggest client), though I knew better than to voice such suspicions. She needed me; I might be able to use it against her in the future. And so I had accepted Gaëtane's invitation, despite the fact that, during the whole of our acquaintance, she had never ceased to question the nature of my feelings for Gém. It was obvious that, deep down, Gaëtane was jealous of the relationship I had with my godchild because I had been there from the start, so to speak. It shouldn't have mattered, but to her it did. Relations between us had deteriorated further after Gém's modeling career took off. A catalogue spread that she did for Baby Dior was the turning point. The photos showed her

lounging around on a giant pouf with several other kids, including some boys, one of whom—Gaëtane pointed out—had
to be at least nine or ten. (Gém was six, at the time.) All were
dressed in tank tops and gauzy foulards, some of the girls held
stuffed animals, but nothing that would make anyone raise an
eyebrow. I had taken Gém to the shoot because Gaëtane herself had been unable to go. Bringing up previous occasions
when I had volunteered to accompany my godchild (because
no one else was available), to photo sessions for so-called art
magazines involving five-year-olds made up like drag queens
and preteens wearing fake garter belts, Gaëtane accused me of
certain unsavory ulterior motives. After that, she began dropping not-so-subtle hints in front of other people, calling me
"Henrik Henrik" and citing my fondness for the novels of Gabriel Matzneff as a sure sign that I was a something-or-other
who should not be entrusted with the charge of young girls.
She had said a number of other things hardly worth repeating
here.

Gaëtane finally noticed me and called out my name. I called
out hers, and she surprised me by kissing me on the cheeks.
The gesture was brusque, almost convulsive, as though she
had decided on it at the last possible second. In the past, we had
always greeted each other with a perfunctory handshake. She
walked ahead, her high heels making a clicking sound, and I
stared at the nape of her neck, which her fashionable haircut
left bare, as she led me outside, past the rose sellers, the lim-
ousines lining the curb (but not a single taxi), and into a cob-
blestone alley I would never have noticed on my own, where
a green Citroën Méhari was parked next to an overflowing
trash receptacle decorated with an effigy of the she-wolf suck-
ling Romulus and Remus. The air had a peculiar, cabbagelike
tang and felt as cold as the air I'd left behind in Paris.

We left the orbit of the train station, and even at this matinal hour there were pedestrians, scooters, buses vying for a place in the narrow one-way streets that Gaëtane seemed to know well, as if she had lived in Rome all her life. I watched her extract another cigarette from a pack of Muratti as she steered with the other (manicured) hand. Next to me, she gave off an impression of both indolence and impatience—a case of suppressed nerves, perhaps. In Paris, I had never once seen her take the wheel; I hadn't known she had a permit. (I myself had never gotten mine.) Several times, I was sure she would hit someone as she took one turn after another—burning a red light at one point—until I was no longer sure if the train station was behind us or in front of us, and I had the thought that she was purposely trying to disorient me, like an unscrupulous driver with a hapless tourist.

"Listen," she said, interrupting the silence, "I know we've had our differences in the past, but I'd like to put all of it behind us."

"Well, I'm here, aren't I?"

We were driving past the university, La Sapienza, where a crowd had gathered for a demonstration of some sort next to a statue of Minerva holding aloft a lance on which sat a lone crow, as though presiding over the proceedings. I glimpsed more crows along the top of several buildings, and I couldn't tell if they were all subservient to the lone crow, or if the latter, for reasons unknown, was being shunned by the rest of his brethren.

"This is hard for me to admit, Henrik, but a part of me always knew that you weren't capable of hurting Gém." She kept her gaze focused on the road. "I saw how fond she was of you, and I became a little jealous. But I shouldn't have reacted the way I did."

"How is she?"

"Her grades are nothing to write home about, and she hasn't made any friends since arriving in Rome. The others make fun of her, according to her teacher, for speaking differently and for being the only blond-haired kid in her class. Who would have thought that she could be singled out for having blond hair, of all things?"

"In Denmark," I said, "I was singled out for not having blond hair. I suppose it's the same thing, in the end."

She honked at a man on a scooter. "What was that?"

"Nothing. It was nothing."

A memory, one I hadn't thought about in some time, came back to me: a kid I had never talked to punched me in the face because—he explained afterwards—he wanted to see if I could see his fist through the slits I had for eyes. That was how it had started; I was eight years old. Soon after that, I left the Kildevæld Privatskole and Copenhagen for the International School in Stockholm.

"She cried when we left Paris," I heard Gaëtane say. "For weeks, she was inconsolable."

I had last seen my godchild a year ago, on the eve of her departure for Rome, when Bors suddenly vanished. The cat liked to hang about in the courtyard of René's building, and Gém had befriended it with pieces of ham, biscottes, even bits of lettuce she carried around in her pockets; the two of them became inseparable. Around me, the animal had always been reserved and circumspect, fleeing when I made as if to caress it, then fixing me with expressionless verdigris eyes from the safety of a window ledge. It was René who had named the cat—all white except for a single black spot on the side—after one of the knights of the Round Table, Sir Bors de Ganis. In the end, unable to console his daughter, my friend had called me—without telling Gaëtane—to ask if I would make the rounds of the neighborhood with Gém (as he himself couldn't be bothered). We had spent several hours looking for the cat, though it was a lost cause. As we made our way home in the rain, she kept pausing, like Petit Poucet, to leave food on the sidewalk. In the vestibule of the building, as I did my best to dry her off, using my fingers to brush back her wet hair, I could see that she was trying hard not to cry. That was when I told her that it was always sad to lose something, but there were some things that could not be lost. A cat, for example. I told her that no one in all of history had ever lost a cat: such a thing simply wasn't possible. Because no matter what happened out there—I gestured behind me, at the rain coming down—she didn't have to stop thinking about Bors, who would stay with her as long as she wanted. And when he did, one day, start to fade away, it would happen so naturally that she wouldn't think to notice he was gone. It would be like the moon, eclipsing itself in stages, so regular and gradual that she wouldn't even know to miss anything. I don't know if she believed me or not.

"Did you tell her I was coming?" I asked Gaëtane. Today was my goddaughter's birthday. At exactly four-twenty-two this afternoon, Gém would turn eight.

"No"—she flicked her cigarette out the window—"you're supposed to be a surprise." The streets had grown smaller, made narrower still by the cars parked on both sides, but Gaëtane handled the Méhari like it was a tiny little Skoda. "René is throwing her a party. I know, I know. But it's kept him occupied until now."

"Last time," I said, "he made all of his colleagues from work bring their kids."

She sighed. "Don't worry. He's let all of his commissions dry up. Ever since the whole movie business, he's stopped translating altogether. He has no colleagues left. The only person willing to work with him now is the Prince of Cannibals."

She slowed to a stop in front of a porte cochère, but didn't get out after she'd cut the contact.

"This Renato Amorese," she said at last, turning to me, "I know his kind. All he knows how to do is exploit people. To him, actors are nothing more than pawns, a means to an end . . . I've been watching his films, and in one of them, *Cannibal Masked Ball*, there's a scene where"—she paused to light another cigarette—"where a sheep is skinned alive with great care, every effort made to avoid sudden movements, as though for the sake of the animal. This is after they trepan a monkey and attempt to cut a sedated rhino in half. It's horrible. But I can't stop watching. The animal cruelty is there only because he could get away with it—back then, at least. He had to fake the human deaths, but he could film the real thing with animals. The thought of someone like that . . ." She shook her head, as though chasing away a thought. "Anyway"—she opened the door to get out, throwing her cigarette on the ground—"I'll walk you to the door. Then I need to be going."

I followed her through a passage paved with cobbles. It was dark enough that I found myself focusing on the click of her heels, a lonely little sound. When she held open the door of the lift—an ancient and ornate thing straight out of Proust or maybe Huysmans—I caught a hint of her scent, the same one she'd worn in Paris.

"So what's he like?" I asked her, as the lift, creaking and grunting, made its way upward.

"Who?"

"The Prince of Cannibals."

"What do you mean?"

"Is he an octopus like Nunzio?"

For several long moments she didn't answer. "I don't know. I've never met him." She was standing slightly in front and I couldn't see her face, only her breath, coming out in faint white puffs. "I've never met him," she went on, as though to herself, "but I feel that I already know him through his films."

She let me into the apartment, then stepped back into the lift. "He's in the bedroom, at the end of the hallway."

I returned her gaze, which was hard, cold. The warmth I had glimpsed at the station was gone. Already, I regretted my words.

"I can't promise you anything," I said.

"That makes two of us."

She disappeared behind the door, and I watched the lift disappear into the ground like a genie in reverse. For a moment longer, I listened to the hum of the machinery and breathed in the aftermath of her perfume. Then I turned and went inside. The apartment smelled of cigarettes, sunlight, potpourri. On the wall was the giant Michelin map of Paris that had been René's for as long as I could remember. It was just like him, a map of Paris in Rome. Every street and square, no matter how small, was meticulously named. How many times had I stood before this map, in René's old apartment, playing little games to pass the time, such as trying to find a street named after a flower or starting with the letter "F," a street with one of those hyphenated names that had always intrigued me, Nonnains–d'Hyères, or Brillat-Savarin, or—failing that—the elusive rue des Silences (which, incidentally, I never found), while René snorted one last line, or while Gém got ready so that I could walk her to school . . . Now I made my way into the living room, past the kitchen and into a somber hallway. I heard rap music, a muffled beat, and recognized NTM's "That's My People." To my right, through a half-open door, I glimpsed

an unmade bed, a pair of leggings slumped over a chair. Gém's
room. She would be at school now. I pushed open the door and
took a step inside. The smell of trapped air, sweet and cloy-
ing, made me pause. Gém was normally very fastidious about
her belongings; back in Paris, every item in her room had its
proper, designated spot. She wouldn't have let things go like
this unless she was acting out, intentionally making a mess,
going against her natural inclinations. Like when she finished
everything on her plate but left the potato purée untouched,
though she loved potato purée, just to see if René would notice. (Usually, I was the only one who appreciated these futile
gestures.) From down the hall, a bit of the rap song reached
me: "*J't'explique que c'que j'kiffe / C'est de fumer des spliffs . . .*"
That's when I saw it, the objects arranged in a neat little line
on her desk, amid the chaos and capharnaum. There was a zip,
a button, a Lego piece, a miniature bolt, a pebble, an earring, a
tiny bulb with the filament still intact. Staring down at the
heteroclite offering, I swallowed something hard in my throat.
Then I backed out of the room. I shut the door, softly. For the
first time, I was glad I had come.

"Henrik! What are you doing here?" René was sprawled on
the bed, dressed in a green loden overcoat with a fur collar,
his head propped up by pillows. He had lowered the shutters,
and the room was plunged into a thick, bluish fog of cigarette
smoke that made the air heavy and dusty. I saw the end of a
cigarette flare brightly, then grow dim again. Multicolored pill
containers—most of them empty—littered the night table.

"Gaëtane picked me up at the train station," I said, trying
not to shout above the music.

René lit himself a new cigarette with the butt of the one

he'd just finished. "No kidding. You're the last person I expected to see here. First she tells me how nice it is to get away from the polluted air in Paris. Now she decides to bring the pollution here—so to speak."

"She asked me to help you."

"And just like that, you agreed? No questions asked?"

"Listen, I can find a hotel if—"

"No, no, no. I wouldn't dream of it, *mon vieux*. The friends' room is all yours. Stay as long as you want," he said, and pushed himself off the bed, the abrupt movement upending the ashtray (which he didn't bother to notice). "Come, walk with me."

I accompanied him out to the hallway and then to the "friends' room." Only the window saved it from being a closet, the dimensions barely large enough for a cot, which was the sole piece of furniture. After a few steps, René came to a stop, causing me to bump into him.

"Hey," he whispered, his lips almost touching my ear, "go to the window and tell me what you see. There's no danger. Really, it's OK. Trust me."

I made my way around the cot. "What am I looking for, exactly?"

The window gave onto an interior courtyard. I saw an agglomeration of parked scooters, some bins for garbage, which I described to him, my attention focused all the while on the sill just outside, on the neat row of trinkets including a paper clip, a nail, another button, along with several objects I couldn't identify.

"Do you see anything else?"

"Should I?"

"The eucalyptus tree, at the other end of the courtyard. From there they have an unobstructed line of sight into the living room and kitchen." He hugged the wall until he reached the window. I caught a whiff of naphthalin and old dust from his clothes. He didn't seem to notice the objects on the ledge. "You see how the branches don't droop?" he whispered. "That means most of them are elsewhere. But not all of them, obviously. There's always one or two who stay behind, as sentries."

"Are we talking about birds?"

"I'm talking about *crows*." He stared at me, pop-eyed. "They watch my comings and goings, not only from the eucalyptus but from other vantage points, from all over the neighborhood. They have access to all the coves and alcoves. As soon as I leave the apartment, they've already spotted me before I can take my third step. I know this because I hear them calling to one another."

The look in his eyes made me pause. I knew that look.

"Are you high, René?"

He gave me an indulgent smile. "No, Henrik," he said, slowly, "I am not high, unless you mean from all the sleeping pills I've been ingesting nightly and the cigarettes you saw me smoking when you burst into the room like a madman."

"I had to ask."

"You and Gaëtane both."

He must've thought I was going to say something, because he held up a hand. "Since I started working on the film, she's been against it. I understand, you know. At dinner, when I'm telling Gém about her character, she feels extraneous, Gaëtane does. I don't mean to exclude her, or act like she's not in the same room with us. It's what the art requires. Because, voilà, I really believe in the project. Renato believes in it. You can't take what she says about him too literally. Those animals weren't really killed, by the way. It's all camera angles and tomato sauce. He explained it to me." René's Adam's apple bobbed up and down. "This is the first time anyone's thought of me as something other than a pen-pushing technocrat. In Renato's eyes, I'm an artist! A legend, he is, and he believes in me!"

He was barefoot, his hair uncombed, wearing his pajamas under the loden coat and looking like he hadn't shaved in several days. How well did he know Gaëtane? I felt sorry for him, but mostly, I felt sorry for Gém.

In a careful tone, I said, "Is Gém OK? The move to Rome must be hard for her."

René made a dismissive sound. "Don't worry, she's really taken to her character. A natural, she is. I always knew that she had it in her when she started modeling for those catalogues. You remember the spread for Baby Dior? Renato saw one of the test shots on my desk and was like, *Che ragazzina!* I can still see the look in his eyes. He's talking about directing the film himself. Tonight he's coming to Gém's party so that he can observe her in her element. This could be it, my big opportunity. Did you know that, in Chinese, 'crisis' and 'opportunity' are the same word?"

"No."

"I suppose you wouldn't." He was lying on his back on the cot and staring dreamily up at the ceiling. "I have to go pick up Gém in a bit, but first I want to show you around San Lorenzo. It's a charming little neighborhood." He sprang up, as though struck by a brilliant idea. "There's a place nearby with merguez—it tastes just like the ones in Paris. My treat, OK?" At the doorway, he turned around, and I barely managed to avoid bumping into him again. "I'm glad you're here, man. It's good for me to get out like this."

Back in the bedroom, he disappeared into the walk-in closet. While waiting, I cleaned up the spilled ash on the bed.

When René came out, I almost didn't recognize him. Or, rather, I didn't recognize him at all. Gone was the loden coat, replaced by a tasseled horsehide jacket and seersucker pants with elephant cuffs. A surprisingly realistic beard—though it clashed with his hair—covered the entire lower half of his face and a pair of oversized frames hid his eyes. Even his eyebrows seemed transformed, more bushy, as if he'd attached hairpieces to them. (I decided not to ask.)

"Renato knows some wardrobe people at Cinecittà. Everything I have on, everything but the horsehide jacket—that's mine—came from them. The Italians have left the studios to film on location, and now there are entire warehouses full of set pieces, just sitting there in the dark, neglected and abandoned . . . These days, it's about making things look as real as possible, but if all of it looks real, does 'real' mean anything?" He waited, as though he expected an answer from me. "Anyways, I have to do this so they don't recognize me."

"The crows, you mean."

"Obviously."

Outside, perhaps it was the disguise, my friend seemed more at ease and even to enjoy his role as my cicerone. He pointed out a fleet of three-wheeled Ape cars in a parking lot, an Alfa Romeo Giulia ("Pasolini died in one") in front of a pizzeria, the street corner where Joyce first had the idea of *Ulysses*, and a hundred-year-old sign prohibiting littering. He told me that a decree forbade the construction of buildings higher than the dome of Saint Peter's, which was why Rome never felt like a big city, more like a succession of cramped villages. Along the way, we ran into two different film crews, and René told me that for every one we saw, there were ten others out there, many of them scouting for potential locations—especially those not requiring permits—which included (but were not limited to) condemned hunting lodges, underground bunkers, abandoned water reservoirs, manor houses once owned by the Mafia, seemingly derelict plazas, memorials of long-forgotten griefs and the shadowy back alleys of municipal parks. All of Rome, he concluded, had become a movie set. I still hadn't gotten used to his altered appearance, and from time to time I caught myself staring at the bearded stranger walking next to me like a vagrant Virgil. Finally, he took me to a café-bar with a maritime theme: expanses of netting (crabs and sea stars caught in them) suspended above our heads, tableaux of ships at sea on the walls, which were painted a sickly, blue-green color. Conque shells lined the liquor shelf behind a counter where the barman, sleeves rolled back, distractedly polished glasses while talking to someone on the phone. He kept the receiver cradled against his shoulder as René bought a bottle of wine from him. "I don't know how many times I've been here," René said as we sat down at a table, "and our good man at the bar has yet to figure out that it's always the same person buying the bottle of red."

He poured our glasses, then with a certain ceremony set down the bottle between us.

"You think I've lost it, don't you?"

I made a noise, and he waved me away as if I had just blown smoke in his face. "I understand, of course. I've become un-recognizable, no longer the René you knew in Paris. The humdrum translator of old is no more. These last few months have seen me experiencing so many changes in my life. Things will never be the same again. But it's me, underneath all this, it's still me."

He drained his glass, and I saw that part of his beard was starting to come loose. "Not long after moving here, I had the most terrible nightmare I ever had. It was the most horrible dream I ever had. Gém was in the courtyard and she was surrounded by crows, hundreds of them. I was standing in the friends' room and I could hear them, cawing and murmuring at one another, like they were enumerating my daughter's crimes. Meanwhile, she stood there, calm and composed, as though she knew she deserved it." He let out a shudder. "I would have thrown myself out the window there and then to save her, but it was like I was nailed to the spot, unable to do anything but watch. When I woke up, I went straight to my desk and wrote down what I remembered. A few days later, looking at my scribblings, I realized that I had a story, or the beginnings of one.

"After that," my friend continued, "I began seeing them everywhere, circling in the sky. You wouldn't believe how many crows there are once you start noticing them! They say it's all the garbage in Rome, but I'm convinced it's all rubbish, no pun intended." He looked around the café, which was empty: we seemed to be the only customers. "Did you know," René said, lowering his voice, "that Rome was founded because of crows? *That's* what they should have on all the trash containers in the city. People used to spend all of their time watching them, listening to their cries, recording everything in a ledger. The smallest variation in flight, in the way they . . ." He paused to imitate, at the top of his voice, several different types of caws, clacks and cackles, and I saw the barman (still on the phone) glance in our direction. "Anyway," he went on, quietly again, "it was very rigorous, very complicated. Everything meant something. The augur had to stand on a deserted hilltop, or lock himself away in his *auguratorium*, where the only opening was above him. Completely alone, day in and day out . . ."

He closed his eyes, and I waited for him to reopen them,

but he continued to sit there like a scarecrow, his lips stained dark with wine. I was beginning to wonder if he had fallen asleep when he said, "Sometimes I think about the loneliness of the augur and I'm filled with a great and unfathomable sadness."

It was almost four in the afternoon by the time we left the café. I realized, outside, that I was drunker than I had thought. René glanced at his watch, swore under his breath and said that he knew a shortcut, the neighborhood Jewish cemetery. The cemetery had no name, and there was no one famous buried there, which meant no tourists either. It would cut down our walking time by several minutes, and walking through a cemetery, he said, helped to clear the mind. Who was I to argue with that? The afternoon sun felt good, despite the chill of the hibernal air, as I made my way down the narrow sidewalks and winding little streets. Just like old times, I thought. René and I had often taken long, meandering walks through Paris back in the day, when we were students at the translation school, sometimes from one end of the city to the other. If we didn't feel like retracing our steps and the first métro was still hours away, we'd climb a fence and wait out the night in one of the parks, whichever happened to be nearest. In that manner, over the years, we had slept in Buttes-Chaumont, Montsouris, Choisy, Monceau, even the square Récamier, and on one occasion the courtyard of Normale sup', during the Fête de la musique. Back then, it often seemed to me that the city itself was one immense park. As we entered the cemetery—our comfortable silence punctured only by the gravel beneath our feet—I felt pleasantly soused, happy to blink back tears of nostalgia. Near the entrance was a plaque with the words QUI TUTTO È FERMO written on it. The cemetery was much larger than it appeared from the outside. I had just noticed the delicate rows of pebbles on top of the headstones, most of them decorated with a Star of David, when I heard a croak, soft and hoarse, to my left. The cemetery was full of crows, unless they were ravens, enormous black shapes along the wrought-iron fence, on the branches of the old trees and in the grass, all of them staring, heads askance.

In a half-whisper, I called out to René several paces ahead. He was standing there, unmoving, with his back to me. It seemed that he, too, had only just noticed them.

"They must've smelled the alcohol in my blood. Corvids can sense that kind of thing. Suetonius mentions it in one of his works. Or was it Livy . . ."

It was one thing to hear him go on about the crows in the courtyard, and another thing entirely to find myself, without warning, surrounded on all sides by hundreds of them. Or what seemed like hundreds. Where had they come from, and how had they managed to get so close without our noticing them? I made a small forward movement, and saw the ravens, or crows, or whatever they were down in the grass, do the same—quick, hopping steps—while their confrères up on the headstones and on the branches contented themselves with pivoting their heads in what I thought was a distinctly scornful manner.

"It's me they're interested in," René said, through clenched teeth. "Not you. They don't know you, they don't care about you."

"What are you saying?"

"You keep going while I double back to the apartment. Maybe I can lose them along the way."

He started taking off his jacket, then the scarves, the sunglasses, tearing off his beard and the rest of the accoutrements (it turned out that he had, in fact, been wearing eyebrow extensions), until there was nothing left but my old friend, the René I knew, transformed back to his recognizable self.

"Are you sure about this?"

René gave a little shrug with one shoulder. "I'll be fine."

"What if some of them follow me to the school?"

"They won't. Trust me." Seeing that I wasn't convinced, he added, "Beyond the cemetery is hawk territory. The crows rarely venture there. They won't follow you." He gave me a pat of encouragement, then hurriedly kissed my cheeks, left, right, left, right, scratching me with his stubble. When he detached himself, I saw that his eyes were wet. "Go on, Gém is waiting for you."

With his jacket and scarves tucked under his arm, he turned and started walking back the way we had come, retracing his steps. He didn't turn around. The crows followed him, either on foot or with their black, beady eyes. The ones perched on the fence flew up to the branches with a felted flutter of wings, as though to better monitor René's egress. I watched as my friend disappeared behind a row of sepulchers.

True to his prediction, they did not follow me. I noticed that there were no crows on the branches of the trees outside the cemetery, as though they really were that scrupulous about the perimeter of their territory and the territory of the hawks, where one ended and where began the other.

A small crowd had already gathered in front of the school entrance—no doubt the afternoon habitués, a sodality of mothers, fathers and older siblings. Unlike me, they were all warmly dressed, with the allure of responsible guardians. In more ways than one, I felt out of place among them, an interloper, maybe even the kind of person Gaëtane, at one point, had accused me of being ("a thirty-five-year-old who ruins six-year-old lives," she'd once called me). And maybe, I thought, as I stood there shivering, she wasn't entirely wrong. She didn't know that when I wasn't at work I spent most of my waking hours at the Forum des Halles or Bercy Village. That was what my weekends looked like since René had moved to Rome with Gém. For a flat monthly fee, I could watch as many films as I wanted, and in a typical day I sat through five or six showings. Revenge fantasies, ensemble-cast romances, Korean anime, Holocaust documentaries, dubbed Hollywood thrillers, it didn't matter. I rarely saw the same movie twice, although I once spent an entire day watching one thing, over and over. By the end, I had no recollection at all of what I had watched.

Kids started emerging, and those who had been waiting outside greeted them with shouts and laughter and accolades. What was I doing here? It was all I could do not to break into a run. Perhaps the anxiety I felt had nothing to do with what had happened in the cemetery. And yet why was I nervous about seeing her again? By now, the sidewalk looked like a gallery opening in Saint-Germain-des-Prés, but there was still no sign of Gém. Had the crows gotten to her? No, I was being ridiculous. A vulgar gathering of birds, that was all it had been, only that and nothing more . . . Suddenly, through the crowd, I spotted her svelte silhouette. She seemed so alone, standing there in the midst of such familial bliss. Had she been waiting like that all this time?

Gémanuelle, my godchild.

I was still drunk; the cemetery air hadn't done nearly enough to clear my head, it seemed. I wasn't thinking straight, or else I wouldn't have taken her, without a second thought, to the nearest establishment—a restaurant of some sort or another—rather than back into the school, where a washroom would almost certainly have been available, a place where I could get Gém cleaned up. Had I not been so shocked by her appearance, I might have done just that, but I feared that the teachers would think me responsible for the torn stockings, the rips in her dress, which was smudged here and there with dirt and various inexplicable stains, as though, on top of everything else, a monumental food fight had just taken place at the school canteen.

The restaurant was mostly empty, only a few customers scattered here and there, sitting at tables set unusually far apart. Everything was too brightly lit. There were thick electric cables on the ground, and I nearly tripped over one of them. Something wasn't quite right. For one thing, there were no servers, and the only person working seemed to be the barman, who bore a striking resemblance to a young Marcello Mastroianni with his dark hair combed back from his forehead. He was engrossed in a book called *La porta sull'estate* behind the counter of the bar, and I made the mistake of asking him where the toilets were. Without looking up, he informed me in English—I had addressed him in my best Italian-accented French—that I couldn't eat here. He had misunderstood me, but I couldn't resist pointing out that most of the tables were unoccupied, and he repeated, more sharply this time, that I did not have the right to eat here.

"I'm asking for my daughter, OK? It's her birthday today!" I avoided looking at Gém as I said this. It had been a long time since we had last played the game; she might even have forgotten about it altogether. My interlocutor, frowning, put down his book, and that was when he saw "my daughter" standing beside me. I watched him take in the sorry state of her clothes.

Then he turned back to me, as if seeing me for the first time as well.

"What has happened to her?" He leaned over the zinc for a closer look. "Her vestments are"—he made a slicing gesture—"*tutti strappati!*"

"She's fine, she's fine. It's for a film directed by"—I paused—"the great Renato Amorese, *il signore dei cannibali.*"

"Is your *girl*, you said?" He narrowed his eyes. "You find her where? You *rapire* her?"

I felt Gém tugging at my sleeve, and my first thought was that she was going to correct me in front of Marcello Mastroianni: no, she wasn't my daughter; no, I wasn't her father. She said my name, and I did my best to ignore her as I explained, in a hodgepodge of French and English, that she had only recently moved here from Paris and was being harassed by her classmates for being different. With that, I pointed to her clothes.

"*Henrik,*" Gém said, loudly, "I want to leave. Now."

Back out in the street, she started walking fast, not looking back, and I practically had to run to catch up with her.

"You didn't have to tell him all that stuff," she said, without slowing down, and the way she had of throwing her shoulders back reminded me of Gaëtane, funnily enough.

"Hey," I said, "I'm sorry for telling him you were my daughter. I know it's been a while since we—"

"That's not what I meant!" She stopped walking and turned to face me. Her cheeks were flushed, her small child's chest heaving. "I didn't fight with the other kids."

"But your dress . . ."

"No one is *harassing* me."

"Then who did this?" I tried not to stare at what looked like a piece of chewing gum in her hair.

"I did it to myself. It's for my character. René says I need to put myself in Maya's shoes if I'm going to play her in the film."

"Maya?" Since when had she started referring to René as "René"?

"That's her name," she said. "Maya the psychic girl."

Across the street, the face of a building entirely overgrown with vines started to move and sway, ever so gradually, as though brought to life by a swarm of invisible hands. I stared in stupefaction for a moment. The wind, only the wind . . .

"So it's fine," I heard her say, "if you want me to be your daughter. I can play that role, too."

"Come on," I said, walking again, afraid I might start crying in front of her. "Let's go find you a lavatory."

We came across a Chinese restaurant whose facilities were not so jealously guarded. There was even a public phone, its orange Bakelite casing scratched and battered. When Gém came out of the WC, she no longer looked like a tatterdemalion; her face was cleaned up, her hair more or less in order. "See? I'm OK. It was just pretend." She made a turn for me, like someone modeling an outfit. I was impressed that she had managed to get rid of the stains on her dress, then realized that she was now wearing it inside out. I thought about what awaited her, the ersatz birthday party, which was little more than a screen test in disguise. In a way, she was already acting in René's film; she just didn't know it yet.

"Are you hungry?" I asked her. "Shall we eat something?"

There were more people than at the pseudo-restaurant we had left, and here they were eating, talking, making noise. The clientele was at least half Asian, always a good sign, for a Chinese restaurant. It meant the food couldn't be all that bad. We chose a table with a view of the street. Near us sat a group of young students, or such was the impression they gave off.

They were Asian, and, listening to their laughter and chatter, I felt a kinship with them, though I didn't understand a word of Italian. Out of the corner of my eye, I watched them as they served themselves from the splayed-out dishes, everyone having a bit of this, a bit of that, rather than each person eating only from his own plate with no sharing, no crossing of chopsticks from opposite ends of the table. When the server came by, Gém ordered for both of us in Italian. She seemed to know exactly what she wanted, and I asked her, as casually as possible, if she had already come here with René.

She shook her head no. "I read the menus when I walk past them," she said. "They're in front of all the restaurants."

I remembered that we weren't far from the school. "René isn't always there to pick you up?"

"Sometimes he's busy. I understand. He's writing my character."

"René would have been here today," I said, "but something came up at the last minute. Really, I'm not making excuses for him. If it hadn't been for your father's heroic act, I wouldn't have been able to come pick you up at all."

As I recounted the run-in with the crows, Gém listened without a word. I thought that she might find the story amusing (she was at that age when she preferred reading to being read to, though in the past she had appreciated my stories, the ones I made up as I went along), but her expression remained resolutely somber as she played with the seasoning containers. When I finished, she didn't speak, a pensive look clouding her features. She had placed the containers, and our plastic cups of water, in a straight line, like the pebbles on the headstones of the Jewish cemetery. I asked her if she was OK, and she shrugged.

"Gém," I began, "the bric-à-brac of things outside the window of the friends' room . . ."

No reply.

"And on your desk . . ."

Her eyes slowly widened. "You were in my room!"

I could see her whole face working: she was trying to decide whether to be upset or not. Someone had finally noticed the mess in her room, someone who understood its reason for being—to serve as contrast with the curated bibelots on her desk.

"The door was open. I shouldn't have. Do you forgive me?"

She sat back and crossed her arms. "Only if you promise not to tell René."

"OK, sure, but why can't I tell him?"

"Because they're not supposed to be my friends."

"Who?"

"The corbies. They like to give me things. Presents."

"The corbies?"

"Tsk, that's what they're *called*." Her tone had grown confidential, like René's at the café. "The ones in Rome talk the same as the ones in Paris. That's why I understood them right away. And why they understand me." She added, quietly, shaking her head: "But they don't want me to do the film."

"The corbos, you mean."

"Cor*bies*."

"Gém"—I looked her in the eye—"you don't have to do the film if you don't want to."

"But I want to, Henrik. Honest, I do."

"Understood. It's the corbies who don't want you to."

"In the film, they're supposed to be the bad guys."

"Is that what René told you?"

Instead of answering, she shrugged in the same one-shouldered way René had, and I realized that she was imitating him. I wanted to tell her that she shouldn't listen to his mumbo-jumbo, but was it really my place? Did I have the right?

When the plates arrived, we followed the examples of the Asian Italians. (Gém had ordered several types of stir-fried noodles, potstickers and soup-based dishes.) Everything was delicious, more than delicious—nothing like the heat-lamp fare at Tang Frères. Never in my life had I eaten Chinese food like this before.

"Much better than the resto we left, right?" I said. "What a strange place that was. And the service! No wonder it's practically empty."

"Henrik," she said, laughing with her mouth full, "it was a *movie set*. Didn't you see all the lights and stuff?"

"Lights?" I remembered the peculiarly spaced tables, but not much else. "Wait. Movie set?"

"It's like the time René and I went down to the RER and the platform looked different. There were all these people doing things, and I saw Mathieu Kassovitz, who smiled at me."

Had I been *that* drunk?

I watched her finish off the last of the fried dumplings, then got up to pay, and when I came back, Gém was playing with the scraps of food left on her plate. Sitting back down across from her, I saw that she was arranging the bits in a neat line. She worked with such concentration that I found myself involuntarily holding my breath. I didn't want to interrupt her, but I thought of René, waiting at the apartment. Dressed in Cinecittà hand-me-downs, smoking one cigarette after another and making last-minute preparations for Gém's so-called party. Was he nervous about Renato's visit? Did he wonder why we were taking so long? As we were leaving the restaurant, I heard a small electronic beep. My watch. It was time. I turned to her and said, very solemnly, "Happy birthday, Gém." She smiled, a shy sort of smile, and in that moment she looked somehow different, if not a bit older. Something about her had changed—there seemed to be less childish fat around the wrists and arms covered with little blond hairs that, too fine to make out normally, now caught the declining light.

Gaëtane had been wrong: Gém did have friends, lots of friends, all over the city. They had feathers and they all knew how to fly.

The sun had already gone down by the time we walked through the porte cochère into the interior courtyard, illuminated by the sole lights of the windows above us. Where had the time gone? In the half-darkness, the eucalyptus was different, the whole tree leaning slightly forwards, as though deep in thought. The crows had returned; they were in the tree, their tenebrous presence weighing down the branches.

With slow, almost hesitant steps Gém approached the tree, and I followed, walking behind her. I could make them out now: black, indistinct shapes huddled close to one another. They looked to be asleep, though it was hard to be sure. I thought she would start talking to them, but she remained silent, and I was reminded not so much of René's dream, or of the way he had described seeing his daughter surrounded by a tribunal of crows; rather, I found myself thinking about the end of "The Seven Ravens," when the heroine is reunited with her lost brothers. It seemed to me that she was communicating with them, albeit without words, the way it's sometimes possible to do in dreams. Or perhaps—a year later, in another city, another reality—some part of her was still searching for her vanished feline friend.

At last she turned away, and in that moment, though there was hardly any light left in the sky, I saw her future more clearly than ever. I knew her better than she knew herself. Nevertheless I had brought her back to René. After all, who was I to stop her from following the river of her destiny? We crossed the courtyard in silence and entered René's building. As we waited for the lift to arrive, Gém asked me how long I planned to stay, and I answered—truthfully—that I had no idea.

"Will you come back and see me?"

"But I haven't left yet!"

"Will you?" she said, her voice breaking a little.

"I promise." I wasn't sure if she believed me, or if she wanted to believe me. Something told me that I wouldn't be the first or the last to disappoint her. Once again, I recalled the day we had spent scouring the neighborhood looking for Bors. In the vestibule, after watching her disappear up the stairs, I had stood there for a long time, long after her footsteps had faded away and all I could hear was the dull throb of the rain coming down on the asphalt. As I was leaving the building, I had seen it, the missing cat, eating one of the scraps that Gém had dropped along the way. Its once-white fur was tangled and streaked with dirt and little clumps of mud. At that moment, it had looked up at me, and even from a distance, something in the animal's gaze told me that the Bors Gém had known and loved was no more. A change had taken place, and there would be no going back to the way things had been. For a long moment, we stared at each other like old rivals. When the cat finally darted into an alley, I made no move to run after it.

He wasn't waiting for me at the station. It was just like René, of course. I'd told him that I would be arriving on the overnight train, the Paris–Rome, and he had promised not to forget. For several long moments I stood there, in the vast concourse of Roma Termini, holding my sac de voyage, still hoping to spot him among the morning crowd. Despite the early hour, most of the benches were occupied, and everywhere around me was movement, chaos, boredom. But no René. I hadn't slept much on the train—I've never been one to sleep in trains—and now I was starting to feel a dull, nameless weight bearing down on me, threatening to cloud my judgment. There was a payphone—possibly the only one—at the far end of the concourse, but when I got there I remembered that I didn't have a card. Or change, for that matter. But nearby was a Relay, and I went in and bought a bottle of water and a telephone card. When I went back, I found someone else, a woman—a fellow Dane, no less—using it. I knew she was Danish because she was speaking Danish. Even without the high heels, she probably had a good few centimeters on me. She was talking to someone, a boyfriend, a husband. "Jens" had screwed up, and she was upset about it. He was to join her at the station, but something had held him up. If he didn't get here soon, they risked missing their train. For a moment she stopped talking, as though she had sensed my presence behind her. I sipped my water and tried to remember the last time I had heard Danish spoken in public.

"I'll tell you when you get here," I heard the woman say. She had briefly raised her voice, before lowering it again. "No," she went on, "I'd rather not say it on the phone." She glanced over her shoulder, and I saw that she was older than she appeared from behind, closer to my age than the age I had initially assigned her. "There's someone behind me," I heard her whisper. "What if he understands what I'm saying?" There followed several "no"s, each more exasperated than the last. "I don't see why it matters. And the restaurant in Munich? Yes, the black girl. The one I told you was eavesdropping on our conversation. You thought I was being paranoid." There was a pause. "Danish isn't a secret language spoken only by the two of us. We need to be careful if—" She let out a sigh. "No, he's not black." She had begun whispering again, though loudly enough that it didn't make her any less audible than someone speaking in a normal voice. "I'm not going to tell you," she said. "I have to go." She walked away without looking behind her.

I picked up the receiver she had been holding; it was still warm, with a trace of what looked like lipstick on the mouthpiece. I dialed René's number, and was not overly surprised when no one answered. Then I remembered him telling me they were filming today, a location shoot in Trastevere. It was possible that he had just left the set and was, at this very moment, on his scooter, weaving through the morning traffic. I felt a hard tap on my arm, and found myself being leered at by a young beggar, possibly North African, though he could have been Italian, I suppose. He was standing close enough for me to make out the darkened pores on his unwashed face. In a farrago of Italian and English, he was asking me for change. To bring this point across, he shook a paper cup filled with coins in my face. I told him I didn't have any money, but he stood there as though he hadn't understood, an expression of dazed contempt on his face. I left him there like that, and moments later, glancing behind me, I saw him approach a fair-haired couple, then continue meekly on his way after the man dropped one or two coins into his cup.

I considered leaving the station, but in the end I decided it was best to stay where I was, just in case. The last thing I wanted was for René to get here and not be able to find me. I looked for an empty seat, but the nearby benches were blocked off by a group of disheveled itinerants sitting on the floor with their enormous hiking backpacks. The situation seemed hopeless. Retracing my steps, I walked past the payphone again, past the Relay, in the direction of the atrium, where a staircase led to the restaurants on the upper level. There were the usual fast foods and cafés, but nothing particularly inviting. Little had changed in the two years since I had last been here. If I kept walking, I would reach the exit, and beyond it the piazza dei Cinquecento. But then, through the window of the aptly named La Fenestro, I saw a familiar silhouette at one of the tables. It was the woman I had stood behind earlier. She was alone, facing away from me. The place looked more expensive than the others, and a glance at the menu under glass confirmed my suspicions. Even a year ago, I would have thought nothing of it, but these days my diet consisted of boiled potatoes—a Danish staple—and cans of ravioli. How had I arrived at this state of affairs? One day, I had started sabotaging my own work, purposely mistranslating documents I was given. No one had noticed—perhaps because my colleagues at the pharmaceutical firm already spoke a dialect of Euro-English—and after a while I found myself wondering if the whole mess wasn't confined to my own imagination, if I really did write "facultative stop" in a

press release . . . "fibrome" instead of "fibroma" . . . or if I only
thought about doing these things. I decided to put an end to
it—whatever "it" was—and told the chief of the translation
department. Finding a permanent solution to such doubts
was, somewhat to my surprise, an unambiguously simple and
straightforward matter, for the department chief.

I let several more moments go by standing at the window.
The dishes in front of her looked untouched, and from time to
time she took a sip of her champagne, unless it was just soda
water (or Danish water, as we call it in Denmark). She seemed
to be lost in thought, and I wondered, not for the first time,
where her companion Jens was, what trouble he could be in.
How long had she been waiting for him? Perhaps he wasn't
even in Italy but in a neighboring country, his movements re-
stricted as he waited for the right opportunity to cross over.
I glanced at the billboards showing the timetables. It could
be that the train she had mentioned on the phone wasn't even
leaving today. Perhaps she had been here, at Roma Termini
station, for several days already. Or longer. In the end, I
gave up on finding something to eat—I wasn't really hungry anyway—and returned to the main waiting area, which
was slightly less crowded than before, as though a train had
pulled in and departed during my absence. I found a vacant
seat among the benches and sat down, between a Buddhist
monk in full regalia and a young woman engrossed in a book
with her feet propped atop her luggage. It had been too long
since I had read anything for pleasure. Whatever book I picked
up I started translating in my head, a habit from my ten years
as a translator, and the smallest ambiguity in the text that I
couldn't elucidate to my satisfaction bothered me to the point
where I soon gave up reading for pleasure altogether. In the
past, I would take with me on my travels whatever documents

I happened to be translating, and once again I had found myself packing my classeur, only to remember that there was nothing in it except for some old papers and my list of frequently translated pharmaceutical terms. I didn't plan on staying very long in Rome, and, accordingly, I had brought only the strict minimum: changes of clothes, a toothbrush, my old mini-disc player and a bottle of pastis bought at a Nicolas near the Gare de Lyon as a last-minute housewarming gift. I'd considered getting something for Gémanuelle, whom I hadn't seen in almost two years. Finally, I had decided against it; I didn't want René to get the wrong idea. In any case, I told myself, she was no longer a shy and studious eight-year-old. How many ten-year-olds still liked what they'd liked when they were eight? Especially a ten-year-old starring in her second film. Perhaps she had already forgotten me.

Someone asked if the seat next to mine was taken, and I said there was no one—the girl with her book had left, at some point—and in that same moment I realized that I had been addressed in Danish. Without thinking, I had answered in French; but it didn't really matter—I had already given myself away. Even before I looked up, I knew who it was.

"So I was right." Sitting down, she gave me a slow once-over. "I bet you've listened to a lot of conversations, haven't you? You and the black girl in Munich. I would've said something to her, too, if Jens hadn't stopped me. I can see why they sent you, given that you couldn't look any less Danish if you tried."

"I'm from southern Denmark," I said, which was my habitual retort to questions concerning my background on occasions when I didn't feel like explaining for the nth time, to a stranger at a party, that I was adopted. But she didn't seem the least bit interested in my background. Instead, she barked out a laugh.

"I've made that joke many times," I said. "But you're the first to laugh at it."

"It wasn't the joke but *you* that I found funny. Now tell me the truth: who are you working for?"

"No one at the moment. Believe it or not, I'm unemployed."

"Who hired you to follow me?"

"I wasn't—"

"Don't deny it. I saw you outside the restaurant." She smiled at my surprise. "The walls have mirrors. You're not very good at your job. I was watching you as much as you were watching me."

"I was looking for a place to eat when I noticed you through the window—"

"So you admit you were looking for me."

"No, I was looking for a place to eat."

"Do you take me for an imbecile?"

I wasn't sure if she wanted me to answer that, so I didn't. She went on, "You despise us, don't you? For what we're doing together. I imagine Karl must have briefed you already."

Us? I realized she meant her and Jens, her Arlesino, her partner in crime.

"I'm sure Jens has his reasons for not being here," I said. "Sometimes there are unforeseen circumstances. You shouldn't think he meant to break his promise."

"What do you know about our promise?"

Even as I told her I didn't know anything, it occurred to me that proving one didn't know something was a lot harder than proving the opposite. That was the whole problem, as I saw it.

She narrowed her eyes. "If I ask you for your name, will you tell me?"

I told it to her—after all, why not?—hoping I didn't sound like a liar.

"You even have a Danish name, possibly the most Danish of all."

"It's my real name."

She nodded, and I wondered if she was only humoring me, playing along. "Mine is Signe." She held out a hand, and I thought about not shaking it. Her hand was on the large side, though the nails were impeccably done—no doubt by a professional—their iridescence catching the light as she held it aloft, waiting. I had a feeling she would wait all morning if she had to. With a sigh, I gave in. Her grip was unexpectedly firm, and I wondered if Signe was really her name or if she had given me something made up because she thought I had done the same. Then again, "Signe" was as common as "Jens," a name shared by half the men in Scandinavia. Perhaps the latter was not his real name, either. I was surprised at how easy it was to think along these lines.

"So," she said, "you stood behind me when I was on the phone with Jens. What did you tell that guy disguised as a beggar? I saw you talking to him. Is he your contact here?" She nodded with satisfaction at my reaction before continuing: "From the mezzanine level I watched you circling the concourse. Then you stood facing the row of benches for a very long time, like someone who has no idea what to do next. I will say this: you are without a doubt the most incompetent agent I have ever encountered. Frankly, I'm surprised you managed to find me at La Fenestra at all—"

"Fenestro," I corrected her. "It's Esperanto. Either that or a mistake."

"Are you trying to imply something?"

"No, nothing at all."

"You then went back to the main waiting area where you proceeded to stare blankly into the distance. Smiling faintly at something, it would seem. Like someone reliving a happy memory, I remember thinking."

"I'm not sure who you think I am," I said, "but I'm not anyone's hired man, or whoever it is you've mistaken me for! I used to work at Sanofi, a pharmaceutical firm in Paris. I was a translator there. I don't know what I am now. Nothing, I guess."

"What are you doing here in Rome?"

Yes, what *was* I doing? I could get up and walk out of the station, René be damned. How far would this woman go? More importantly, where would *I* go? I concluded that, for the time being, I was stuck here, like a stateless person in an airport.

I told her that I had come to see my friend and his daughter.

"And where is this friend of yours?" she asked, surveying the concourse the way I'd done earlier, as though expecting to spot him among the travelers.

"I don't know. That's what I've been asking myself. He's had his hands full lately because his daughter is in a film."

Why had I told her that?

"Your friend is an actor?"

"No, his daughter is. She just turned ten." I thought she'd ask for her name, but Signe seemed lost in thought.

Suddenly, she said, "This isn't your first time visiting him."

"How did you know?"

"Watching you earlier, I couldn't help thinking to myself,

There's someone who knows his way around, but still seems hesitant in his gestures. *Like someone retracing his steps . . .*"

I was starting to wonder who was spying on whom at this point.

Signe went on, "I told you earlier that from the mezzanine I saw you smile. What were you thinking about?"

"I don't remember."

"Oh, I think you do. The look you had then, it was the same look you had in your eyes just now, when you mentioned your friend's daughter."

"You don't miss a thing, do you?" I couldn't decide whether to be impressed or irritated by her powers of observation and deduction. "If you must know, I was accused of something. Of pretending to be something—someone—I wasn't, with my godchild. In any case, he's forgiven me." Or that was what he claimed, though sometimes—like today—I couldn't help but wonder . . . Had he forgotten on purpose? Had he changed his mind about letting me see Gémanuelle?

"No," I went on, in reaction to her questioning expression, "it's not what you think." I knew that no one would have questioned our closeness if she had been my daughter. We understood each other, Gém and I, in a way that René, though he had given her his genes, didn't. But the fact remained that she wasn't my daughter.

"If you didn't do anything, why does your friend—"

"I don't know."

"You don't know? Or you don't want to tell me?"

"There's nothing to tell." I added, "He's always been jealous of my closeness with Gém, or that's what he claims."

"Your closeness."

"We used to play a game where I would pretend to be her

father. But it was just a game. That was all it was, really. I understand her, Gém, in a way that her biological father never will."

"You understand her, sure, but does she understand you?"

"What are you getting at?"

"Have you talked to her about any of this?"

"Of course not. I'm not crazy."

She made an ambiguous sound. "And your friend? Does he know that you're in love with his nine-year-old daughter?"

"She's ten. And I'm not in love with his daughter!" I glanced around, but the Buddhist monk appeared to be asleep. No one else was paying us the smallest attention. My outburst had gone unnoticed, and even if someone had heard me, would he have understood the Danish words?

"One day," I told Signe, "I found her practicing the lines René had written for the character she was to play in her first film. This was two years ago, here in Rome, at René's place in San Lorenzo. When I walked into the room, Gém had her back to me, and at first, she didn't notice me next to her. The script she was reading from didn't resemble the one my friend had shown me. He had changed everything in such a way that Gém wouldn't be exposed to any of the violent elements in the film. René had managed to write another, completely different plot, just for her. The rest of the actors were in one film, and she was in another, all by herself. But my friend had made the two versions intersect in such a way that, on camera, it was like they were one and the same."

In the version he had written for Gém, the crows— enemies in the film—were now her friends. It didn't take long for me to see that he had written his own version of "The Seven Ravens"—not the original story told by the Brothers Grimm but the adaptation staged at the Crous where I had taken her. René must have gone to see the puppet show for himself. At the time, Gém had gone on tirelessly about how much she liked it, and whereas I had thought it had fallen on deaf ears, he'd been listening all along. He had made her the heroine of her own puppet play.

"A part of me always thought that he wasn't a good father to Gém, but for the first time I realized that it didn't matter what kind of father he was. It was enough that he was her father."

"*That* was your grand revelation?"

I ignored the irony in her voice.

"It was like something fell into place for me, watching my godchild reciting the lines that René had written for her. She seemed so vulnerable, and at the same time untouchable. None of the violence in the film could touch her. It was there, all around her, within hand's reach. But René had protected her from it. For the first time in years, I started thinking about someone I had once known, long ago, when I was a student in Paris. Her name was Fumiko. I'm not saying that Gém reminded me of her, or any such thing. They were . . . are . . . nothing alike. For starters, she was Japanese, the girl I knew. Like my biological parents. All these years, she's haunted my dreams. Sometimes I think I'm still in love with her."

"Wait a minute. What does this girl have to do with your friend's daughter?"

"Nothing. That's just it: I don't know what made me think of her all of a sudden. Maybe it's the guilt I've always felt about . . . what happened to Fumiko. We'd been going out for a year when she locked herself in her room one day. It wasn't even the first time. I thought she would come back out soon enough, I really did. But she never did."

I had never told anyone—not even René—about Fumiko.

"She killed herself?"

"Yes. And I let it happen. Gém deserves someone better than that, no?"

"Why didn't you call for help?"

"I don't know. It's a question I've asked myself more times than you can imagine."

Every time René did something like this, forgot to return a call, failed to meet me, I was left wondering if there wasn't a deeper, hidden meaning behind his actions; if he wasn't telling me, without telling me, that he suspected something. Perhaps, without fully realizing it himself, he had always known that I was a menace, a danger, to those around me. That anyone I got close to would come to a bad end, sooner or later.

"All right," Signe said, leaning back in her seat. "As stories go, it's not bad, not bad at all. A convincing performance."

I stared at her. "Why would I lie about this?"

"To make me think we have something in common."

"*You* were the one who wanted to know about my friend's daughter!"

Would I ever convince her that I was telling the truth? For several long moments, neither of us spoke. I felt exhausted, and at the same time, strangely relieved. An emptiness descended on me, as though someone had taken away the last ten years of my life.

"I believe you," she said at last. "Everything that you've told me."

"Then why . . ."

"To test you, to see if I might be wrong about you." She nodded, as though to herself, her gaze focused on the timetables. "I had to make sure I had chosen the right person to hear the story of Signe and Jens."

I was too surprised to say anything, much less protest,

when she started telling me about the two of them. Jens, it turned out, was her brother, a brother she hadn't known existed until two years ago.

Later, I came to the conclusion that her skepticism, the brigade of men hired to keep tabs on her, all of it had been an invention, a pure formality: she'd needed a reason to continue talking. Out of everyone at the station, why did she choose me? How could she have known? We were like two spies in a movie who meet at the drop-off point to exchange information. After spotting each other, we put down our briefcases; I reach for hers and she reaches for mine. We go our separate ways. She doesn't look back, and neither do I.

These are the contents of her briefcase:

"I was born in Vejle, though on my birth certificate it says Haderslev. My mother was fifteen when she had me, and immediately afterwards I was given up for adoption. She came from a prominent family who knew how to contain its scandals. Eight years later, my mother—by then respectably married—had my brother, Jens. He grew up thinking he was an only child. He was twenty-nine when we met, here in Rome, at a gala given by the Danish embassy. I was there with my then husband, who was the cultural attaché. When Jens looked at me from across the room, it was like my world crumbled to dust. Until then, I had drifted through life in a daze of indifference and dullness—that's what I realized that night, for the first time. As though we had planned to meet like this, each of us made our way to the exit. We walked to the Sofitel a few streets away and checked into a room. I don't think we exchanged a single word.

"We lay on the bed, fully clothed, holding hands and staring into each other's eyes. I think we spent the entire night like that. It was the happiest night of my life. Even the feel of his hand in mine was almost too much. I couldn't get enough of his smell, his face, the sound of his voice, the shape of his feet. Everything about him was more beautiful and more perfect than I could have imagined a person could be before meeting him. In the beginning, neither of us knew who the other was. How much simpler it would have been if we had never found out! Somehow, his wife—and not long after that my husband—discovered what we were doing. Jens's wife is heiress to a large family fortune, which complicates everything. The father-in-law—Karl—told Jens that it's either the inheritance or me. For the past year, we've been meeting in secret when we can, in hotels outside Denmark. Jens uses his business trips as an alibi, but I've always known that our days together were numbered.

"One afternoon, at a restaurant in Salzburg, I noticed a man at the next table hanging on our every word. I knew he was Danish from the way he spoke German to the waiter. Jens thought I was seeing things that weren't there. To me, it seemed exactly the kind of thing Karl would do. He certainly has the means. Since then, I've been seeing his men everywhere. You're the first I've confronted, and it turns out that you might be the only one I was wrong about. Then again, maybe Jens was right all along."

She mentioned some other things, and there were a few digressions, but that was the gist of what she said, as far as I can remember. Suddenly, she stood up. "I'm sorry. I have to go." She surveyed the waiting area. Earlier, I had caught her glancing at her expensive-looking watch. "Your friend will show up with his daughter." She looked down at me and smiled. It was a wistful, melancholy smile. "I have a feeling."

"Where are you going?"

"To catch my train."

Though in that moment I wasn't sure there was a Jens at all, I said to her, "He might still come." But she shook her head.

"No, I've waited too long as it is. I won't wait any longer."

In no time at all, she was swallowed up by the crowd. Where was she going, I suddenly wondered, scanning the main hall. Back to Denmark? What exactly had she and Jens planned to do in Rome? I considered going after her. But to what end? She had made her decision. Now I had to make mine. I began walking in the opposite direction, towards the exit. René's apartment wasn't far from the station; I could take a taxi to the via San Quintino and wait for him there, at his front door. I would camp out all night if I had to. Just then, I saw a man making his way through the moving bodies. I'm not sure how I knew it was him. In truth, I didn't. (I still don't.) But he had her face, her dark-blond hair and hollow blue eyes. I thought about calling out to him, but I hesitated too long and he ran past me, oblivious. I saw him disappear down the corridor marked AI TRENI. At that moment, someone shouted my name. It was René. He was standing at the other end of the waiting area, a white helmet balanced under his arm. And with him, two years older but still recognizable, was my Gémanuelle.

The Specialist of Death

The other week, on French television, they'd shown my god-child Gémanuelle's second film, *The Specialist of Death*, directed by Renato Amorese, a.k.a. the Prince of Cannibals. My initial impulse had been to avoid watching it altogether, but I couldn't pass up a chance to hear her voice again (she had dubbed herself in French), though I turned off the television before the final, climactic scene. It was only a film, and not a terribly original one at that, but the sight of Gémanuelle's—or rather, her character Maya's—lifeless body was more than I could bear. Even with the original Italian version, I'd never been able to get through the ending.

Despite the spring evening—unexpectedly warm for Paris—I was in a funk by the time I arrived at my friend's new place for the housewarming party. René, after selling the old apartment near the place des Vosges, had recently moved into a modest two-bedroom in Belleville. The lack of furniture, the bare white walls, the unopened boxes made everything resemble a not-quite-built set. I hadn't told him about the television broadcast, hoping it might have gone unnoticed.

I spent most of the night picking up after my friend—half-finished bottles of beer, the watch he kept taking off, even his wallet (a continuity Polaroid of Gém dressed as Maya in the little plastic window)—all the while making sure he hadn't left a dwindling cigarette in the crack of a sofa. When René finally brought it up, I was standing near the doorway, outside the zone of attention, like an usher or a waiter or a ghost.

"Did any of you see it? *The Specialist of Death*. My daughter's second film."

René was addressing the group gathered around him—former FAO colleagues of his, acquaintances from his many social circles, a few of Gaëtane's friends who hadn't defected to her camp in the aftermath of the separation. I wondered how many of them had watched the film and were keeping quiet.

"What? No one?"

He glanced around him, waiting, and I could tell from his posture that he was already drunk. By the time *Specialist* came out in Italy, Gaëtane's liaison with Renato (who had directed all of Gém's films) was already public knowledge, third-page fodder for the Italian gossip rags. My friend had moved back to Paris while Gaëtane had stayed in Rome. Now he was living off the revenues from his daughter's films (where he was credited as "associate producer"), though his share didn't include royalties from the syndication rights sold to the M6 Group in France and Switzerland.

The silence was total. Months earlier, at one of Renato's parties, he had broken down weeping in front of the guests, and I was dreading something similar tonight. It had started out innocently enough at the time. With the aplomb of a first-rate actor, René had praised *The Prince of Cannibals*, Renato's latest work and the sequel to *Specialist*, making comparisons to Antonioni and Argento—and then, in the same breath, to Uberto Lenzo and Regolo Deodati—burying the film under so many elogious and dithyrambic names that no one was likely to find it again. Those who hadn't seen the film had probably come away from my friend's performance telling themselves that the only thing better than a masterpiece was an unrecognized masterpiece.

"Not one person?" René said, surveying the room now. "You can't expect me to believe that not a single person here has seen the film that killed my daughter?"

René had seen all of Renato's films, including the ones made during the cannibal craze that swept through Italy in the late seventies and early eighties. His *Cannibal Garden Party*, with its astonishing cinéma-vérité realism, the first tablet of a triptych alongside *Cannibal Masked Ball* and *Cannibal Wedding Ceremony*, had nearly gotten its director dragged before a tribunal. Even after his actors came forward and proved that they were alive and well, accusations of animal cruelty involving tortoises and monkeys continued to plague him to this day. Activists spray-painted his house, left death threats on his answerphone. He had spent most of the eighties and nineties trying to wash out the blood, rid himself of the stench of viscera, churning out a number of comedies, musicals, Westerns and pornos. At the start of his collaboration with René, he hadn't made a film in over twenty years.

For a time, the two men had gotten along. After all, it was René who had brought Renato out of retirement, that purgatory of obscurity. They had met at a strip club off the via Veneto. (No use hiding it now.) The next morning, René had brought him a script that he'd written, and Renato liked it, wanted to film it, perhaps because *The Impossibility of Crows* was an amalgam—minus the cannibalism—of his previous works, which my friend knew by heart. Finding investors, thanks to his network of contacts and his innate talent for gathering others to his cause (Renato himself being a case in point), was not nearly as hard as convincing Gaëtane of the film's merits, or that it would be good for their daughter's budding career. Renato's sulfurous reputation as the Prince of Cannibals didn't help matters any, of course, but the promise of a starring role in a real film with a real director—a once-in-a-lifetime opportunity, as René put it—wound up swaying her, and she even forgave him for taking Gém to the audition without telling her. (She didn't yet know about the strip clubs.)

In the beginning, my friend was at the set every day, sitting in on shoots, watching the rushes, eating catered meals with Renato in his caravan. He insisted on addressing Renato as "maestro" until the latter told him to stop. Their camaraderie was bolstered by their names, René and Renato, each "reborn" in his own way through the film. René took a permanent leave of absence from his post at the FAO to act as producer for *Impossibility*, and Renato dreamed of making his big comeback. Their first film together did well, showing at festivals in Shanghai, Abu Dhabi, Knokke-le-Zoute and Pyongyang.

Then, during the filming of *Specialist*, their second collaboration, Renato offered my friend a small nonspeaking part playing one of the henchmen who kill Maya's parents. According to Gaëtane, he had done it in order to keep René occupied and out of his hair. The role was hardly a role, but it involved several minutes of camera time and this might have gone to René's head. While in the background of a shot, he would check his gun repeatedly, or start wiping it down with a cloth, which led to a tiff with the identical twins playing the main villains Hugin and Munin, who (both) accused René of trying to steal their scene. Though Renato had to step in and arbitrate, wasting time placating a pair of disgruntled actors in identical crow masks (which made me question the utility of hiring twins in the first place), he forgave René—Renato

was the forgiving type, according to Gaëtane—but then René
told him that it didn't seem right to be part of a group of men
trying to kill Gém. She was his little girl, after all. Renato
reminded him that in the scene it wasn't Gém who was killed
but her parents. (Renato later told Gaëtane that, on realizing
his lapsus, he had immediately corrected himself: ". . . *Maya*
who was killed . . .") Exactly, René had answered, it's like
I'm killing *myself*. Did you know that Fernandel refused to die
in his films? Not, he added, that I'm comparing myself to
him. It's not real, Renato tried to explain, you're playing
a role, your daughter is playing a role, we're all playing a role.
At which point René looked up from the prop gun he'd been
cleaning and asked what role, he, Renato, was playing with
Gaëtane. Laughing as though he'd made a joke, my friend then
asked to play Gém's father in the film. Renato, ignoring the
barrel of the gun pointed at him, refused. René accused him
of being ungrateful. After all, who had wooed the investors?
Who had gotten Joey Starr to make a cameo appearance? The
two men parted on less-than-good terms. That night, René
felt a familiar tingling in his big toe, and by the next morning
he was unable to leave his bed. The slightest contact with the
sheets was agony. It was his gout, a hereditary condition in
which the attacks were few and far between but, alas, unpredictable. (Prolonged tension and stress could also set it off.)

A few days later, without René there to object, Renato
decided to change the story's ending. In René's script, Maya
emerges from the battle with Hugin and Munin wounded but
victorious, and the last shot shows her, dazed and dirty, clothes
torn, hair streaked with blood, standing before an abandoned
shopwindow where an enormous birthday cake evoking the
Vittoriano is displayed alongside a *steak-frites* with a stream
of gravy tracing the path of the Tiber, a macédoine of fruits

representing the seven hills of Rome and a *pot-au-feu* in the style of Arcimboldo's paintings (*Summer*). Renato, unhappy with the ending, wanted Maya to be killed by the two *corvi* (as agents of Corvus are called, plural of *corvo*). He thought what René had written too sentimental, and lacking the tragic tone that he, Renato, envisioned for the story. It was only later, after the fact, that I learned what he had done. By then, of course, it was too late to change anything.

"I saw it," I called out from the doorway. "I watched the film." Everyone in the room turned to see who had spoken. A grimace, like an expression of panic, traversed René's face, and I was reminded of an actor onstage forced to react to a line not in the script.

"Henrik, *mon ieuv*," he said, recovering. "Well, obviously, you've seen it. But, you know, I was asking the others here."

"No," I told him, "I'm talking about the television broadcast. I watched it too, René. I haven't forgotten the deal Renato made with M6, the one he cut you out of."

René's smile flickered. "You see what he's doing?" He appealed to the crowd, as though to take them as witnesses. "All evening he's been following me around, keeping an eye on me. Because that's what a good friend does. Isn't that so, Henrik?"

Heads turned from René to me, then back to René.

"You're making our guests uncomfortable," I said, calmly, as he took a few unsteady steps in my direction, spilling his drink.

"'Our'? Since when are they *your* guests?"

"René," I said, "your daughter is still alive."

"Are you trying to steal my role? Is that why you're here tonight? I thought *I* was the only one weighed down with guilt over the death of—"

"She's not dead, René. You can't go around telling people that. It puts them on the spot."

"What can I say?" He leaned forward so the others couldn't hear. "I'm not like you," he whispered. "I can't simply turn the page and move on to the next chapter."

"Is that why you cannibalized my life?"

"What are you talking about?"

"The character of Niko."

His surprise seemed genuine.

"Niko and Maya," I went on. "You changed the names, but it's obvious . . ."

"You're crazy."

"Am I?"

"It's a common trope. The old veteran and the young ingénue. Haven't you seen *The Professional*? *La cité des enfants perdus*?"

"René, I'm sorry that things turned out the way they did. Really, I am."

"I don't need your apologies. Or for you to look after me. Any more than I did then. It was Gém who needed you. She was your godchild, and you let her down. You turned your back on her. She trusted you, Henrik! You were more of a father to her than me!" If he hadn't been so drunk, I might have thought he really meant it this time. Turning to his audience again, he said in a normal voice, "This is Henrik, one of my oldest friends," presenting me to the others as if I had just arrived, while everyone pretended not to see the tears streaming down his face. "He was there during the filming in Rome. Gém used to say that he was her bodyguard. The Italians thought he was one of those Hong Kong action stars. I told them, No, he's from Copenhagen, believe it or not. You'd never think it, looking at him, but he grew up in Denmark and has a real way with kids!"

After René's gout had him nailed to the bed, I began to accompany Gémanuelle to the studio at Cinecittà. In the beginning, a car came for us every morning, a black Mercedes 6.9, along with a uniformed driver whose resemblance, down to the *ébouriffé* white hair, with an engraving of Schopenhauer was like something out of a dream. Through the window of the living room, I would see the car parked in the courtyard, waiting there like a giant black bird. By then, Gaëtane had already left for work; it was just Gém and me at the table. I told her that in Danish breakfast was called *morgenmad*, "morning food," making the mistake of writing it down first. Despite hearing me say the word out loud, she continued to add an extra syllable, so that I finally told her we could call it *brækfest*, easier to pronounce and which meant, literally, "vomit party." (She found that more to her liking.) Then, with no explanation given, the Mercedes disappeared—and the driver, too, naturally—and I had no choice but to take Gém to the studio myself. René had his scooter, and there was the old Citroën Méhari—used mostly for weekend trips—but as I didn't know how to drive, Gém and I took the tramway.

We must have made a strange couple. It would seem that, even in a city as dense as Rome, we often stood out. In the tram car, I would glance around and find at least one passenger openly eyeing us. Everywhere we went, we drew stares, some of them nonplussed or openly hostile. Gémanuelle's hair was very clear, very blond, and mine, well, was not. Did it look like I was kidnapping her? Once, a uniformed *carabiniere*

approached us and, ignoring me, asked her in bad English
if she was lost. Answering him in Italian—which she spoke
perfectly, without the slightest trace of a French accent—she
explained that she had only dyed her hair, which was in reality black, the same as her friends (pointing to the crows in
the plaza). She hadn't forgotten our little game. As we were
walking away, she asked me if René and Gaëtane were going to divorce and who she would live with, in that case. I
was thankful, for once, that she didn't have Maya's telepathic
powers.

At Cinecittà, I would accompany her to the dressing rooms
where she had her own little corner, a canvas chair with her
name printed across the back. I was just supposed to make sure
she was being taken care of, but I usually stayed longer, if only
to observe Gém in action. She had a gift, no doubt about it: I
saw her get through intense, dialogue-heavy scenes without
losing concentration, holding her own among actors several
times her age. She wasn't simply parroting the lines she had
memorized but really listening and *reacting*, like a seasoned
professional. Even though René had done his best to keep her
ignorant of the true nature of the film, with the story he had
fabricated especially for her, I am now convinced that she was
perfectly aware of what she was doing, of all the violence and
death and mayhem she was causing with her telekinetic powers. (How could she not wonder why she was being told to
imagine "something sad" or "something scary" or "something
really terrible" while a fan blew her hair back and a makeup
artist applied fake blood to her nostrils?) Her talent as an ac-
tress became all the more apparent during her scenes with
Niko, the movie version of myself, as I had come to think of him,
though I might have been the only one to see the resemblance.
After all, the actor who played him looked nothing like me,

and one might say that, physically at least, he was my diametrical opposite. Niko is a drifter who, after the death of Maya's parents, becomes her guardian and mentor and friend. He is the one who teaches her to hone her powers so that she can use them to her advantage against the evil minions of Corvus. A few times, I caught members of the crew blinking back what could only have been tears. I alone knew what she was doing: it was like watching the two of us together, pseudo-father and pseudo-daughter, when René wasn't around to spoil the fun. Maya and Niko's first meeting—in the ruins of the Basilica Santa Maria, involving fifty cats on a soundstage—needed to be done in one continuous take, and the atmosphere on set was tense. Knowing that Maya cannot yet control her powers, Niko wills himself to remain calm, emptying his mind of excess thoughts: she must grasp, without interference, his deepest intentions . . . The sequence, which ended with Maya collapsing into Niko's arms, had everyone cheering and applauding as soon as the cameras stopped. But no one thought to bat an eye during the scene—later deleted—where Maya asks Niko if he will become her father when all this is over and they've defeated Corvus. To which Niko replies that he always wanted a daughter, a family, which he'd been deprived of, growing up in an orphanage. ("We're both orphans," Maya says. "We can choose each other.") When the cameras stopped, I had to leave the room and splash cold water on my face, which seemed to me, in the lavatory mirror, the face of a dead man, a ghost.

It was decided at the last moment that the ending with Hugin and Munin would be filmed at a location in Paris, a cheaper alternative to building a large-scale set at Cinecittà, and which had the added benefit of René's absence. I was to accompany Gémanuelle there, but I let Gaëtane convince me

that she should go instead. Of course, it made more sense that
she be with Gém, the two of them sleeping in the same hotel room, in the same bed, sharing the same pillow—she was
her mother, after all, whereas I was . . . nothing in particular. I would stay in Rome and look after my friend, who still
couldn't leave the bed on account of his gout. (I didn't know
that Renato had rewritten the ending.) I remember telling
myself that I was doing the right thing—René was having a
hard time, he was my oldest friend and he needed me—but I'm
not sure if I believed this, even then. To this day, I can't help but
wonder: if I hadn't backed out at the last minute, then Gaëtane
might not have gone, she and Renato would never have become lovers, and maybe, just maybe, René might not have lost
custody of Gém.

One of the last times I saw her on the set at Cinecittà, the
light technicians were setting up, the mic operator still getting into position and the ground beneath me a mess of cables.
At the center of it all was Gém—or should I say Maya—
illuminated from several different angles. Her blond hair
was glowing, slowly pulsing, a few strands starting to rise, as
though charged with static electricity. I looked around to see if
anyone else had noticed, but I seemed to be the only one looking directly at her. I wondered if the effect was intentional, or
if I simply happened to be standing in the right spot—a trick
of the light, a trick of the mind. Not only her hair, but even
her skin seemed infused with the same mysterious incandes-
cence, like a manifestation of her telekinesis, I thought, not
what had been written for her character but real magic, ema-
nating from her body and with which she could annihilate us
all in the blink of an eye. I hadn't yet told her that I wouldn't
be going with her to Paris, and I found myself wondering
if, somehow, she already knew. I waited for her gaze to cross

mine, but it was as though she couldn't see me with all the lights shining in her face.

The morning after René's housewarming party, I took the 1 Line all the way to the terminus, La Défense. I walked around a bit, until I came to a terrace overlooking a courtyard surrounded by shops and cafés and high-rises. Behind me was the Grande Arche and the commercial center. Below me, in the courtyard, was a group of kids engaged in a game of football. Around me, the buildings, their façades once white, or almost white, had gradually yellowed and blackened over the years. Farther on, beyond the line of high-rises, I could make out the skyscrapers of the business district.

The Wall Street Institute—where I taught Wall Street English, four times a week—had a branch nearby, but this was the first time I had ventured into this particular complex. (Until now, I had avoided it altogether.) It wasn't hard to see why Renato had wanted to film the climactic scene here. With only minor adjustments, some clever camera angles, the cluster of residential towers could be made to pass for a futuristic redoubt in a post-apocalyptic world, among the curved pathways and marmorean walls.

I hadn't seen her since she had left with Gaëtane, Renato and the rest of the crew to finish the film. Soon afterwards, Gaëtane and Renato had moved in together, and now she lived with them in a well-to-do neighborhood of Rome. A quiet little street, I am told. Somewhere near the piazza del Popolo, with cobblestones and ivy-covered balconies, one of the few spots in the city where the clamor of traffic can't be heard. In a few days, it was going to be her eleventh birthday. My father had once told me that eleven was the age at which one was least likely to die, coming as it does after the dangers of early childhood but before the vicissitudes of adolescence.

From the terrace, I continued to watch the kids, and suddenly one of them stopped running after the ball and looked up at me. For a moment, it seemed like he was going to do something, make a sign, a gesture, but in the end he went back to his game as though nothing had happened. Only then did it occur to me that he might have been staring at something else altogether. I made my way down to the courtyard, giving the players a wide berth. This was where it had happened, the final confrontation against *i due corvi*, Hugin and Munin. In my head, I tried to reenact the scene. Maya is taken by surprise, despite her ability to sense the presence of other humans from their psychic signatures, despite everything Niko has taught her during their all-too-brief time together. Once again, I ran through the scene of her demise, her death, which I had imagined so many times that it was like I had already seen it, countless times, in an endless succession of screen tests and failed outtakes.

At one of the cafés—Le Fleurus—I walked in, greeted the proprietor, and ordered a coffee, which I drank standing up at the counter, taking my time. Afterwards, I asked the proprio if he by chance remembered an Italian film crew in the area about a year ago. He didn't seem in the least surprised by my question, as though I wasn't the first to ask. "Afraid not," he answered after a moment's reflection. "I wasn't around then." He gestured with his chin at the restaurant across the courtyard, Le Chien de Fusil. "Momo might be able to tell you something. Unfortunately, he's not here, and I can't say when he'll be back."

Outside, I peered into the restaurant he had pointed out. The interior was dark, as though abandoned. What was I looking for, exactly? The kids were gone, having finished their game; the late-morning air was brisk, mistral. I turned, slowly, in a circle. Just barely visible from where I stood was the Grande Arche de la Défense, and I tried to recall the name of the architect—a Dane—who had designed it. But the name refused to come, and in the end I gave up. Someone I had met at René's party last night had told me that the voices of those once closest to us are the ones we forget the fastest.

Forgive me, Gém.

The last time I came to pick her up at Cinecittà, she wasn't waiting for me at our usual spot in front of the headless Roman statues. Was I running late? No, I was on time, as always. I looked around. Empty lots, neglected props, expanses of green lawn. All was calm and silent. Not a soul to be seen, not even a solitary crow circling overhead. René had told me, showing me around the first time, that the outdoor sets were most often used by big foreign productions, who came and built everything from scratch, then left it behind—huge set pieces, thereafter forgotten and decaying. Italian film crews had their own studios elsewhere or shot on location, as it was both cheaper and more modern. The era of Fellini was long gone.

I found her among the remains of Pompeii, which had been used for a Spanish television series that had won a lot of awards. At the stone archway with its artificially weathered concrete, we stared at each other in silence. She was upset with me—that much was obvious, even if I couldn't see inside her head. How had she found out I wasn't going? Had Gaëtane told her? (I had made it clear that I wanted to break the news myself.) The look in my goddaughter's eyes said that I was

abandoning her, letting her down—all because I was afraid of
what I might see, the charred and blackened casserole of my
inner self reflected, this time, not in the secrecy of a lavatory
mirror but in the openness of her ten-year-old's face. Confronted by her unwavering gaze, I became convinced that she
could hear my every thought, and as I struggled to fight down
my panic, it occurred to me: the trick was not to empty one's
mind, which in any case was impossible, but instead to *fill* it
with more thoughts, all kinds of thoughts, crisscrossing and
converging. Like typing over a word with another word, then
with another, again and again, until there is only an indeci-
pherable jumble of letters, I thought to myself, as I gave her a
smile that reflected none of the chaos and turmoil and sorrow
inside of me.

Acknowledgments

Thank you: PJ Mark, Mitzi Angel, Molly Walls, Ian Bona-parte, Yves Jaques, Laura Efron, Frances Hwang, Nathalie Fer-rier, Margot Livesey, Kevin Brockmeier, Thisbe Nissen, Lan Samantha Chang, Ethan Canin, Frank Conroy, Anthony Swof-ford, Jim Crace, Cressida Leyshon, Deborah Treisman, Jaimy Gordon, Gabriel Louis, and—most of all—Bosie.

I'd also like to thank the Fine Arts Work Center in Province-town, where I finished writing this book during the most produc-tive (and therefore happiest) seven months of my life as a writer.

Thanks, as well, to the Crous de la rue de l'Abbaye and the workshop of Dominique Barbéris at the Sorbonne. A shout-out to Grégory Bouak, Daniela Bambasova, Namtran Nguyen, Tiburce Guyard, Perrine Rideau (merci de l'avoir lu à ma place, mon texte sur José Bové), Philippe Laurichesse, Lu-cille Dupré, Marie-Pierre Borniche, Tatiane Thiénot, Sandrine Jacquemont, Ivan Berlocher, Kim Estivalet, and Nate Hoks.

"Crow the Aesthète" is modeled after the poem "*Das äs-thetische Wiesel*," by Christian Morgenstern. Henrik's speech to Gém about her lost cat, Bors, contains echoes of Rilke's letter to Balthus about his vanished cat, Mitsou. I first encountered the word "kærestesorg" in a poem by Henrik Nordbrandt.

Fumiko's message, in its entirety, reads as follows: "Un revenant dans ta chambre peux faire disparaître le silence"—in addition to the error described in the book, she also left out a "tu" before "peux."

David Hoon Kim is a Korean-born American educated in France, who took his first creative writing workshop at the Sorbonne before attending the Iowa Writers' Workshop and the Fine Arts Work Center in Provincetown. His fiction has appeared in *The New Yorker*, *Brins d'éternité*, *Le Sabord*, and *XYZ*. *La revue de la nouvelle*. He writes in English and in French.

Paris Is a Party